I0747570

SCAR

DARK ISLAND SCOTS, #3

Jolie Vines

WWW.JOLIEVINES.COM

Copyright © 2022 by Jolie Vines All rights reserved.

No part of this book may be reproduced in any form or by any electronic or mechanical means, including information storage and retrieval systems, without written permission from the author, except for the use of brief quotations in a book review.

Editing by Emmy Ellis at Studio ENP.

Proofreading by Lori Parks.

Formatting by Cleo Moran / Devoted Pages Designs

Cover design by Natasha Snow.

Cover photography by Michelle Lancaster.

Cover model: Anthony Patamisi.

To all those thriving despite deep scars

BLURB

A scar tore his face. Mine would carve his heart.

I'd do anything to save my missing sister, even sell my body to the highest bidder.

Until he steals me from my buyer's mansion.

Camden rescued me, but he won't let me walk away. Especially when I discover he's my buyer's son.

And the strange thing? I can't even be angry at the sweet, gentle, scarred Scotsman for the terrible thing he did.

Chasing after me will hurt him. And loving him will only leave me with scars.

—

Scar is the third episode in the wildly popular *Dark Island Scots series*. As with the previous brothers' stories, this is darkly delicious and may raise eyebrows. Check the note inside the book for warnings. Remember Camden is a tattoo artist? Just wait and see where he lays down his...skills.

Let Camden and Breeze leave you emotionally scarred!

READER NOTE

Dear reader,

Thank you for picking up Scar. This book is third in the Dark Island Scots series. You should probably read Ruin and Sin first to understand all the drama and goings on.

Please be aware this series contains darker themes, including tattooing...places, blood play (unintentional), violence to a child (historic), and sexual assault. Plus all kinds of danger. A full list is on my website -

https://jolievines.com

If you're an audio fan, you'll delight in the story as told by narrators Zara Hampton-Brown and Zachary Webber. Delicious!

Happy reading,

Jolie

1

Breeze

In the company of dangerous men, I stumbled through the forest. The night air swirled up to my ass—I was naked under my borrowed t-shirt, everything left behind in the burning house.

A twig dug into my heel, and I hissed in pain, too aware of being pursued to cry out.

The man beside me slowed. "Let me carry ye."

His tone was kind, if fierce, but I wasn't fooled.

In the space of an hour, I'd gone from being the willing fuck toy of a dirty old man to the prisoner of his son. Way to go, me. Take a sexy, half-naked bow.

I'd come to the mansion to find my missing sister. The people around me now had raided the place for other reasons, and the end result had been disaster. Old McInver was dead or dying, collapsed in a heap somewhere. At least one man had been murdered. Fire ate the building, set by another of the gang who'd taken me now.

Police and firefighters swarmed the dark, remote land

we were escaping.

Whatever these men had been trying to do, their actions had cost me my chance to track down my sister. With McInver dead, I'd never find out where she'd been taken. Never be able to get her out of the mess she'd found herself in.

Grief broke over me in a wave.

I couldn't answer his demand.

"Breeze?" my so-called rescuer tried again, squeezing my cold fingers. "What's wrong?"

"Just pick her up, Scar," his brother snapped.

Scar. When we'd first met a few days ago, he'd given me the name Camden. The nickname was a cruel one, as he had a deep scar down the left side of his face.

Whoever he was, he lost patience with me and scooped me up with his arms around me and under my legs.

I tucked my head against his broad chest. Bare, too, as he'd given me his shirt when he'd unchained me from McInver's chair.

Saved me, for certain. If I'd been left, I'd be roast human by now.

We charged through the forest, emerging into a lane where two cars were parked.

Camden made a sound like a growl, setting me on my feet. "That must be Burn's car, which means he hasn't made it out. We need to go back for him."

His brother, a huge, hulking, scary man glared back into the trees. "The cops are right behind us. If we leave now, we'll have a chance at getting away."

"We can't go without Burn," Camden snarled.

"Do ye think I want to?" The bigger man wheeled around.

The curvy blonde woman with him opened the door of an old grey Ford, the closest vehicle.

From deeper in the forest and the open park the other side, shouts came. The police, probably. Hunting for the arsonist and anyone escaping the scene.

"My family is falling apart at the fucking seams," the big man continued. "Cassie taken. Struan in hospital. Now Burn is out there somewhere. Trust me, I don't want to do this, but I won't risk my lass or ye. Burn drove here of his own accord. He'll find his way back to us."

Camden glowered at him. "Ye and Lottie take Breeze and go. I'll stay."

"No fucking chance."

The woman, Lottie, I gathered, intervened.

"Sin's right. We need to get away before we're found and every one of us arrested. After what McInver did, Sin could be jailed. We need to hide."

Old man McInver had grabbed the shotgun in his son's hand and pulled the trigger. Together, they'd killed a man.

Fuck.

I stole backwards, my trust for these strangers at zero. But my options were limited. I was almost naked and had no phone or money. We were in the middle of nowhere, and even if I had the chance, there was no one to call who could come rescue me.

I couldn't afford to get caught by the police. My fingers trembled, and I twisted them together.

Camden abruptly spun around and marched to the car, setting a possessive hand on my back and preventing my escape. "Fine. We'll abandon him and hope he resurfaces. Let's go."

He guided me into the car, and I went without a fight. He dropped heavily next to me while the couple climbed into the front, Camden's brother driving. Headlights off, we rolled down the lane.

Shadows concealed us, and we edged slowly towards the exit.

Urgency danced through me from the need to escape, despite the company I was in. People had died, and a fire blazed. Anyone caught up in it, even a mostly innocent person, say an unused prostitute like me, would be in danger of copping blame. And I was stuck splat in the middle.

Rock, hard place, meet Breeze.

Flashing lights broke the night. Ahead at the end of the lane, a police patrol car cruised past, lights on but sirens off.

As one, we all ducked, the Ford halting with a shudder.

My breathing sped. The patroller's blue lights flooded our car's interior, and we all snapped to absolute silence.

The police stopped, too.

For a long moment, all that moved was the blinking light.

It didn't get closer or move away. They were watching us.

I peeked across the back seat at Camden. Hunched over and with his jaw tight, he flicked his gaze to his brother, giving me a chance to stare.

My first impressions were messed up. I'd thought him

kind, but that was before I knew who he was. Or who his daddy was.

What kind of monster hid under his skin?

In the blue light, his scar stood out, the ridged edge of it more obvious along the side of his face and slashing his eyebrow. He must've been in one savage fight to have earned that.

Aside from that, he was pretty, his face evenly proportioned, a cut jaw line, light stubble, dark to match his thick, black, slightly too-long hair. His bare chest and thick biceps had no further scarring, but black tattoos had been inked into his skin.

I took a moment to imprint him in my mind. Whatever he wanted from me, and I knew it wouldn't be good, I was glad not to know.

He swung his focus to me.

Caught me staring. I tamped down the little shock of eye contact and refused to look away.

Then Camden did the strangest thing. He slipped out his hand to take mine, a fleeting upside-down smile of reassurance playing with his lips.

He was...comforting me?

I didn't dare withdraw my fingers.

"Oh my god. I think they're going," Lottie whispered.

The lights moved away, the flashes ceasing.

Cautiously, we all sat up, peering out into the black night.

"How could they not see the car?" she asked.

"I bet they did," her guy replied. "But they're looking

for people running."

"Which means they'll note its position and be back around here soon," Camden concluded. "Get us out of here, Sin."

His brother gave a gruff nod and slowly pulled away again. Out of the lane, we joined a wider country track, heading the opposite way to the patrol car. The farther we travelled, the more we picked up speed. I withdrew my hand from Camden's and peered out the rear window, expecting the cops to burst from every dark corner.

No lights followed us. No siren wailed.

After some distance, we made it to a brightly lit highway. I didn't know this part of Scotland all that well, but main roads were scarce, so we had to be somewhere along the edge of the Cairngorm mountains.

The others in the car all seemed to heave a sigh of relief. Camden stretched to grab a spare t-shirt from a bag behind him while his brother put his foot down, and the distance grew between us and the burning house.

It was only when we turned off into a mountain road then arrived at a cabin that I realised we'd made it.

Escaped the man I believed knew all about Summer's disappearance.

A tremor of emotion rippled over me. No matter the fact that I was free, she was still a prisoner somewhere. Or worse, she'd been killed. I wouldn't stop until I knew the truth.

Camden climbed from the Ford and held out a hand to help me. I swallowed but took it, resigned to whatever awaited me in the cabin.

Everyone here had seen me naked. McInver had paraded me like a prize then secured me open-legged to a chair. He'd crowed out loud that I was there for his son to fuck.

He'd meant the bigger guy, I guessed. Sin. But he had a girlfriend, which meant that Camden had claimed me for himself.

I'd been around the block too many times to think anything different. Men looked at women for one of three main reasons—as a saintly mother, a fuckable whore, or with bone-deep hate.

If I was to survive this next part of my fate, I had to put myself into the middle category.

For Summer's sake, I had to live.

2

Camden

We entered the mountain cabin, a refuge we'd used previously after escaping prison. The space was dark, but no one moved to put on the lights.

Sin took up his phone. "I'll make sure we can stay," he muttered, then dialled a number. "Gordain. I need to ask a favour."

Gordain owned the land we were on. He was a friend of a friend and had helped us in the past, even once giving us a ride in a mountain rescue helicopter. If he turned us away, we had nowhere else to go.

Worse, no way of Burn finding us.

I had his phone, and our sister had mine. If he didn't follow us here, I had no clue how he could track us down.

To my left, Breeze shifted on her feet, drawing my attention. Standing in a pool of moonlight from an open window, she was pale, her yellow chin-length curls silvered. My black t-shirt swamped her, ending at mid-thigh. Like a movie star on the run in an action film.

She held herself taut, obviously afraid.

Really fucking beautiful.

I locked down the burst of warmth that flooded me. It wasn't her fault that never before in my near twenty years of life had I been attracted to anyone. Yet one glimpse of her naked and spread out for McInver and my hormones had decided to wake up. Had my dick hard and my blood running hot.

That was fucked up. I wasn't like him, into hurting people. Abusing women.

"Lottie," I summoned Sin's girlfriend. "Breeze needs clothes. Do ye have anything she can wear?"

Lottie snapped her gaze off Sin who paced the lower half of the open-plan room, still on his phone. "Thea's things are in a holdall in the car. She won't mind Breeze borrowing something. She's skinny, too, a better fit than me."

Sin finished his call. "We can stay. Gordain asked to see me. He wants to know what's going on."

I snapped on a lamp, and my stomach tightened.

Blood spatters decorated my brother from his arm up to his neck. The fallout from him shooting Augustus Stewart. Except it had been our father's hand pulling the trigger. Sin had only held the gun.

Breeze sucked in a breath. Fear flashed over her features before she hid it.

Sin stared at the drying blood. "I need to tell Thea I killed her da."

"It wasn't your fault," I said fast. "McInver forced ye."

He didn't reply, his attention moving to Lottie.

"He was my father, too," Lottie replied softly. "So I can say that he deserved that death, but I agree. It wasn't by your hands."

"I was holding the gun. I wanted him dead."

"Still, it wasn't your decision in the moment," she decided.

An expression of discomfort played out on his features. For the first time ever, my stern, capable brother appeared… unsure.

In the not-too-distant past, he'd stood here and asked us to trust him to lead us. Right now, he needed someone else to step up.

"Go scrub yourself clean then burn those clothes," I ordered. "I'll go to Gordain and hold him off."

Sin nodded slowly. "What will ye tell him?"

"The truth? I hate lies."

My brother's jaw tightened. "I never wanted to involve him."

"Pretty sure we've lost the luxury of choice." I swept my gaze across him and Lottie, making them pay attention to my words. "Tonight was fucked up. Too much has gone down to even start making sense of it, but the priority has to be getting our family back together again. I'll tell Gordain enough so he can warn us if anyone comes looking. If he wants us to leave, we can go. It'll give us time to hide the evidence painted all over ye."

To my surprise, Sin only jerked his head in agreement then made for the stairs, commenting that he'd text Gordain that I was on my way. Lottie placed gentle fingers on Breeze's shoulder and guided her in the same direction, murmuring about finding her some clothes.

"There are spare bedrooms," she told her. "You're safe with us."

A brief stiffening of Breeze's muscles was my only clue that she didn't agree.

"I'll sleep in with Camden," she uttered.

I stared at her and opened my mouth to refuse. It was better if she didn't. It was better for everyone if she wasn't in my bed.

"I'll feel safer that way," she added with her gaze down.

Holy fuck. I couldn't say no.

I also couldn't read her at all. Couldn't tell if she felt obliged to stay with me because I'd rescued her or if she genuinely felt safer around me.

"Pick a room for us," I said instead. "I'll be back soon."

I charged out of the cabin and into the night once more. This estate was as remote as McInver's, but in comparison, tranquil and calm. Thick evergreen forests edged mountain slopes. Gordain McRae lived in a castle that I'd only seen in passing, but it was close enough for me to sprint to.

A light glowed above the arched entranceway. Others sprang to life as I approached. The door opened ahead of me, and Gordain emerged, arms folded.

I lifted my chin to him. We'd met briefly in the past, and I respected the older man.

"I'm Camden, Sin's brother. You've probably heard the others call me Scar."

He flicked his gaze over me in a fast assessment, as if in his mountain rescuer role and checking for injuries. "Good to see ye, Camden. Take a walk with me."

He pulled the door closed behind him and descended the few steps to the gravel. I fell in with him, and we slowly crossed the car park.

I picked over my words, trying to work out where to start. "We're grateful to have somewhere to stay."

He snorted. "There's a stately home on fire thirty minutes from here. The owner is on his way to hospital."

Hospital. Then McInver wasn't dead. "News travels fast."

Gordain kept on walking, his pace easy. "It does. The Cairngorms community is tight. There were rumours about the owner of that house. Some might say he earned his fate."

An echo of what Lottie had said about her da.

"Some would be right."

I closed my mouth. I doubted Sin had admitted anything to this man, but he knew enough. His nephew was friends with Struan, my brother who was in hospital. Max had come when Struan called for help, bringing his uncle and the mountain rescue team to the island where we'd been imprisoned. The men responsible for keeping us there were both dead. Our prison keeper, too. There had been a gang of islanders after us for the money.

The last part, Gordain had seen. They'd been paid off by McInver, but before that, they'd chased us around Scotland.

A conclusion hit me. Any confession came with admitting guilt. As much as I believed us victims, we'd also committed crimes. Struan had drowned a man. Sin had held the gun that killed another. I'd offed our prison keeper.

And Burn had started the fire that people were gossiping about.

Gordain continued, breaching the silence. "The initial police reports say they believe the fire was deliberately set. They also state that McInver's guards had left him outside then ran for it. They chased them down, but it doesnae seem like they caught any."

He stopped where the castle's car park met a road, a wide river meandering the other side.

His attention fixed on me. "I told your brother that the police can be a useful tool if ye need the law to work in your favour. Sometimes they're the opposite. Sometimes it suits me not to ask too many questions or to be indoors with a man whose clothes might smell of smoke."

I stared at him, instantly conscious of the fresh air and of his subtext. If he didn't know, he couldn't be forced to tell.

He didn't want my truths.

"Instead of wondering too much about some old pervert's house, I might get distracted by a group of hikers who stumbled onto my estate and had nowhere to stay," he intoned.

I got with the program. "Those hikers would be very grateful. None are injured, but they need shelter."

Gordain nodded once and sharply. "Good to know. My son-in-law is putting together a box of food they can collect from the castle steps in a minute. I'd be interested to know if any...wildlife might've followed them here."

He meant had we come in hot. "No. They were cautious."

I was rewarded with another nod.

Gordain stretched out his arms, tattoos decorating both, and swung his gaze around us. "Hiking can be exhausting. I'd recommend lying low for a few days. The cabin is theirs for as long as they want it. If in future those hikers feel they need better advice on routes and equipment, I'm here for that. Otherwise, I assume they'll do what others have done in the past, and up and leave when they're ready."

I nodded acknowledgement. We'd done a runner on him before. Still, he was ready to help us.

The older man pointed to the door, held up a finger to indicate me waiting, then turned and walked away.

I'd intended to be honest with him, but I got his position. He didn't need to know. At least not right now, and probably based on his interactions with Sin in the past. My brother kept his cards close to his chest.

But I couldn't let him think the worst.

"Gordain," I called, and he stopped. "Those hikers didn't get lost on purpose. They never even wanted to go on a fucking walk."

"Aye, lad. That's more than apparent." He disappeared into the house.

A minute later, a younger man set a box on the doorstep. He glanced up, seeking me, gave me a chin lift, then went inside.

I sighed, relieved that we had beds for the night and some degree of safety, then collected the food and trudged back to our temporary home.

At the cabin, no second car had appeared. Burn had presumably stolen his, so I entered with a small hope that he might've ditched it and still have made it here.

Sin sat in the window seat. In clean clothes, and with the blood scrubbed off him, he'd reset himself. Dark energy coiled around him.

A fire smouldered in the wood burner, the smell of singed cloth barely detectable.

"No sign of Burn?" I checked.

He unfurled his long legs and stood. "None. I'll keep watch until he shows. Lottie messaged Thea and Struan, so they know the latest. If he somehow chooses to go to them, Thea will call us." He spotted the food box and gave an unhappy laugh, looking away. "Fucking Gordain."

I carried it into the kitchen, and he followed.

"He's okay with us being here and didn't ask any questions." I unpacked the milk, butter, and bacon into the fridge, leaving the rest of the produce on the counter. "I would've told him everything, if he asked, but it was clear he didn't expect it or need to know."

My brother watched me. "And then he just handed over food. Can ye imagine having someone like that in your life growing up?"

He didn't elaborate. He didn't need to. None of us had had a consistent parent who'd cared for us. Being decent. Supported us regardless.

"No," I admitted, tamping down an unexpected and unwanted burst of regret. "Where are the lasses?"

"Upstairs. Go on up. Get a few hours' sleep then take over the watch."

He turned away, effectively dismissing me. Sin needed time to process the night. I didn't know half of what he'd been through, only what I saw at the end. That was fucked up enough.

I climbed the stairs, stuck on another, bigger distraction. The lass I'd brought back here with me. Breeze had suffered God only knew what at McInver's hands.

She'd been naked, chained to a chair. I hated with violence the fact that she'd been on display for any fucker to stare at. To hurt.

I needed to know who she was, why she was there, how the fuck Burn had recognised her. Beyond that, she needed care and someone to give a shite.

With my history of a broken childhood where my mother had been used by men and had sold herself over and over to any arsehole with cash in his hand, I couldn't bear it.

The fact my father had kidnapped Breeze.

The fact I wanted her. Desperately. It hadn't eased.

I'd be her guard if she needed someone to watch over her. Stand outside the door.

But sleeping beside her was out of the question.

3

Breeze

A rap came at the door. I shot up on the bed then forced my muscles to unlock in a pretence of relaxation. Lottie had found me clothes and toiletries, and I'd taken a quick shower, towel drying my hair, but otherwise leaving it in loose, damp locks.

Then I'd perched on the edge of the bed with only the towel around me and awaited Camden's return. He hadn't kept me long.

"Come in," I called.

The door opened, and he entered, his expectant expression flipping to one of shock. He shut the door and closed his eyes.

"Shite. You're not dressed. I'll go."

Weird reaction. I patted the bed. "Don't be silly. Sit down with me."

While he'd been gone, I'd run over all the things I knew about surrendering to a man. The tricks I'd heard used by others.

In a heartbeat, I regretted the fact I'd never put any of them into practice. I needed that experience now. I needed to be able to bend this man to my will. To stay alive as a minimum.

Camden cautiously opened his eyes but didn't budge from his position. Cautiously, he scanned the room. "Did Lottie give ye something to wear?"

I gestured to the chair where borrowed clothes waited in a pile. "She did. She's been very kind."

He nodded slowly. "Put on underwear and a t-shirt then get beneath the covers."

If this was a kink request, it was a new one on me. Slowly, I stood, keeping my gaze on him. Scar turned away, one hand shielding his eyes even though he faced the other direction.

I dropped the towel, baring my naked body with a pointed toe and my shoulders back. Lottie had given me moisturiser, so my skin gleamed. I looked good, I hoped. Boobs out, pussy completely bare. I palmed my tits.

"I'm out of bed."

He didn't peek.

No burst of energy. No shoving me onto the quilt, face-down, while he crammed his dick into me.

"That's step one," he said. "Now for the clothes."

Utterly puzzled, I padded to the chair and sorted through the items. Thankfully, Lottie's friend had brand-new underwear, so I slipped them up my legs.

"Little blue thong on."

Camden made a funny sound. "T-shirt. Bed. Steps two and three."

The white t-shirt clung to me, my nipples visible through the material. I sank back against the pillows and drew the blanket over my legs. "Done."

He swivelled and lifted a finger to check then joined me, taking a position at the bottom of the bed.

For a moment, I just stared at him. If he was gentle, this wouldn't be the worst thing in the world. Better than his creepy father pawing at me.

Scar watched me in exchange, something in his gaze I didn't recognise. Then he spoke.

"I have a few things to say. I wanted to repeat that you're safe here with us. We need to lie low, but if there's somewhere ye want me to take ye, I can do that in the morning. Also, I need to apologise. Sin and I were there the night of your kidnapping. I saw ye get carried into McInver's house, but at the time, we weren't sure that it was a person. You're small," he said with a gesture up and down my body. "We couldn't be certain."

True. I was on the short side, though with a round ass and enough boobs to make me perfect for the job I'd taken on.

But I wasn't quite understanding him. There was no way he was just going to let me go. He might think it, but if I demanded he release me, it wouldn't happen.

Not without taking payment from my flesh.

"It's my fault ye were there for so long," he continued. "After I saw ye in the bedroom, I made an anonymous tip-off to the police, but obviously they didn't find ye."

I held up a hand. "Wait. It was you who called the cops? My guard was pissed off about that. But listen, you've got the wrong idea. I was there of my own choice. McInver bought me."

Might as well tell him the facts. Lay it all out there.

Camden straightened from his lean on the bed frame, his apologetic expression morphing into a frown. "Bought ye?"

Right. I needed to be explicit. Set the stage for how we were going to go on. "I'm a prostitute."

Fresh shock stole over him. His mouth dropped open.

"McInver won me in an auction. His terms included how I was to be brought to him. By way of violence. He wanted me to act afraid, like I was just a girl snatched from the streets."

"That's sick."

Probably, but I hadn't let it faze me.

The most important thing I needed to do now was win over Camden and get out of here alive. Which meant moving on to the next part. I stiffened my spine.

"Get into bed with me?" I asked.

His gaze travelled over my face, but he gave a slow shake of his head. "That isn't a good idea."

I widened my eyes, trying to look innocent and cute, even as mild nausea clamped my belly. "I really need you close to feel safe. Please?"

Camden pressed his lips together but again shook his head.

Shit. Maybe I shouldn't have told him the prostitute thing. But how was I supposed to know his deal unless he told me?

McInver had given specific instructions. Beyond fearful, he'd wanted me docile. I wasn't supposed to look him in the eye or flinch if he hurt me. I'd been prepared to endure it all in order to find Summer. I'd planned to question him the moment he'd done the deed. When he was happier and doped up on sex hormones.

It had been my last resort. I'd tried asking the guards, but no joy. If they'd seen my sister, they wouldn't say.

That didn't help me any now.

What was I supposed to do with this man? Like father like son?

Did I spread myself out and ask him to chain me up?

The hint of nausea I was trying to ignore turned into panic. The most natural way to start this would be to kiss him, except I'd already decided that lip-to-lip action was off the menu. It was one thing I probably wouldn't have to do, at least according to the professionals—ladies who'd been doing this their whole adult lives. Men would put my mouth to better use than that, they said.

None of which explained why I had the urge to lean in and kiss the alarmed look from Camden's face.

Okay, okay. Focus. If I couldn't do that, then I needed to reach back, strip my t-shirt, and crawl across the bed to him. Tease my fingers over his waistband then lower his zip, free his dick, and slide my tongue down it. With any luck, he'd rear up and just fuck my mouth so all I had to do was suck.

Knees open wide, back arched, tits perky. Optimum blow job position.

Except I still wasn't moving, and sitting here thinking about it blew no dicks.

Camden leapt to his feet. "Ye need rest. I'll sleep outside on the hallway floor so no one will disturb ye. Lock the door behind me."

"Wait," I said through a thick throat.

But he was gone.

I gaped at the door. What a fuck up. He'd been sitting right there, chatting away, and all he'd had to do was grab me and fuck me. Except he hadn't.

It didn't make any sense.

And even more messed up? A well of hurt rose inside me, generated by this stranger's gentle rejection.

The following morning, Lottie's voice outside my door woke me.

"Breeze? Are ye awake?"

"Hang on," I mumbled, putting away the bad dreams and broken sleep from the night.

In the early hours, I'd chosen a book from the shelf across the room. *Wuthering Heights,* with its mystical, dark feel and characters who acted nothing but horrible to each other. It had sent me to sleep eventually, but exhaustion still held me in its grip.

Quickly, I dressed from the rest of the clothes pile. Lottie's friend, Thea, was taller than me, but otherwise a good fit, and I let each item become armour, protecting me from the painful world and bad choices. I had a cute pair of frayed denim shorts, my white t-shirt, no bra, but I could live with that, and a light cut-off hoodie. She'd even found a pair of flip-flops.

I flicked the lock I'd engaged on Camden's orders and opened the door.

The blonde woman stood on the other side. She grinned at me and flicked her gaze over the clothes. "Oh good, it all fits. Want some breakfast? I'm cooking bacon."

My belly growled. I needed to get out of here, but eating sounded good.

"Um, maybe."

"Will ye come downstairs?"

I hesitated, and Lottie's expression softened. "Or not. You've been through an ordeal. Relax a while longer. I'll bring something up for ye."

Never in my whole life had anyone waited on me. I didn't deserve her kindness, but I nodded anyway, and she left me.

Once she'd cleared the hall, I trailed after her but paused out of sight at the top of the stairs. Voices came from the living room below, and I peeked around the corner at Scar and Sin on the sofas, talking to someone on the phone with the loudspeaker on.

I wasn't going to use Camden's real name from now on. We weren't friends. I couldn't confuse that.

"Have the police been there?" Scar said to the person on the line.

A woman's voice returned. "They have, but it's different than in Inverness. They don't seem to be so interested. Remember they thought Struan might be Burn? I haven't heard any of them say that now. It felt more like a safety check by the hospital staff because Struan refused to give his name."

The two men exchanged a grimace.

"Any news on when our boy can get out of there?" Sin asked.

"They said he needs these specific antibiotics for three days. After that, he'll be allowed home under strict instruction to keep his wound clean so it doesn't get infected again. I told the nurse he'd been in the sea, and she called him an idiot boy. They don't seem that worried." The woman made a hiccupping sound like a sob. "I thought I was going to lose him."

Both men leaned towards the phone.

Scar swallowed and set a hand on the table. "Listen, Thea. He's going to be okay. The medics said so. We'll take better care of him this time."

I'd seen the same care in his eyes when he first met me. It had been there on the car drive and last night, too.

A shuddering breath came through the line. "I know. Ignore me. Struan wants to know about Burn. How are we going to find him if he doesn't have a phone?"

Sin tapped the table. "He'll come here. Where else would he look for us? Tell Struan to stop stressing. We'll find him. Then we'll get Cassie back. None of us will rest until it's done."

With a few more words, they wrapped up the call.

Who Cassie was, I had no idea. Maybe another girlfriend.

Damn. Perhaps that was why Scar didn't want into my bed.

The brothers reset their expressions to the same dark frown.

"He should be here by now," Scar said.

"Agreed," Sin replied. "Which leads me to assume one of two things. Either he's stuck somewhere, and therefore can't get here. Maybe hiding in those woods, or if the car he stole won't start."

"Or he got taken," Scar concluded the second point.

"Exactly."

Both went silent for a moment. Then Scar spoke again.

"Gordain might be able to tell us. He seemed to have knowledge of the police's actions last night. But if he doesn't..." He scrubbed a hand over his face, tiredness showing.

He really had spent the night on the floor outside my bedroom. I knew because I'd heard a buzzing sound when I'd been reading and had peeked out into the hall. He'd been sitting on the floor with a lamp next to him and a tattoo gun in his hand. He'd calmly worked on his inked sleeve, only raising his gaze to show me he knew I was watching. I'd dived back into bed and let the low drone lull me to sleep along with the book.

"McInver's in hospital," Scar added. "If we wait a while, the police won't be crawling over his grounds anymore. I'll go back to search."

Sin gave a sound of protest. But whatever his reply, I missed it because I was stuck on that first point, my heart hammering.

McInver wasn't dead. I could still get information from him. In a hospital bed, he wouldn't be a threat to me. If I could find out which hospital and get access, I could ask my questions about Summer and see his reaction. I'd have a clue.

All I needed now was to find him.

Another burst of inspiration hit me. His mansion would probably be empty. It was a big place, so if the fire had been caught in time, it might not all have burned down. Maybe he had an office there. Maybe his bedroom had survived the blaze.

Okay. I had places to start.

Downstairs, Lottie called to the men to get their food. I sucked in a breath and crept back to my room before I was seen.

My strategy with Scar hadn't worked, but if he was going to McInver's estate, I was going, too.

My plan to seduce him just by sitting there had been weak. Next time, I was going in dirty.

4

Camden

On Gordain's advice, we laid low for most of the day. He'd promised us news on the police investigation when he had it, but if Burn was in custody, it hadn't been made public.

And our younger brother still hadn't shown up.

I waited out the day then, after night fell, sat alone in the dark living room.

We needed some kind of family protocol for the future. A precaution in case something like this happened again. A place to meet or a memorised number to call. But we didn't have that now, so all we had was my alternative plan.

At dawn, I'd return to the mansion.

I mulled over my choices.

Going there too early in the evening felt risky. If police or security guarded the place, they'd probably be more hyperaware and watchful overnight. But an hour or so ahead of the early sunrise felt less obvious. It was a risk I was willing to take.

Footsteps on the landing stole my attention.

Earlier, Breeze had emerged from the bedroom and come downstairs. She'd peeked at me but mostly kept her eyes downward. She'd spoken with Lottie, but I'd left them to it, heading out for a jog instead, scoping the land around the cabin, keeping my eyes open.

When I'd got back, she'd hidden herself away once more.

We hadn't been alone together. I'd been meaning to go up to her, but I felt like a fraud.

She'd wanted me to stay. I'd told her no. She'd sat there looking so lost, seriously fucking gorgeous, but I'd repeated in my head that she was a victim, and walking away had been easy.

I'd done nothing other than obsess over her since.

Taken two cold showers to cool my overheated blood while hating myself for the erection that wouldn't go away.

Everything was fucked up.

But it wasn't Breeze wandering around. My brother appeared on the stairs. He stomped down and dropped onto the adjacent seat. I'd left a single lamp on low, so could pick out his features in the dark.

"When are ye leaving?" he asked.

"Half an hour or so."

He acknowledged that with a grumble, flexing his hands on the arms of the chair. Sin didn't like my decision, but I couldn't rest until we found Burn. It had been twenty-four hours now. Longer.

I couldn't get an image out of my head. Of secret possibility number three—that he had been injured and was lying somewhere needing help.

Out of all of us, I had the least heat on me, so the responsibility was mine to go find him.

Though saying that, we were all killers, or at least accessories to murder. There had been witnesses to Struan's and Sin's acts. Probably the same for Burn's arson. The woman I'd killed had been partially an accident. Our vicious, cruel prison keeper on the island had been my victim, and I regretted nothing.

We buried her in a deep grave in the grounds of the hostel, and as far as we knew, nobody knew or cared where she was. We were still driving her car, which was a risk we had no choice in taking. None of us had the cash to buy a new one. Thea had been spending her inheritance on us, and her borrowed car was our only other set of wheels.

"Why are ye up?" I asked Sin.

He brought his gaze back to me. "Couldn't sleep. I want to go with ye."

"But you're not going to. I'll be safer and quicker alone."

He heaved a sigh that sounded like agreement. "Just keep me updated so I don't lose my mind."

"Ye know I will. Keep an eye on Breeze for me."

His gaze turned curious. "How's she doing? Lottie said she isn't talking. She's hidden away reading for most of the day."

I gave an uncomfortable shrug. "We spoke a little. She said McInver bought her. She was there voluntarily."

He shook his head, adamant. "No way. She's been trafficked. Before ye arrived, McInver said she was a virgin. That he'd checked. There's no way she walked into prostitution at age eighteen or whatever she is and sold herself to a man like him."

My thoughts came crashing down on themselves. A virgin? I didn't even want to consider how McInver had checked that. It made me want to break things.

My rage simmered, and I tried to focus on what I knew.

She'd twice mentioned a sister. Outside the house, with the fire blazing, she'd wanted to go back in because McInver was the only person who could tell her about her sister.

I slammed my eyes closed. How had that skipped my memory?

I hadn't asked her about Burn recognising her either. Lust and staying away from her had messed up my head.

"She could've if she had a really good reason," I muttered back.

A door creaked upstairs.

Sin eyed me, then stood. "Ask her. I'm going to take a walk."

"Wait." I paused him. Tension tightened my shoulders and hung around me in a haze. "How safe are we here?"

His lack of sleep, his patrolling, the watches we kept.

Sin stilled. "What do ye think?"

"That we're not. Nowhere is safe. The moment we have Burn, we're gone."

He nodded then let himself out, and I stared at the door. Life kept on dealing blows. One after the other.

Footsteps came, and Breeze peered down the stairs. "Can I talk to you?"

She'd removed the hoodie I'd briefly glimpsed her in earlier, and her t-shirt rode up to reveal a sliver of her belly. It also outlined her tits in a way I'd tried to ignore last night. Coupled with the short shorts, I was in trouble again.

I gritted my teeth against my frustration. "I'd like that."

She joined me downstairs and curled her slender legs under her at the other end of the sofa.

"Tell me how my brother knows ye," I asked.

"Your brother?"

"When we fled the fire, Burn asked what ye were doing there."

She gave a small shrug. "No idea. I never met him before. I assumed he was mistaken."

Damn. I believed her, which made this a dead end. "Okay, then what happened to your sister?"

She watched me but didn't reply.

"Outside McInver's, ye said that if he died, she died, too. I figure she wasn't in the house, or you'd have fought harder to get back in, so what is it? Did she work for McInver? Was she in some way indebted to him? Did he buy her, too?"

She folded her arms, still not answering.

I tried again. "Ye said you're a prostitute, there voluntarily, but the dirty old bastard McInver told my brother and the whole fucking room that you're a virgin. Ye sold yourself to him because of something to do with your sister, correct?"

Breeze clenched her jaw, and I knew I'd hit the mark.

The frustration I was trying to hold in rushed at me.

In theory, every woman on the planet had a right to work any career they chose. It was none of my business. If being a hooker made her money, that was her decision.

Except this wasn't a choice.

Breeze was desperate. Right at the point of no return. One shove into that shite life and she'd never find her way out. There was no glamour to the career, even for well-paid escorts. It was a dangerous and ugly life.

I knew that all too well.

"Don't think you know a single thing about me," she said carefully.

"I don't. That's why I'm asking."

"Likewise," she continued. "I don't know a single thing about you. Other than the fact you're McInver's son."

I tilted my head. "Which means what? You've already judged me based on him?"

Her gaze remained steady. "Then it's true. How far did the apple fall from the tree? Did you know that kinks run in families? Whatever his likes, I bet you share them."

I sat up, my mind spiralling, and annoyance adding to my mix. Because she could be right. McInver had tied her down. That legs-spread position had been when I'd first seen her. My first ever blast of sexual feeling had come from seeing her like that.

I wanted to see her in that pose again.

Fuck.

"You're a virgin prostitute," I bit out. "Which means that something has to be really screwed up for ye to sell your first time to a man like McInver."

"Men are all the same. What difference does it make which one messes up my body?"

I glowered at her, not willing to free my own personal demons. "It's a shite choice."

"And mine to make." She closed her eyes for a long moment as if reining in her temper, then settled her blue-eyed gaze on me with resolve. "If you're trying to be helpful, there's somewhere I need to go. Back to McInver's. I know you're going there tonight. Take me with you."

"No."

She took an outraged inhale. "Yes! Or am I a prisoner here like you think I was there?"

"Want to leave? Go right ahead. The door's right there. But I'm not taking ye back."

We glared at each other.

How the fuck had this happened? I'd gone from being worried about her to wanting to provoke her. She was a stranger to me, yet every single one of my buttons had been pushed.

And for fuck's sake, I was hard again.

Breeze's gaze dropped to my lap.

With no pause, she rose to her knees and dragged off her t-shirt, her golden curls falling with little bounces.

My gaze snapped to her tits.

Round, perfect, fucking ripe.

She popped the button of her shorts and wriggled out of them, leaving herself on her knees and in only the tiniest thong.

I couldn't speak. All day, I'd pictured this. Her naked.

My sexuality hadn't just woken up, it was screaming for release, dominating my thoughts. So much that I couldn't speak to stop her or prevent myself from gawking.

I gripped the sofa back and arm, my knuckles proud.

Breeze crawled closer, setting a hand on my thigh.

She kept her gaze on mine and reached for my jeans button. Opened it. Drew down my zip.

All I could do was watch. Let my blood rush lower.

I couldn't breathe.

Then her hand was around my rigid cock, and she ducked to enclose it in her mouth.

Hot. Wet. *Fuck.*

I gave up a pained groan. My hips moved of their own accord.

"Wait," I finally managed.

But it was weak. No real opposition.

She licked me, then sank lower, her fist around the base of my cock. Her tongue flattened around my length, the heat of her mouth combined with the incredible suction.

Nothing had ever felt so good. I was instantly addicted to the rush. Her touch. Her every move. Chemicals washed over me, changing me.

She rose and sank down again, killing me with heat.

Needed more. To tie her up. To fuck her hard. Make her scream my name.

No, a voice in my mind crashed through.

I broke my hold on the sofa arm and dug my fingers into her hair, gripping harder than I should've. Breeze gave a tiny sound of shock but kept moving, bobbing her head up and down.

For an almost orgasmic second, I controlled her actions.

More thoughts crashed and collided. To snap up and push her onto her back. Squeeze her tits, suck her nipples, and fuck her right here on the couch.

Christ, I had to stop.

"No," I forced the word out loud.

Breeze slowed then came off my dick, still holding me in her fist. "Tell me how to satisfy you. I'll do anything. You won me from McInver. I'm yours to have in any way you please. Just do what I ask."

What a fucking image.

Horror mixed with shame slammed into me.

I'd only just found out my father was a dangerous pervert and someone who wouldn't hesitate to take Breeze up on her word. I *wanted* to do it. To fuck her. To come in her. To take that first time and all those after.

My train of thought disgusted me.

By painful degrees, I regained control of my mind and hauled up from the sofa, dislodging her grip on me as I staggered away. Breeze dropped back, still basically naked. Still the most beautiful thing I'd ever seen.

"Put your clothes on," I ordered, cramming myself back into my jeans and fastening the button.

My dick pulsed, hating me.

"You're stopping me mid-blow job? Are you for real?"

I closed my eyes for a beat and centred myself. She

needed help, not anger.

"Completely for real. Don't do this. Don't use yourself like that."

"Seriously? You reject me then lecture me?"

"Aye, I do! I know what it is for a woman to think she has control but to be putting her life on the line. Using your body like that makes it all people see when they look at ye. A hole, not a person."

Tears of humiliation shone in her eyes. "Like your dad did?"

Fuck that. "I'm leaving. You're not coming with me. If there's something ye want me to keep an eye out for at McInver's house, I'll do that, but I won't put ye in danger. Tell me now."

"Who are you, my fairy godmother? I don't need you to care about me. All I need—" She took a steadying breath, her cheeks burning red even in the soft lamplight. "I need to talk to McInver. The details of that conversation are no one else's business."

"I'll try to find out where he is. Will that do to keep ye off your back?"

Her lip curled in disgust. I felt it, too. I couldn't stop being an arsehole.

Breeze leapt up and stormed away.

I snatched the car keys and my phone and headed out the front door.

Sin emerged from the darkness as I climbed into the driver's seat.

"Thought I told ye to wait for me."

"Yeah, well, you're here now. Do me a favour and don't let Breeze leave," I snapped.

My brother looked me over. "Did something happen?"

Yeah, my first sexual experience was basically an assault. Problem was, I didn't know which of us was the perpetrator and which the victim.

Without answering, I slammed myself into the car and sped away into the pitch-black night.

In the depths of the woods, the scent of burning hung heavy in the air. I prowled through with stealth, circling the perimeter of the grounds, my dangerous task scouring away the last of my horny state. Assuming the cops had a description of our car, I'd stuck to back roads to get here and left the Ford a distance away, making the rest of the journey on foot.

The roads and tracks were empty. Dawn had yet to break the purple-blue sky, but as I entered the lane where we'd parked up on our last visit, I didn't need the light to see what I hoped couldn't be true.

Burn's stolen car was still here.

With my ears open for any sound, I trod over the bed of soft pine needles, approaching the vehicle.

Dread clamped my stomach. I wanted to see him asleep in the back. The car broken down. Him awaiting rescue.

But no. The interior was empty. The car sat in the same position he'd left it, tucked in at the edge of the lane, half concealed by thick bushes.

Disappointment gutted me.

If my brother had left the estate, he hadn't driven away himself.

Maybe he'd stolen a police car. I suppressed an almost panic-stricken laugh. Burn would do that. My brother flirted with the wrong side of crazy.

Chances were slim, though. Which led me to my next thought. The possibility that he was holing up in the house somewhere.

He was more than a little obsessed with fire. He'd come here to burn it, and if I thought about it, I remembered a conversation when he'd wanted the specifics of the layout of the mansion. He'd asked about the kitchen, particularly.

Looking for an incendiary point.

The blaze had been spectacular, with a side of terrifying. If he'd wanted to admire his handiwork, or even been stuck and unable to pull himself away, that explained why he hadn't run with us. He could even have gone back inside.

My darkest thought was of him lying on the floor somewhere inside the house, barely breathing from smoke inhalation, or knocked out by falling timber and unable to get out.

Or dead.

I couldn't think like that or the hope driving me on would evaporate.

Turning from the abandoned car, I hiked through the woods, eventually emerging at the edge of the park. Down the wide expanse of grassy slopes, McInver's house lurked, a hulking grey shape in the landscape.

Still standing.

It was dark enough for me to approach without being seen, but I took my time, using stands of trees as cover. The first tendrils of light piercing the black sky enabled me to scope the empty car park. No fire engines and police cars now. Not a single vehicle in sight.

As I got closer, the devastation to the building became clearer. The entire right-hand side was blackened, crumbled, or collapsed. The farthest point to the right a mound of rubble on the ground. An entire three-storey wing of the structure had just gone.

Yet the rest of it had survived. The firefighters had managed to save a good portion of the building, with the centre to left-side windows still intact and the scorch marks on the stonework fading. I gazed at the un-ruined side of the mansion.

It gave me somewhere to explore on my brother hunt.

And there was no time to waste.

Breaking cover, I darted for the central entrance. Previously, I'd broken in using a side door that led to the kitchen. That was completely gone now, and I needed to get inside before the sun edged up farther.

Police tape blocked the entrance. I ducked under it and pushed the heavy door. It swung open with ease.

No one had thought to lock it. Which meant no one was taking direct responsibility for McInver's property. That was encouraging.

Inside, a shadowed entrance hall waited, the staircase still standing, running up to the left. Dead ahead, the doors to the great hall had been left wide open, and through them, broken stonework lay on the polished marble floor. Faint daylight revealed where the roof had collapsed.

Ash danced in the air.

I tasted it on my tongue.

There was no dead body where Augustus Stewart had fallen, his brains blown out. Someone had moved it. Maybe the guards before the fire started.

A shiver ran through me. Not only did the place have the air of desolation, but I had the crushing sense it could collapse at any moment, the remaining walls and rooms groaning and breaking, sliding into a heap of dust and stone on top of what had already fallen to ruin.

Still, I had to take the risk. If the building fell, and Burn was in here somewhere, he'd die.

My heart thundered for a second time tonight, and for entirely different reasons.

I couldn't let anything happen to my brother. I'd only just found a family after years of having no one.

Steadying my nerves, I got on with my hunt.

5

Breeze

My thoughts twisted, tormenting me no matter how I tried to make my mind blank. Scar had left hours ago, and I couldn't rest. Never once had I expected him to refuse me. What man turned down a blow job?

The way he'd looked at me, been hard for me...he'd wanted me.

But then he'd walked away.

I stared into space, and my awful thoughts reached a conclusion. Had I just assaulted him?

Under the quilt in my room, I cowered, darkness consuming me. After a lifetime of being looked at by Mum's friends as a whore in the making, their words, not mine, I refused to be a victim. I'd gone to McInver's fully expecting to feel some loss at entering the industry I despised so much but with the strength to pack it away.

In doing so, I'd somehow managed to flip the narrative.

Ignored signs that Camden, Scar, hadn't instigated anything. It had all been me and I'd missed the mark so badly.

God.

I owed him an apology.

I needed to leave.

Except his brother was downstairs, and I didn't fancy my chances of getting past that man mountain. Making a run for it felt sketchy.

Also, Scar had promised to hunt for information at Mc-Inver's. If he was a man of his word, he'd be the only one I'd ever met.

Everything about him ruffled my nerves. Despite myself, I'd argued with him, the man who was effectively my captor and protector. I'd replayed every word of our interaction. I didn't get him. Not at all. He'd seemed truly outraged at the plan I'd made and he'd so easily guessed at. Fuck him for judging me.

I wrapped my arms around my legs. The only other person who'd ever given a damn was Summer. We had each other's backs.

Thoughts of my sister constricted my belly.

We were so alike when we were younger, people often mistook us for twins, though I was eleven months older. Same features. Same blonde hair. I'd cut mine short and permed it as a mark of my own identity.

We'd changed as we grew, though. She was curvier than me now, and taller, but our personalities were where we really differed. My sister acted as if driven by a dynamo. She grasped ideas and ran with them. Took risks based on the strength of her passions. I was the planner, and I thought everything through. I needed to get things right where she needed to get them done.

We shared a sense of humour down to a tee. I smiled at the memory of one of the last times I'd seen her, where we'd laughed over dumb shit and enjoyed ourselves with no hint that something was about to go wrong.

As I examined that memory, an idea sprang into my mind.

Something I hadn't checked in all the time I'd been searching for her.

On that final, fateful night, we'd played a game. One we'd invented as thirteen-year-olds. Both of us had been jaded by our childhoods and the way we saw men treat women. Summer had downloaded a dating app, and we'd made a profile, using a picture of her processed through multiple beauty filters until she resembled a supermodel rather than a scrubby teenager from the streets.

We made up a pretty name and a bullshit profile, then watched as the notifications pinged in.

That's where the fun started. Neither of us ever planned to meet the jerks who hit up our fake account, instead, we used a series of stock phrases to reply to their comments and DMs.

Is your pet real or did you stuff it yourself?

I need three tons of scrap metal to make a boat.

This is getting out of hand. I'm going to the caravan to calm down.

It was a test to see exactly how far men would go for a pretty face. How much they'd engage in a nonsense conversation because it flattered them that an attractive woman was replying.

It was ridiculous, hilarious, and a secret we shared.

The replies brought us both to tears of laughter every time.

I own a dog, but he's real. Can I get your number?

I like metal. Meet me and I'll show you my piercing.

I'll come to your caravan and blow your mind with my giant dick.

As soon as they bit, we'd stop responding. Until the pictures arrived. Around one in five guys would take our fake account's silence as some kind of come-on.

A dick pic was inevitable.

Then came our masterstroke. We saved all the dicks and sent them back as a flood. Send us one? Get thirty in response. If they supplied their phone number, we'd send them there, too.

Stunted, pale dicks, or banana-shaped, angry-looking ones. Sometimes they'd have embellishments, like a cock ring or a piercing. It was a whole tasting plate for us girls to hand out.

It never got old.

As the years went on, we kept up our game. What had begun as childish fun turned into a routine bonding exercise.

One we'd missed for the first time ever now she was missing.

My breath caught in my lungs. Summer didn't have her phone. Or so I assumed, as since starting my panicked hunt, my calls and texts had gone unanswered. She wasn't a huge user of social media, but the accounts she'd had had gone silent. Her boss said she hadn't showed up for work, the few friends I knew had nothing. Dead end after dead end.

But I'd never checked the dating app.

It was a long shot, but I burst from the bed and jogged downstairs. I knew the login. All I needed was a phone.

Scar's brother snapped his head up from his position on the sofa. His glower fell on me, and I swallowed, sidestepping out of the room and into the kitchen to where Lottie poked through a box of food on the counter.

"Do you have a phone I can borrow?" I asked fast.

She paused and blinked at me. "God. I should've offered that already." She pulled the phone from her tunic pocket and handed it over, unlocked.

"Thank you. I didn't take anything other than underwear to McInver's." Why had I said that? I didn't intend to share anything else. The less people knew about me, the safer I was.

Lottie's gaze clung to mine. "Holy fuck. That's intense."

Brief panic rushed in me. I stammered to change the subject. "Thanks for lending me this."

"It's actually Struan's, that's the oldest brother, the one in hospital. Go ahead and make your calls. Just let me know if any messages come in. We're still waiting for news from Scar, though I'm pretty sure he'd call Sin first rather than this line." She blew out a breath. "He's having kittens out there. We're both so worried."

"Four brothers," I said, distracted. Struan, Sin, I guessed next, then Scar, and the last had to be the one they were all looking for, Burn.

"Jamieson is the youngest brother. That's Burn. You'll get used to the nicknames. Ruin, Sin, Scar, and Burn. Struan, Sinclair, Camden, and Jamieson. Then there's Cassie, their little sister. She's missing, too."

"Violet," Sin called from the living room.

Lottie gave me a lingering, still curious look, then slipped away.

No, I wasn't going to get used to the nicknames, including how she was Lottie but her boyfriend called her Violet. What was up with that? Instead, I scurried to the kitchen table and sat, pulling up the phone's browser. Navigating to the web version of the dating site, I logged in. It took forever, the signal out here weak. Finally, the message tab loaded.

Dozens of new notifications from guys filled the screen. I flipped through each, ignoring the occasional dick to find any recent replies. But the farther I went down the list, the more my heart fell. All were from over two weeks ago, when we'd sat together and laughed about it. Summer hadn't replied without me.

It was yet another no-go.

Misery gathered. My expectations had been low, but it had still been a burst of inspiration that fizzled out.

I twisted the phone in my hands then brought up a draft message in the app.

If you're out there, please let me know. I'm so worried, I sent it to our own account. I'm staying with a guy called Camden, he's searching for his missing brother, Burn, or Jamieson, as they all have nicknames. I don't know why I'm telling you this because all I want is to find you. Please, Summer, talk to me.

I sent that, too, then closed out of the site with a heavy sigh.

It had been days since I'd been home, not that I wanted to return to my place—that didn't feel safe anymore, but it was possible that Summer might've reappeared on her own. With less energy than before, I dialled our mother's number.

It rang out.

I sighed and sent a quick text, saying it was me and to answer. The second time, she picked up.

"What's happening? What time is it?" Mum croaked, her voice thick like I'd just woken her.

I glanced at the kitchen clock and winced.

"Five AM. Sorry, I've been up a while."

"Is everything okay?" Mum said.

"Who the fuck is it?" a second voice sounded.

I rolled my eyes. Mum's boyfriend, Jack, was the biggest waste of space on the planet. She worshipped the ground he walked on and had moved us all from Manchester to Edinburgh to be with him.

Mum answered him, and he mumbled a long stream of curse words.

"Have you heard from Summer?" I asked over his complaints.

A long pause came. "No, baby. She hasn't been by. Why?"

"It's been two weeks since I last saw her, Mum."

She didn't share my concern over Summer's disappearance. Or at least wouldn't acknowledge it.

"She's off with a boyfriend or having fun somewhere."

My temper frayed, but I swallowed the need to snap. "No. She'd have told me, or would at least have her phone on her. You know where she went, and where she hasn't come back from. I'm scared that she's missing."

Mum sighed. "Summer's a big girl. She can take care of herself. She'll be back when she's back. Will you be coming around today? I could use seeing you."

I loved my mother. She'd been through the worst of life and come through it protecting her daughters, but the moment we'd become self-sufficient at seven or eight years old, it was like she'd been released to fall into a hole. I'd only just dug her out of one, and it was too raw.

"I'm not sure," I said.

My mother told me she loved me and hung up. I growled, stabbing to exit the phone's dialling screen.

A figure appeared in the kitchen doorway.

Lottie entered, her eyes wide. "Is your sister really missing?"

Shit. I hadn't checked my voice.

In an alternative reality, I might have trusted this woman. She'd been nothing but kind, finding me clothes, even bringing me food when I was too weirded out to face the world. But I didn't know her. I didn't know any of these people.

The kindest, most gentle-hearted person could turn on you in a heartbeat with the right motivation. I'd seen girls preyed on by women who knew they could sell them either for cash or favours from dirty men. Not that I tarred Lottie with that brush, but I knew the world, and I wasn't about to lay my trust at a stranger's door, no matter how badly I wanted to spill my story to her.

Or to Scar.

Especially not to him after what I'd done.

I gulped back words I couldn't say and handed over the

phone. "I'm sorry. I can't talk about it."

She nodded. "I understand. I went for years never telling anyone my darkest secrets. Believe me, it's liberating when ye finally get it off your chest. And if it helps, I found out I have a sister just recently. Thea, who you'll meet if you're still here in a few days. The bond runs deep."

She held my gaze for a moment, marking her words. Then she gestured towards the living room. "Scar's on the phone. He hasn't found Burn, but he wants to talk to ye while he's at McInver's."

God, I hoped he hadn't told them what I'd done. I ducked my head and followed her.

On the sofa, Sin held his phone.

"Scar," he said into the loudspeaker. "Breeze is here. I'll let ye talk in private, but do what ye need to do then get out of there. We need your arse back here in one piece."

He jumped up and disappeared with Lottie upstairs, leaving the phone on the table.

"Breeze," Scar said on loudspeaker.

I waited for the others to move out of earshot then carried the phone to the window seat. "I'm here."

"How much did ye hear?" he asked.

"Nothing. Lottie mentioned you haven't found your brother. I'm sorry."

"So am I. But I did find something that might interest ye. The house is still partially standing, and I've been exploring. As I was talking to Sin, I found an office on the ground floor. I'm in there now."

My pulse quickened.

He continued. "Besides finding out where he is, tell me what I'm looking for that could help ye."

I closed my eyes and pressed the heel of my hand to my forehead. I wasn't about to spill the details of Summer's disappearance, but there could be a clue in that room.

"McInver was a regular user of prostitutes," I said. "Is there anything about which girls he bought, like a list of names, or the brothels?"

Rustling came from the other end of the line. "Can't imagine he'd leave records of that around, but I'm checking. There's piles of envelopes unopened on his desk. Official stuff, I think. The drawers are locked."

A crack followed.

"I managed to open one. Hunting around inside now."

I pictured him in McInver's opulent space, rooting through his possessions. I bet the guy had a leather desktop and some big boss chair. Probably priceless heirlooms on the mantelpiece and fancy paintings on the wall.

If Scar was caught in there, the cops would assume he was a thief.

"Don't pick up anything expensive," I said in a rush.

He gave a short laugh. "Wasn't going to. Are ye worried about me?"

"Don't flatter yourself," I said, my cheeks warming for unknown reasons.

Something about this phone call felt…intimate. At least how I guessed intimacy with a man to be. The real version, not the dick-in-unwanted-mouth variety I'd created.

I had nothing to compare it to, though. I'd never had a father or brother. I'd even avoided male friends at school.

Summer had been different. More open than me. She was often on her phone chatting with someone, though there had never been a boyfriend.

Another crack told me Scar had broken into the next drawer. Then again with a third. Each time, he gave a brief overview of the contents as he found them. Envelopes. A cash tin. Some ledgers about land use. No lists of women.

"Sorry, nothing of any use in here. There's a filing cabinet," he said. "It's unlocked."

A drawer slid out with a metallic sound.

My gut churned. "You're right. Unless he had reasons to keep sex records, I can't imagine he'd have a filing system of women he's messed with."

Scar gave an unhappy chuckle. "And you'd be right. This is fishing and hunting licenses for the past hundred years."

"Jesus," I muttered. "Your father is a walking antique."

A clang came, and I guessed he slammed the cabinet drawer shut. "Don't call him my father. Technically he is, but when ye say it, it's like you're making me his even more. I don't know the man. Never met him until recently. I don't want to again either."

His tone came out harsh, and I swallowed my surprise. Perhaps he wasn't the little rich boy after all.

Then he spoke again, the same urgency in his voice. "What's your phone number?"

"Uh, this isn't my phone." Mine was left at home.

"I know that. Your real number. I have a pen and an old envelope to scrawl on."

Maybe it was the fact I was still wondering about his words, but I opened my mouth and recited my number. My actual phone number, that I was pretty sure I'd never given to a boy before.

"Is it real?" he said, low.

"Yes."

"If I dial it, you'll have mine, too."

I didn't reply. The moment stretched out, somehow warm and...interesting.

"Oh, hello," Scar said suddenly.

"What is it?"

"There's a light flashing on an answerphone. I didn't notice it before because it's in the corner, and there's a stack of papers in the way. I've never seen a phone like this before except for on TV."

"Can you get it to play the message?"

"I'll try."

A long beep came, then a voice filled the air. "This is Julian from *Heathcote hospital,* just confirming we're in receipt of the details from your insurance company..."

Julian rattled on, but that detail lodged in my mind. Heathcote hospital. I'd never heard of it before, but that probably meant it was a private one. Trust old man McInver to have some snooty private medical cover.

Better still, now I had a name, I could find him.

The message ended, and Scar came back on the line. "Did ye catch that? I—"

A hiss of breath came followed by a bump, like he'd stumbled.

"Scar?" I said.

Silence followed, loaded and alarming.

"What is the meaning of this? You're trespassing on private property," a stranger's voice suddenly rang out.

I gasped at the phone, a lightning spike of fear piercing me.

Hitting mute, I listened in, trying not to give him away in case he was hiding.

He had to escape. Please.

Reality hit me in the face. *No.* I couldn't care about what he did. He was the opinionated son of a pervert. He'd judged me with zero information. I'd assaulted him. We had no common ground.

"Sin, Lottie," I yelled to the stairs, backing away from the phone.

He was theirs, not mine.

Scar said something I couldn't make out, then the line went dead.

I stared at the phone, panicked and afraid.

He'd been caught. And it was all my fault.

6

Camden

I gunned the engine, the sun up and McInver's estate far behind me.

The last hour had been wild. From the man grabbing me, to the reason he let me go. None of it made sense, and I hadn't even started to process it.

Utterly confused, I sped on until I reached the estate we were hiding out in. Like Sin had done two nights ago, I paused in a wooded lane for a while, just to be sure I wasn't followed, then trundled on to the cabin.

My brother burst out and jogged to the car, yanking my door open. With a scowl locked and loaded, he stared down at me. "Fuck. Are ye okay?"

I climbed out, still in shock. "Fine. Amazed I'm not in a jail cell."

Sin's shoulders came down an inch. "We would've busted ye out. Get inside, tell us everything."

He led me into the cabin, but I hesitated on the threshold and thumbed back at the Ford.

"I left the keys in the ignition."

Sin snorted a grim laugh. "Who's going to steal a car out here?"

I relented. In the living room, Lottie ran over and threw her arms around me. I patted her back.

"I was so worried," she said. "Are ye hungry? Let me make something."

"Need caffeine. I'll grab a coffee." I peered around the room. "Where's Breeze?"

Sin pointed upstairs. The urge came over me to go straight to her. Check she was okay after what happened on the sofa.

But I needed to share my story with my family.

It was too unreal to delay.

I ignored the Breeze-shaped instinct and strode to the kitchen, Lottie and Sin following. A pot of coffee waited on a warmer, so I poured myself a cup.

"Who was the man?" Sin asked. "Ye only said in your text that he wasn't a cop and he was letting ye leave. Some kind of security?"

"Naw. McInver's lawyer. He started out hostile, and with rights considering I shouldn't have been there."

"I'm amazed he didn't call the cops."

"Same, except I didn't lie to him. When he asked me who I was, I told him McInver's son, and his whole attitude changed. I'm not kidding. He fucking smiled. But the really weird thing was—"

The front door creaked, and we all froze.

"What was—?" I started.

A car door cranked open.

I ran.

Out of the cabin, I burst into the fresh air just in time to see the Ford moving, a slight, blonde figure in the driver's seat. Breeze stared at me through the glass then accelerated.

I clasped my hands behind my head and bellowed after her, "Stop!"

"Where's she going?" Lottie spluttered, arriving at my side.

Sin snarled. "She stole our fucking stolen car."

I took off, sprinting along the gravel road. Dust rose in Breeze's wake. The Ford punched forwards and disappeared into the tree line, far from me now.

I staggered to a halt.

I'd lost her.

I'd probably never find her again.

*S*car: *What the fuck?*

Scar: Talk to me.

Scar: Where did you go?

The next several days dragged.

After Breeze's vanishing trick, we kept to our plan of lying low. I messaged my little thief, but she never replied. My mission to find Burn had failed, but we held out hope that he was somehow making his way home to us.

With every night that passed, that hope faded.

I couldn't be idle. Borrowing a car from Struan's friend, Max, for an evening, I returned to the last safe house, but it was empty. Boarded up to prevent squatters like us. I'd drawn a blank.

Burn was gone. Breeze, too.

Likewise, we couldn't locate Cassie.

Our sister had been taken by force back into foster care, and the phone we'd hidden in her plushie toy dog rang with no answer. None of us had a clue how to track it. Eventually, it would run out of power.

For now, we'd lost her, too.

The only hint of a silver lining was in the fact that nobody seemed to be looking for us. Gordain kept tabs on the police investigation into McInver's house fire. He couldn't discover if they'd arrested anyone, but he was certain they weren't actively searching.

Of the long list of people who'd been hunting us, many were dead, and the only others we'd worried about were the villagers from Lottie's island, the place we'd been imprisoned. McInver had paid off her father, and by the looks of things, he'd run off with the cash. Lottie had spoken to her mother who said she'd seen nothing of him, and that the other villagers had given up and settled back to normal life.

None of which made us feel safe, but it gave us a short reprieve to stay in the cabin while we worked out what the fuck we could do.

I didn't like to wallow. It wasn't a natural state for me, but having my family around me had felt like winning, and I needed to get that back.

Just as urgently, I felt the almost obsessive need to

chase down Breeze. Except I didn't have the first clue where to start.

Running flat out, I skirted the hillside, the July sun beating down on me.

Every day, I jogged, sometimes for hours in order to distract myself and use up the energy that needed out. It also gave Sin and Lottie alone time to get up to stuff I really didn't want to overhear.

Sweat trickled down my face, following the line of my scar. Sin had told me that McInver had made some comment about knowing who'd cut my face.

That fact bothered me.

Almost enough to take up the lawyer's offer of returning for another chat, but that had its own dangers.

I drove my feet into the barely there gravel track, crossing a glen on the side of the mountain that climbed behind our temporary home.

No one was around. Only deer on the opposite slope and me. Wild open space yet still not big enough to contain the emotions rising in waves.

Frustration was one.

Unending, relentless horniness was bigger.

My obsession with Breeze wasn't limited to her story, but also to how she'd made me feel. The memory of her mouth on my body.

My guilt remained, but anger had joined it.

I wanted her. I couldn't have her.

And now I was running with a fucking hard-on again.

A thick forest lay ahead, so I put on speed and charged

into it. Deep inside the trees, I let out a yell, scaring away whatever creatures hid within.

Then I slumped against a tree and slid to the ground.

Nothing moved around me. It was so quiet here. So calm. My blood rushed south, and I palmed my dick then groaned.

The pressure in me needed release. It needed a little devil lass to return to me with something real to say and genuine attraction.

That was out of the question.

There was nothing but me, endless fir trees, and all-encompassing lust.

I ran my thumbs under my shorts waistband and lowered them to free my dick. A quick glance around gave me the all-clear, and I squeezed my shaft then pumped it with my fist.

Breeze's soft, pink lips.

Her bending over my lap, naked, so fucking sexy.

I jerked myself faster, picturing kissing her. Laying my hands on her perfect skin.

The outline of her tits had imprinted in my mind. I wanted to play with her nipples, suck on her until she moaned my name.

As happened every time I went there with my dirty thoughts, the scene turned darker. I'd extend her arms out and secure each to a bedpost, using chains, cord, or whatever was to hand. Then I'd do the same with her legs so she was spreadeagled and unable to move.

Unable to get away from me.

To run away again.

Her body would be my plaything, and I'd get access to every part of her, watching her reactions as I drew my lips over her belly. Up the inside of her thighs. Taste her.

Eventually, I'd give up teasing her and give in to her begging and fuck her. Thrust into her tight virgin pussy which would be dripping with arousal.

I'd slide inside her and nearly come with how good it felt, but I'd get myself under control and work her until she lost it. No matter how warped my fantasy, I only wanted to give her pleasure. Have her consent as well as her screaming for me.

But I wanted her constrained and maybe even a little afraid of what I'd do. How far I'd go. Even if I'd never hurt her. I couldn't get away from the image, and I ignored my guilt and fucked my fist harder, so fucking hot for a woman who didn't want me.

In my mind, she did, though. She'd cry out my name. Demand I fuck her faster, harder, make her feel good. Then when I did, and she was squeezing my dick, so close to release, I'd tell her that I was going to come inside her, both of us losing our virginity in the most vivid and real way. No barriers, no control.

My breathing stuttered, and my dick swelled harder still.

It bothered me how badly this secret fantasy turned me on.

It bothered me that I wanted her unable to touch me back.

I pictured sliding into her bare pussy over and over.

Her tight tits and her arched back. The chains rattling. Her orgasm hitting so hard she cried out in shock.

I jerked up onto my knees and came onto my fist and the forest floor. Ribbons of cum intended for a woman who wasn't there. Whose restrained, naked body had kicked off this unending need in me and who'd made it far worse by stripping and sucking my damn dick.

I pressed a hand into the pine needles and spoke her name, breathing hard.

But it was just me there to hear it. She never would.

Not unless I took action.

As I cooled down, I made a decision. I wouldn't rest until I found her. I had no car, no money, no fucking clue where she'd gone, but somehow, I'd find Breeze again. I had to know she was okay. I had to end this suffering.

An hour on and I neared home, lost in thoughts that were shaped like a wild, blonde bombshell. I'd washed and drank from a cool mountain stream, but even dousing my hot head in the chilly water hadn't eased my constant heat.

Our cabin appeared across the open slope. My gaze locked on a car outside.

For a heart-stopping moment, a fraction of a second, I thought it was her, come back to see me. But no, it wasn't the Ford.

This car was Thea's.

My brother was back.

I sucked in a breath and charged across the hill to half fall through the front door. Struan raised his gaze from the sofa.

"Holy fuck," I bit out, then I paced the room and knelt to hug him.

Struan wasn't a hugger, but he threw his arms around me and thumped my back, Thea leaning to join in the hug, too. Sin and Lottie watched on from their seats.

"We weren't expecting ye." I sat back and looked at him.

My brother had been in hospital for days after a knife wound he'd taken escaping the island became infected. He'd collapsed on the floor of our last safe house, moments before the police raid that saw us evicted and Cassie taken.

Now, he was pale but healthier-looking. Not holding himself with tensed muscles like he had done.

Thea cuddled up carefully next to her boyfriend. "We just got back. He's free!"

Struan snorted a laugh. "Last ye saw of my miserable self, I was half dead."

I echoed his smile and jumped up to take a spare seat, no small relief filling me for having them back. "But you're okay now?"

He brushed his fingertips over the grey t-shirt which concealed the injury to his belly. "With any luck. They kept me in for longer than necessary, just to make sure I didn't fuck myself over again. I'm supposed to rest and take pills, but other than that, I'm sound." The easy humour left him, ebbing away as his demeanour changed. "Not being here has driven me insane. Everything's gone wrong since I've been away. Thea didn't want me to have the full story about Cassie and Burn when I was in that hospital bed, but I made her tell me."

"I didn't want you to leave and get sick again, that's why I gave you the option of not knowing," his girlfriend replied quietly.

He breathed through his nose, the dangerous side of him not far under his tattooed surface. "And they're still out there somewhere, fucking lost."

Sin's black eyebrows furrowed. "Don't ye think we've tried? Scar went out to search for Burn. I have Gordain monitoring the police, waiting for any sign that he's been picked up. We've called Cassie's phone, we've tried speaking to the social care people."

Struan uttered a low growl. "We need to do more. They're our family, and we've left them out in the cold."

"For fuck's sake," Sin gritted out. "We didn't leave them."

"Then where are they?" our brother retorted. "How can Burn have just vanished? Can ye imagine how scared Cassie is? She's six years old. She'll think we abandoned her."

"We all feel the same," I said, hands out to stop the brewing fight. "It's made us all crazy, but riling each other up won't help anyone. Don't forget we were worried about ye, too."

For once, I had things worth fighting for. But the past few days had seen me mostly stuck here and unable to take action. Breeze taking the car had been one of the worst things she could have done. With no way of getting around, at least no easy way, it had cut off our options.

Struan dropped his head back on the couch. "I know. I've just felt so fucking useless."

All three of us brothers shared that.

"Well, we're here now," Thea said. She placed a hand on Struan's knee and shook him as if in warning to hold his temper. "Lottie kept us up to date with all the things that had happened. So what's next?"

I already had a plan in my mind. "If ye let me borrow your car, I have more places to check for Burn."

She nodded instantly. "It's all of ours. You don't need to ask. Where will you try?"

"Burn came from Aberdeen. I'll head out there first. Sin can tell me the right haunts to check. I'll trawl the city." I considered the next idea, not all that comfortable with the thought. "The last place I can imagine him to be is Torlum, but equally I don't want to rule anything out."

All of us stilled.

I never wanted to go back to that prison island again, but I would for my brother.

Sin and Lottie exchanged a glance before Sin spoke.

"On the subject of Torlum, Lottie and I have been talking, too. We have an idea regarding Cassie, but first, Lottie's ma needs help."

"Is she okay?" Thea asked.

Lottie offered a small smile to Thea. I was still getting used to the fact they were sisters, but now I knew it, I could only see the similarities.

Lottie took a steadying breath. "In a word, no. I called

her and told her what happened the night of the fire. About Da taking the money and running, which she seemed relieved over, but then I told her about Augustus."

Thea's father, now dead. Shite, Lottie's biological da, too.

Thea swallowed. "God, was she upset?"

"Devastated. Brutally so."

"I had no idea they were so close," Thea whispered.

"Me neither, but Ma must've loved him. It's not good for the baby, her being so upset, so Sin and I are going out there. We're going to move her out of Da's house to somewhere safer and hope the change helps."

"To Granny's house?" Thea asked.

"If the offer still stands?"

"Of course it does. By rights, that big Victorian house belongs to you as much as it does me, so your mum is welcome to it. I'll give you the key." Thea lifted her bag and rummaged in it.

Sin looked at me. "If you're heading out on a drive, take us to the ferry crossing."

A shiver ran down my spine. That dark island haunted my nightmares. But I nodded slowly. "I'll drive ye there. I don't envy ye going back. I can't help picturing Keep's grave, or Jenkins' dirty expression every time he looked at Burn. Torlum's full of ghosts in my mind."

Struan curled his lip. "What if the islanders see ye? Or worse, catch ye."

Lottie reached out to take Sin's fingers in hers. "My parents' home is remote enough that we can get Ma out with a few bags and go. We'll take Thea's boat over so we can land away from prying eyes and leave the same way, too. If we go at night, chances of anyone seeing us are low. Besides that, my mother says that without a ringleader, the islanders seem to want to put the past behind them. It does have risks, but I have to know she's out of that house and feeling safer." She flicked a glance at her boyfriend. "Besides, Sin won't let me go alone."

He gave a hard, unfunny laugh. "I don't want ye anywhere near danger, and definitely not alone. If you're going, I'm there, too." He switched his gaze to the rest of us. "But if an islander did find us, what are they going to do? Without their head honcho, they have nothing on us anymore. We, on the other hand, know they sat back and enabled our abuse and imprisonment. Took money for it. Proving it would come with a shite ton of questions we don't need, but at some point, we have to stop running. I've sat here for a week and waited for Gordain to tell me the cops were looking for the person who killed Augustus Stewart. That hasn't happened. What if it never does?"

He rolled his shoulders back. "Which brings me onto the next part of my plan. Do ye remember what the policewoman said when they took Cassie away? If we can prove we're related to her, we might get visitation, and if we have a settled home, we could even get custody."

"What about it?" I asked.

"I'm going to ask Gordain for work. Real work, on the books."

Surprise danced over me. Sin was talking about going legit. I understood it, but I still carried a sense of danger with me and needed to keep control.

Meanwhile, he'd been making plans to face off with

the world.

"We still don't know what lies have been told about us. What evidence people are waiting to use," I argued.

"And we're never going to find out unless one of us asks," he replied. "I'm not saying this is the right path, but it's the one I'm starting on now. I'm going to work, earn money, get a reputation that looks good on paper, then tackle the rest as it comes. If someone is chasing us, they'll find us and I'll handle it. What else is there to do? I'm done with running. We'll never see Cassie again otherwise. Besides…"

He glanced at Lottie, and she flushed red.

"For many reasons, I want a settled home for Violet. For the rest of ye, as well. I want an address for us all, and to pay my way. Most of all, to make a safe base to raise bairns."

If he meant more than just Cassie, he didn't elaborate.

Struan watched him, some thought process going on behind his eyes. "I've never had a real job. How does that even work?"

"For ye? It doesn't right now. We'll discuss it again in a couple of weeks when you're fit, but from now on, I want to fix this mess we're in. We're all going to struggle over making a life for ourselves," Sin said, directing us in a way we'd all agreed he could. "But I'm setting Violet and myself at the hub. Cassie said she saw us as her parents. We will give her that back. We'll find our sister, bring her home and raise her."

He'd made his point, and we all had things to do now. I'd continue hunting for Burn, and secretly for Breeze, too. Sin and Lottie would build a base with the hope of bringing Cassie to it. Struan and Thea had their lives to sort out with him getting better first.

If this was how a family worked, I was ready to try.

Even if our foundations were on very shaky ground.

A few hours later, Struan found me sitting outside the cabin, trapped by the last of the daylight. Sin and Lottie weren't due to leave until tomorrow evening, while I was buzzing to go.

At nightfall, I was driving.

I'd cross off at least one location on my list and be back in time for tomorrow's trip. Something was pulling at me, like I had to get out there. And I suspected it was to do with Breeze.

Struan eased himself to sit on the bench next to me and gazed out over the landscape. "Tell me about the lawyer who caught ye."

He knew the basics, but I repeated what had happened, still not quite making sense of it myself.

"He walked in on me as I was standing in McInver's office. Thankfully, I wasn't holding anything expensive, and all the drawers I'd rifled through were closed, otherwise I'm pretty sure he would have thought me a thief. He asked me who I was, and I told him McInver was my father. His hostile expression just dropped, and he became, I dunno, excited. He gripped my arm and shook my hand, saying he'd heard of me. McInver had mentioned me in meetings and also left him a message saying he needed an inheritance organised. According to him, our father was desperate to name his heir."

I reached for my phone and took the white business card from the pocket on the case, handing it to Struan.

He peered at it. "Mr Golding, lawyer, property and estate management." He switched his gaze back to me. "Did he think ye were Sin?"

I shrugged. "I told him my name was Camden, and he didn't say anything. But he did wring his hands and said he was so sad to tell me that following the fire, my father had been taken to hospital. He had no clue that I'd been there that night."

My brother turned the card over in his fingers. "Then he just let ye go?"

"He did, but not before telling me that I had to call him urgently to arrange that blood test. He was going on about decisions that needed to be made, bills to be paid, things like that. I was just desperate to get out of there. There was no sign of Burn, and as far as I was concerned, this lawyer guy was a heartbeat away from changing his mind and getting me locked up for trespass."

"Ye were lucky to get away."

"Sin said the same. His view is that McInver's toxic, and if any of us go near him again, we risk jail."

Struan rubbed his stubble. "Yet he was the one who kept going back."

"Sin needed to know what happened to his mother. McInver forced Augustus Stewart to reveal that he'd killed her, right before he grabbed the gun in Sin's hand and then shot Augustus dead."

He went quiet for a moment. I knew he would've heard

the story already, but it wasn't easy to process. He and Sin were half a year older than me, with my birthday passing in the week just gone, making us all twenty at the same time. A strange legacy from our messed-up father who'd gone on a late-life fucking-for-pregnancy spree. Their birthdays were only days apart, but where Sin was serious and steady minded, kind of like me, Struan was wilder. More like Burn.

A powerful ache hit me of missing the youngest of my brothers.

Struan tapped the bench. "This is why Sin wants to go straight. He's got his answers. He's content to let it go."

"I'm not," I said quickly.

"I'm fucking not either," Struan said, his tone dark.

"What keeps sticking in my mind," I said, "is that part where the lawyer said decisions needed to be made."

My brother caught on fast. "Implying that McInver can't make them and he doesn't have the authority."

"Exactly." My thoughts stewed. "The heir thing, the need for decision-making, the excitement, he's looking for someone to take over from McInver. Isn't he? Why else would he be so enthusiastic?"

For a long moment, Struan worked this through. "If Sin agreed to be the heir, he'd have the money he needs to officially take on Cassie."

"He won't do it. Without even asking, I know his answer. He's dead against McInver and his money. Think about what he just went through. He's probably traumatised."

"If you're asking do I want to do it, the answer is fuck no. That man abused my mother."

"He abused all of our mothers."

Struan choked out an unhappy laugh. "Besides that, McInver chose Sin. Ye told me yourself how impressed he was with his tall, strong son. We don't get to opt in to his murky-as-fuck world."

That scene had stuck in my mind. McInver made that claim at the same point he rejected me for being broken and scarred.

Something else said that night broke through my thoughts. I nudged Struan.

"Augustus Stewart told us Charterman wasn't dead when the islanders pulled him from the water. He finished the job himself. You're not a killer."

Struan's mouth opened, then he swore softly and looked away. "I need to tell Thea."

He stood but paused, still facing me. "If you're thinking of becoming McInver's heir, think again."

"For fuck's sake. I wasn't considering it, just working through the option."

"Good. Because no amount of money is worth ignoring all the ways he screwed over everyone he knew."

I snorted agreement, relieved to know he felt the same. "We'll find ways between us. None of us need shite from him."

The front door opened, and Sin walked out, shock in his eyes. "Gordain's on his way to see us. He has news."

"About what?" I jumped up.

It had to be the police.

We needed to get out of here.

"Of Burn," Sin answered. "He thinks our brother's in

jail."

7

Burn

A clang came from outside my cell, and I counted in my head, the pace of the police station becoming regular to me after days and nights locked up.

Six...seven...eight.

On cue, the little shutter on my door slid aside, and a pair of eyes peeked in.

Propped up on one elbow, I waved. "Hey, Charmaine."

"It's Officer Munter," the woman grumped, performing her sweep of the room.

Not that there was anything in here to check other than me. A dirty metal toilet, a sink, the bolted-down bed. There was no window in my cell, nor any other inmates nearby to talk to, so I figured they were low on prisoners to torment.

"If ye say so." I grinned at her. "Any sign of that charge sheet yet? Or a lawyer?"

"Ye know what you've got to do, Jamieson."

I gave a baffled shrug. "Oh look, it's not just me getting names wrong. Who is this Jamieson, and why do ye think

I'm him?"

Her gaze deadened in disdain, and she slid the shutter closed with a metallic rasp.

"I'll be waiting when you're ready to let me go," I called cheerfully after her, then continued counting until her footsteps faded.

Once I knew she was clear, my bravado slipped. I'd been avoiding this for a long time. *Jamieson* had an outstanding warrant. *Jamieson* had committed worse crimes than simply setting fire to a building.

Jamieson was a murderer.

If they could prove that I was him, which was pretty fucking likely because…I was, then I wouldn't see real daylight for a long time.

I had to hope that there wasn't the evidence to back their claim. As things stood, I was so far only detained, not yet arrested. We'd long gone over the twenty-four hours they were allowed to hold me, and they hadn't said a word. I pictured them scrabbling to make a case against me.

All they had was me running through the woods near a burning building. The officer who'd taken me to the ground claimed I smelled of smoke. The whole fucking place smelled of smoke from the fire that devoured the mansion, so I knew that couldn't stand up in court. I didn't have matches or a lighter, as I'd ditched everything at the scene, and they couldn't prove a motive. Without knowing exactly who I was, they had nothing.

They knew it, and I knew it.

I slumped back into my thoughts. Since I'd been here, I'd wallowed in guilt and misery. It was my fault my family had lost the beach house we'd been staying at. I'd set a fire on the beach when Sin had told me not to. Drawn eyes our way.

I could only hope they'd found somewhere new to settle and that Cassie wasn't missing me too much.

But that paled to the one person who dominated my mind.

Summer.

Seeing her outside McInver's place on the arm of my brother had thrown me for a loop. It hadn't felt real. I'd demanded she explain herself, but the woman had stared at me like I was a stranger.

Not the boy she'd made a pact with years ago.

That hurt as much as being grabbed by the cops.

Summer, or whatever fake name she'd given to Scar, had been my living dream while I'd been on the prison island.

Obviously in that time she'd not thought about me. She'd moved on in a way I never could. Done things I thought impossible from when I'd known her.

It scalded me from the inside out. Scorched and burned up the obsession I'd had with the girl I'd talked to endlessly but never met. Not until the day she blanked me.

She'd given up our agreement, so I had to as well.

An hour passed before further footsteps sounded outside.

This time, my cell door opened.

"Oh good, breakfast," I sang, just to be annoying.

A hulking, miserable-looking cop entered—the second of the two who were the only ones to check on me. He'd been the arsehole that grabbed me at McInver's place.

He grimaced at me, a printout clutched in his hairy hand.

My broken heart skipped a beat. It was my mug shot, taken at age fifteen when I'd been at a foster care centre. Luckily for me, in three years, I'd changed a lot. Back then, I'd worn my hair buzzed short, like Sin did his. I'd been skinny, and small, too, my height coming in the two years after.

Now, I had long hair on top and the sides shaved. An angular face with defined cheekbones. A muscular frame from hard work. Nothing like the kid I used to be, at least I hoped not.

"Who's that?" I gestured at the paper without getting up.

"Ye, ye little shite."

I snapped out a laugh. "Is it in the cop etiquette book that you're allowed to talk to inmates like that?"

The big lump didn't break a smile.

I tried again. "Come on, cunt-stable, ye have to let me go. Your time was up days ago. Shit or get off the pot."

He raised his gaze to me again, some dangerous look in his eyes. "If you're not willing to talk, I'm in no rush. We have all the time in the world to process ye."

"Ye had twenty-four hours. It's only longer if ye think I murdered someone, and from what your friend said, all they accused me of is setting a fire while I was out for an innocent jog."

His lip curled in a sadistic grin. "That timer depends

on the date you're checked in. Maybe the chief decides we picked ye up this afternoon on patrol at the stately home ye burned down. Maybe it was tomorrow morning."

I stared at him, all of a sudden my control slipping.

They hadn't taken my fingerprints. Nothing to suggest I was in their system. With the limited number of people that came to my cell, was I being kept a secret? How could that be possible?

He raised a shoulder, anything but easy. "On top of that, the terrorism act gives us up to two weeks to hold ye here while we construct your charge."

Two weeks? My blood ran cold.

"That's bullshit. I'm no terrorist."

"Then give me your name."

I balled my hands into fists. "Ye can't just keep me here like that. People will be looking for me."

"They'll have to give a name to do that."

Fuck this guy. "Ye haven't even told me officially what ye suspect me of. What are my rights? Where's my lawyer?"

He took a second piece of paper from under the photo printout, dropped it on the floor, then turned to leave.

I snatched it up. "What's this?"

I wasn't about to tell him I couldn't read. I'd never admitted it in school or to any of the staff in foster care. They all just thought I was ignorant. But someone might've guessed. It could be on my rap sheet and the clincher to him deciding my fate.

The cop slammed the door and locked me in without another word.

I squinted at the meaningless squiggles, and panic set in.

My family had no idea where I was. I had zero ways of contacting them, and the cop was right—they wouldn't come here and ask for me by name.

There was no way of getting out.

I was well and truly fucked.

8

Breeze

Low on energy and at my wits' end, I pressed on the video phone doorbell outside my mother's flat.

It was an out-of-place piece of technology in one of the most notorious blocks of flats in Edinburgh's Leith district. No one called here unannounced, unless it was a drug raid or social workers.

Mum lived here with her boyfriend. Summer and I had stayed with them on and off when we were younger but more frequently were taken into care when Mum couldn't look after us.

Now, my sister rented a bedsit two floors up in the same grey tower block while I had a room in a shared flat in town.

My sister wasn't home, but Mum should be.

I pressed the bell again, holding my finger on it.

"Come on," I muttered, eyeing the dark hall where the overhead lights had failed and no one had been by to fix them.

We'd had a couple of text conversations since I'd been back, but from wanting to see me, she'd changed to avoiding me. I'd been busy searching for Summer and also trying to track down McInver's private hospital, but I'd had no luck with either. It had been at the back of my mind that I really needed to see my mum.

"Look what the cat dragged in. Hello, Summer," Jack's voice came through the doorbell intercom.

I started, peering behind me. I was alone.

"It's Breeze," I muttered, my pulse racing from his slip-up. Dude had to be high. My sister and I hadn't been confused with each other since we were kids. "I need to talk to my mum."

"She isn't here."

Something in his voice sounded off. Shaky.

My heart dropped. "Where is she?"

He didn't reply.

I buzzed the bell again. "Jack. Where's Mum?"

"Christ alive, she's persistent," another voice came.

I cringed. It was one of Jack's friends, though I didn't know which.

"Come in, if ye want to smoke with us, or do us a favour and leave off that fucking bell. Choose, little whore," the friend said, following it up with a hacking laugh.

Another person answered him with a hyena cackle, followed by Jack choking on his own mirth.

I gritted my teeth and ignored the party of idiots. "I'll go if you tell me where my mother is."

"She's working," Jack returned. "Wait, have ye got any

money?"

"No."

"Then piss off. Call back in an hour."

I caught the tremor in his voice that time. He had the shakes. If Jack was withdrawing, he was using the hard stuff again, which meant Mum would be, too.

I knew exactly what kind of work she was out doing.

"Argh." I thumped the door with my fist and stormed away, trying to not feel the tear inside.

My sister and I both gave her money so she didn't have to walk the streets. We helped her stay off the drugs. Encouraged her in every way. But everything had fallen apart since my sister's disappearance, and now I knew why Mum was so chill about it.

She was self-medicating.

I should've gone to her sooner.

Just like Summer deserved my help in finding her, Mum deserved my loyalty in forgiving her each time she fell. She'd suffered more in her life than most people could survive. From the age of thirteen, she'd lived through hell. The world owed her an easy ride.

That couldn't stop my hurt from growing as I stomped upstairs in the block.

Two floors up, I used my key and let myself into Summer's place.

Brushing my fingers over furniture, I wandered around my sister's bedsit, scanning aimlessly for a clue. Anything. No one had been here in weeks, aside from me.

Here, we used to spend countless hours together.

Watched films on borrowed Netflix accounts. Made agreements to never sleep with anyone we didn't love.

Pain and desperation built inside me, and I sat heavily on her bed. I missed her so much. Could she be dead? The thought was impossible to bear.

I'd searched the tiny flat multiple times for anything that could give a hint on my sister's disappearance, but there was nothing. All I knew was what Mum had told me. My sister's last act that had given me my only place to look.

The route that had led me to sell myself to McInver.

As I'd done more often than I could admit, I opened my text app and stared at the messages from Scar.

Another had come in last night, and I had to fight myself not to reply.

Scar: I don't care about the car. I know you're seeing these because it taunts me that I've been left on read. I just need to know you're okay.

Unfamiliar emotion rocked me, and I lay back on Summer's quilt.

He had the knack of making me feel like this. Somehow different. Not so alone in the world.

If he knew where I was, he'd probably be bossy with me. Try to help. He'd get in the way, too.

My phone whooshed, another text landing.

Scar: What's up with all the dick pics on Struan's phone? He found a dating app website open with your picture on it and loads of dick sent to guys.

Ohmigod.

My heart pounded, and I cursed myself for not closing

that down and deleting the history. It had all happened so fast.

Before I could stop myself, I tapped out a reply.

Breeze: Careful, or you might find a dick flood on its way to you.

Instantly, the dots showed me he was typing back.

Scar: Jesus fuck. You're alive, then.

Why did I like it so much that he cared?

Breeze: To be fair, the men we sent dicks to started it. We only ever reciprocated.

Scar: So it's a game?

Breeze: Exactly. They send an unasked-for pic. We reply: 'What's wrong with it? Ohh, wait, my ex had that problem.' Then they get the flood. It's pretty hilarious.

We were talking. I wanted him to say more. Anything to distract me from my life.

Scar: Bonding time for you and your sister.

I stared at the words. As if he knew he'd stumbled into unacceptable territory, he sent a fast follow-up.

Scar: Some of those dicks are fucking weird.

Breeze: You have no idea. We used to rank them from bad to worse.

Scar: Getting a little worried in my masculine pride here.

He had nothing to worry about with his pretty dick. I gave a surprised laugh then jumped up from the bed, trying to get my mind off his penis. It was none of my business and better forgotten.

Out the window, I gazed down on the dank street below the tower block.

A woman rounded the corner. My mother.

Messages forgotten, I flew into action, needing to catch her without her joining Jack's little party.

On my way out the door, I snatched Summer's long cardigan from a hook. I'd barely been home in days, and tonight was cooler.

The cardigan had weight to it.

I pulled a phone from the deep pocket.

"Oh fuck," I whispered, locking up and sprinting down the stairs, half on autopilot.

My sister's phone had been switched off for weeks. I figured she'd lost it as I'd hunted for it endlessly, but no. It had been there the whole time.

At the exit to the tower block, I pressed the button to start the phone up. It remained dark. Out of power. Later, I'd charge it, but now, I needed to have this conversation.

The Ford I'd stolen was parked by the side of the road, so I perched on the bonnet, watching Mum's slow progress down the long road. I'd got here a lot faster than her.

"Mum," I called when she was close enough.

She spun around. Her eyes widened. "Breeze? What are you doing here? Jack said Summer came around."

"He made a mistake. It's just me."

She deflated, like I had at Jack's error.

For an attention-stealing moment, I got stuck on an idea.

No one could confuse Summer and me. Not unless they were fucked in the head, like Jack, or if they'd only seen a picture of us from the neck up. Scar had asked how his brother recognised me outside the mansion, and at the time, I'd assumed it was a mistake. I'd never seen him before in my life.

Likewise, he'd assumed the dating app pic was me.

What if my sister had met Burn online and not in person?

My mother tottered closer, and my stomach rolled.

"Where have you been?" I asked.

She fluttered her hands over her tight, hot-pink top and strip of a skirt that left nothing to the imagination. Bruises decorated her arms, and her skin had a yellowish tone.

"I had no choice," she mumbled. "Don't come at me."

Hurt rose in a hot wave. When I'd sold myself to McInver, it had been with the intention of finding my sister. But the money had been put to good use, too. Mum and her boyfriend had racked up debts to a drug dealer. The entire amount had been paid off by my ordeal.

She'd promised with all her heart never to go back. Cried over it. But the only reason she'd be selling herself now…

Mum sucked in a breath. "Police," she hissed.

Sure enough, a patrol car eased down the street. I swallowed and stepped away from the Ford, linking my arm through my mother's as if we were out for an unlikely evening stroll.

"Is that car hot?" she whispered.

I clutched her bony arm. "Yep."

I shouldn't have been driving it. I should've abandoned it after I'd run from Scar, but it had come in useful. I kept walking, Mum keeping pace.

"Explain," I demanded in a low tone.

"I owe money again," she confessed. "More, this time."

"How is that possible?"

"Jackie and me... We had a plan. We were going to sell. We would have made so much from it."

I closed my eyes, letting my mother guide me across the road, not daring to peek back at the patrol car.

Jack had struck again. He had any number of great moneymaking ideas that never paid off. He and his friends would sit together and boast about their criminal undertakings, each trying to outdo the others. It was the backdrop to several years of my childhood and probably the reason I liked to lose myself in a book. It had been my escape from listening to them.

"So let me get this right. Jack decided to become a dealer, took delivery of a ton of drugs, and then what happened to it all?"

Mum didn't answer. She didn't need to.

They'd partied. Used the lot with their friends.

"Is there anything left?"

"No. He was shaking tonight, and we only had weed. I had to go out."

Both were using again. Both would get sick if they went without their drugs for too long.

"I'm sorry," Mum started. "I didn't want to."

I ran my hand down to hers and squeezed her fingers, trying to stop myself from crying. "I wish you hadn't."

"Me, too, baby."

Except she couldn't. She'd tried over and over, but her past, her current trauma, or her shitty boyfriend always tripped her up.

"How much do you owe?"

Mum's gaze sank to the floor. "A lot. The dealer's a nasty one. He already came around a few times."

God. A fresh resolution settled in me. I could never walk away from my mother. Never abandon her to the hell she'd made for herself. As long as I lived, I'd do whatever it took to help her. She and Summer were all I had.

Which made my next decision easy.

I flicked my gaze back up the road where the police car sat adjacent to the Ford. Looked like that was lost now, too.

"Listen. If I help you this time, you need to leave Jack. Kick him out of your flat. I know you love him, but you're never going to get better if he stays. Every time you make progress, he drags you back."

I'd never asked her directly to end her relationship, but it had reached the point of no return.

In her tight clothes and smudged lipstick, Mum ducked her head. "You're right. When Summer gets back, everything will be okay. I'll get better for my girls, I promise."

I gave her hand one final squeeze, then released her, walking away.

"Where are you going?" she called after me.

I didn't reply. She was messed up, and Summer wasn't coming back without help. For their sakes, I had a bus to catch back into central Edinburgh and my fate to seal once again.

*A*cross a meticulously tidy desk, Vanessa, Baby Girl's manager, narrowed her eyes at me. "What the fuck happened?"

It was here, over a week ago, that I'd run in desperation, searching for my sister. Summer had come into this place, too, a nightclub with hidden services. Had the same conversation I did. It was hard to believe, considering our background, that she'd sell herself to the highest bidder, but the facts were plain. She'd told Mum her plan in a short, infuriating note.

It was the last anyone had heard of her.

I mangled my fingers together. "I did everything I was asked to do."

"So where's my client?"

"It isn't my fault the old dog collapsed and his house burned down. He had people after him. I barely got away with my life."

Vanessa pushed her ass-length black hair extensions behind her ear, the beads tied in the ends clacking. Her lips pursed. "Watch your mouth. He was one of my best paying customers. Now look at him."

"It's not like I rode him into a coma. He didn't even get it up."

She rolled her gaze up and down me, her green contact lenses alarming. She styled herself like Catwoman, which worked for a woman who ran a cat house.

"Are you saying he didn't fuck you at all?"

He'd pawed at my body. Stuck his finger in me. But that

wasn't what she was asking.

"Nope."

Her look intensified, her Northern English accent getting stronger too. "You're here because you want a second go."

"I need the money."

"Why should I let you? I'm a client down. You had one job and you failed." She jabbed a sharp finger at me. "You were supposed to uphold my reputation. Instead, you hospitalised a respectable man."

"That was nothing to do with me," I argued.

I had to persuade her. Vanessa and her club had the access I needed.

My mother had worked at Baby Girl for a short stint. I remembered coming to this place when I was young and thinking it amazing.

It didn't take many more years to see through the glossy exterior and closed doors. It was a nightclub on its legal side, a strip club in a grey area of Scottish law, and an exclusive vendor of women's bodies on the very much illegal side. Prostitution wasn't against the law, but pimping was. Vanessa was very choosy over who she took on, and she only catered for a subset of very well-off men.

Like McInver.

Like whoever bought Summer.

In a twisted way, I was lucky she'd accepted me as a commodity. Vanessa didn't trust lightly. Ironically, it was Mum's name that got my face in the door.

Anxiety swarmed in my stomach, but I'd done this once and I could do it again. "I want you to put me up for auction to the same group of men. Explain to them that my first buyer didn't have the cash. The next one gets a needy girl."

The hostility in her simmered, and she ogled me for a long moment. Then she tapped her lip. "We could sell that. Show your disappointment at how Daddy didn't want to play. Really up the pity angle in how desperate you are to have some gold-plated dick tear you up on that precious first time."

My stomach clenched, but I nodded with fake enthusiasm.

She hummed, warming to the idea, then picked up her phone and tapped out a message. "Okay, I'll bite. You have that innocent prissy little missy thing going on that I know some of my buyers snap up. Let's see if we can find you someone a little more vigorous with that sob story. After that, you can go onto my books, but you won't earn anything like the same, understand? These sweet virgin deals are special."

"I understand." I'd already asked about Summer once but I had to try again. "When my sister came here..."

"Hmm?" She raised her eyebrows but didn't look up from her screen.

"What happened at her auction?"

"Can't discuss business, you know how is."

"But the buyer picked her up, right? She went through with it?"

"I already told you that. Are you after some kind of guarantee? I don't take lightly to criticism of my establishment."

"She hasn't come back." I tried to hide the wobble in my voice.

This got me her full attention.

Vanessa set down her phone and folded her arms. "What of it? The client buys a package deal. It's up to him and the girl if they extend it. It happens all the time."

It was over three weeks now. Three weeks of not hearing from her, of zero sightings and radio silence.

"I'm worried about her. Can you just make a call?"

"No."

"Can you at least tell me the client's name so I can check in on her?"

"Out of the question. Are we going to have a problem here?" Suspicion played out in her tone.

I was facing the same brick wall I'd hit before. No one here would speak. My only option had been to go into the system that had swallowed my sister. Infiltrate it, with the unfortunate loss of my virginity along the way, and get to know at least one of the men. Then I could ask my questions directly to him and persuade him to pass me around.

Or, I could walk away and hope Summer returned all by herself. But the chances of that were getting slimmer by the day. She'd gone into this for reasons I couldn't even begin to understand, and I had to see it through for her sake.

There was no way in hell she'd done it for the money—I knew Mum hadn't mentioned her debt to anyone but me, which meant Summer was in trouble.

I felt it deep down, the sister connection powerful, just like Lottie had said that time in their mountainside cabin.

"No problem." I swallowed every bit of my resistance

and offered a meek smile.

Vanessa grumbled but lifted her phone and took a shot.

Moments later, a tap came at the door, then a half-naked exotic dancer peered inside. Her nipple tassels jiggled as she moved, and her hair fell in bold red twists around her face. "What's up, boss?"

Vanessa beckoned the dancer into the room. "Divine, Breeze needs some advice." She gestured between the dancer and me. "She's going to audition for the List."

The List.

That had to be her exclusive, rich client base.

I hadn't heard the term before and squirrelled it away, along with the fact that this dancer was in on it somehow.

Then her first words took shape in my mind. "What do you mean audition?"

The door opened again, and one of the bouncers from downstairs entered.

Vanessa gestured to a two-seater couch across the room. "Neville, sit on the sofa and keep your hands to yourself. It's your lucky day."

She took hold of a small tripod, fixing her phone into the frame, then angled it at the couch where the bouncer sat, his hands on his knees and sweat breaking out on his brow. Then she took headphones from a drawer, pressed something on her computer that made music blare from them, and handed them to him. "Don't take them off."

He obeyed, flinching at the loudness of the music but otherwise sitting still.

"Already once, you've been through my hands," the boss said to me. "You were face to crotch with a generous and respectable client, but from what I can see, only let him down. Divine is going to train you in how to please a man. If you do well, I'll book you in again. If you fail, bye, bye."

I took in a rushed breath.

Before I could speak, Vanessa held up her hand. "I have a reputation to protect. It is not enough to be nineteen and intact. You're going to work for your money this time. You only made the cut before because I was low on numbers and needed a body that evening. Now, I can be pickier. Sit next to Neville and pay attention to Divine's demonstration. Be grateful for the opportunity or you can see yourself out."

I switched seats, cringing to keep an inch of space between myself and the hulking bouncer. Divine drifted closer, brushing her fingertips over Neville's knee. His gaze locked on her round tits, and his trousers tented.

Ugh.

I wasn't worried about seeing other people screw, no matter my inexperience, but I hadn't expected to audition. I'd been prepared to lie back and let some buyer fuck me seven ways from Sunday, but not to perform. Definitely not in a room with other people watching and a camera on me.

My mind shot back to my encounter with Scar on the sofa in his cabin. Back then, I'd wished for this level of experience so I could seduce him. Now, all I felt was horror at what I'd done.

He was decent. Kind.

I hadn't been able to stop thinking about him.

Right now, I needed him far from my mind.

Divine kept her gaze on Neville, but her words in a gentle English accent were for me. "The customer is never wrong in what he says or does, so long as he pays for it. Always agree on the terms upfront, including the charge for anything above. Know exactly what you've been paid for and what you can demand as extras. Those little bonuses can really add up, sis. Believe me, these men will pay. What we earn is chump change to them."

She stepped away from the couch, a couple of feet in front of me and Neville. Her movements were different now she was on display. Sinuous. Purposeful.

She set her hands on her tight waist, her fingertips grazing her skin.

"Never let them see you powder your nose, if you know what I mean." One manicured finger tapped her inner arm. "Don't shoot up anywhere visible. Any mark on you and Vanessa will sack you on the spot."

"Damn right I will," Vanessa muttered.

"I don't take drugs," I spluttered, but no one cared.

Divine continued, grazing her hands up her body and into her red hair, pulling it back to drop it again in a wealth of bouncing curls. "They're paying for a show. Even if it's just you and them, they expect you to know what you're doing, at least in following orders. If they tell you to bark like a dog, get your yap on. If they want you scared, whimper at every touch and produce a tear, just be sure you keep up the illusion that every minute of it is getting you wet."

Beside me, Neville adjusted his crotch, his hairy arm pressing against mine.

"They will lead, but you can do your bit to help the seduction. One, the purposeful look at first sight. Think of this as a triangle. Glance at their left eye, then down to their mouth, then back up to the other eye. Just a couple of seconds, give them a small smile, then look away. It's simple, but it has them hooked and shows them you're interested."

As she spoke, she drifted her gaze over the bouncer's features. He swallowed.

"Second is in the way you move. Every action should be graceful and designed to show off what you've got. Can you dance?"

I grimaced. "Not like I imagine you can."

"It's easy. Stand next to me." She directed my gaze to her feet. "Heels flat to the floor, bend your knees a little, then wind a figure eight with your hips."

Divine acted out her description. In turn, her hips rose and fell in small circles, showcasing her long legs and drawing attention to her bare belly and below to the centre of the movements. Crazy sexy and almost hypnotising.

The whole time, she held Neville's gaze, and heat rolled off him.

I clumsily copied the move. "That is not easy. You're super skilled."

"You're so sweet. They won't care so long as the intent is clear. Now, men blow their load easily," Divine said with a snort of a laugh from Vanessa. "They want value for their money and will lose interest the second they come, which means delaying that as long as you can. Play the game. Make sure they know it is inevitable, and that you're dying for it, but draw it out. Watch for their signs, and work those hard, so by the time your mouth is around their dick, they've already had a good time. Ninety-nine percent of the time, they'll wear a condom to go inside, but some will pay more to bareback you. Make sure to take Plan B after. Don't assume they'll pay maintenance for their brat. It's a small group, and they're in with the family court judges—"

"Enough of that. Move on," Vanessa snapped.

Divine jerked her head in a nod, wincing like she realised she'd said too much. "How are your blow job skills?"

Cold clamped hold of my belly. I thought myself immune to this, but I'd been wrong. "I don't have any," I said, then instantly regretted it.

Divine spared a glance for the clock on the wall. "I need to be on stage in the peep show rooms soon, so we're going to need to speed things up a bit." She gestured to Neville.

The man snapped forwards, his t-shirt damp with sweat down his chest and under his armpits. He whined, his gaze fixed on her tits.

From her desk, Vanessa pointed at me. "On your knees, pretty girl."

I had to do this? Every part of me revolted.

I didn't want this. Not at all.

But I was trapped.

The boss tutted. "Hurry it up."

The thought of touching the sweaty bouncer horrified me. Even though I'd forced myself on Scar, his dick in my mouth had been strange but not bad. I hadn't felt revulsion, more determination to get him hot, followed by guilt over him not wanting me.

Why couldn't I do this now?

I couldn't perform sexual favours for strangers.

Yet I had to.

Panic rinsed over me, icy and directing me to run. My heart sped, and a sour taste flooded my mouth.

Neville wrestled with his trouser button, and Divine tutted, placing a finger on his to pause his movements, mouthing, "Let us."

The two women and the sweaty bouncer all waited on me to get on my knees for him, pressure growing with every second.

If I wanted to see my sister again, I had to follow her into this hell.

I perched on the edge of the couch.

With shaking fingers, I reached out and popped his button.

Neville whimpered and finished the job, sliding his zip down. He freed his dick, purple and stunted. I recoiled.

This was over. I'd failed.

I couldn't touch him.

He shifted faster than I could process. In a burst of movement, he snapped out a hand and grabbed Divine. "Take her top off. Press your nipples into hers until they're hard then suck her tits. I want girl on girl. Your tongue in her cunt. Then you can both have my fat cock."

He pawed at her then dragged her towards me. I caught her before she fell.

Divine steadied herself on me, her eyes wide in shock.

Neville yanked off his headphones. "Come on, bitch. You heard me." He snatched at her again, this time clutching her between her legs.

I pulled her behind me and backed us to the wall.

Vanessa drew herself up, her expression pure anger. "You did not just go there, you fucking moron. Get up."

In a flash, the atmosphere changed from Divine's sexy setup to utterly hostile.

"Seriously?" Neville swung his gaze from Divine's chest to the boss.

"Yes, seriously. At what point did you think you had any control here?"

"Because... I mean, she's just a whore. What does it matter?" He swiped his fingers through his hair, his hands shaking as realisation set in.

He'd fucked up.

His unimpressive erection wilted.

Vanessa's rage grew. She rounded her desk, her black hair whipping with her move. "All you had to do was keep your mouth shut. You never, ever grab one of my girls like that."

"She was touching me. It was a lesson, right?"

"How the fuck did that turn into the Neville show?"

"Shit. I just wanted to help the kid." He pointed at me.

"And you lost yourself your job."

Neville stared at Vanessa. "You can't be serious."

She angled her head at him, a viper about to strike. "I'm going to say this once so your single brain cell has a chance to understand. You're fired. Get out."

His face flushed as purple as his dick, but he stuffed himself back into his jeans and stomped to the door.

I watched him go with a mix of relief and wonder. Vanessa left the room presumably to see him off the premises.

Divine gently moved me out the way from where I was still blocking her. She rubbed her arm where Neville's fingers had left faint red marks. "I don't think anyone has ever stood up for me before."

"Vanessa is fierce," I replied.

"I meant you, babe. I've had doormen order punters off me but never anyone get in between." She peered at the clock again. "I really do have to go get on stage, but if you ever need help or advice, come find me sometime."

She went to leave, but I stalled her with a hand out.

"Wait. Did you ever meet my sister? Her name's Summer, and she looks like me, at least in the face."

She paused, her red lips open, then shook her head. "Sorry, I don't think so."

"Can you tell me the names of the men on the List?" I added fast.

Divine slapped her fingers to my lips. "Hush or Vanessa will hear. Every girl who goes into this signs an agreement not to talk, me included. If you're afraid, don't do it. If you're tough, you'll be fine. See you on the flip side, honey."

9

Camden

Night had long fallen as we pulled up to the dock, the sea inky black against a darker sky. Sin and Lottie climbed out of the car, and I joined them, taking a long inhale of sea air. Tonight, they were heading back to Torlum.

Now we knew where Burn was, in a police station awaiting charges, according to Gordain's contact, we didn't need a widespread search for him anymore.

In theory, I could go with them.

I glanced back to the road that headed out of the deserted car park and down through the Isle of Skye. But Burn wasn't the only person missing in action.

I had somewhere else to be, and a plan my brothers wouldn't like, but it was my turn to step up. Sin and Struan both had girlfriends. I was the lone wolf who could sacrifice himself without hurting anyone.

My brother took a rucksack from the back of the car, then slammed the door. Before they left, I had something to share with him. A worry that had been brewing in my mind.

"Keep's grave is bothering me," I told him.

Sin's eyebrows furrowed, just visible in the faint light. Then he lifted his chin, realisation clear. "Because Breeze stole her car."

We'd buried Keep, our prison keeper who I'd murdered, in the grounds of the youth hostel where we'd been locked away. We already knew the police had been out there, as the address had been used as Cassie's original foster care home. They'd found nothing, which suggested we'd done a good job in concealing the site. Then we'd been driving around in her car ever since. It had been a problem Breeze had taken off our hands.

"If ye want to go straight," I told him, "that dead body in a hole in the ground is a risk."

Slowly, he nodded. "If the cops picked up Breeze in the Ford, what's to stop her talking about us?"

I'd already considered and rejected the idea. Instinctively, I knew she wouldn't give us up. Besides, we were working on the assumption that the police had nothing on us now. From what we could tell, there were no outstanding murder warrants, no dead bodies waiting for identification. Struan had walked out of hospital without question. Gordain had kept an ear out and heard nothing about the rest of us. Which left Keep's grave as our only smoking gun.

"Breeze won't say anything," I decided. "But they could take a second look at the hostel, and there's a chain of evidence leading to us from that grave."

My brother and his girlfriend swapped dubious expressions, but time was running out. They needed to get on a boat and over to Torlum under cover of night if they were to help Lottie's ma.

"I'll check it out," Sin confirmed.

He and Lottie set off down the slope to the water's edge where the smaller boats were moored.

I got back into Thea's car and started my next trip.

In the morning, I was meeting McInver's lawyer. If Gordain was right, and our brother was in a jail cell somewhere, presumably they'd charge him with arson. Which meant McInver would be entitled to an update. Gordain couldn't find out anything about Burn, so we knew our brother wasn't talking, but the cops would respond to a request from a wealthy homeowner.

Or someone asking on his behalf. Say, a son.

I had no idea if my plan would work, but I was going to do it anyway.

In a few hours, I'd made the drive from Skye to Inverness.

It wasn't a city I knew well, as I'd grown up in Stirling, far to the south, but it was where I needed to be, come morning.

In the city centre, I parked up and found my phone.

Since our short text conversation, and before, I'd been unable to stop picturing Breeze tied up in McInver's house. Her determination to sell herself. The fight we'd had about it.

From my pocket, I extracted the envelope with her number scrawled on the back, something I kept with me as if it was a connection to her. On the back was the stamp of whoever had written to McInver. It had been torn, so only the second part was visible.

...ick Manor.

'Ick' seemed right, and appropriately named if they were friends with the old man.

Putting away the paper, I wrote out a new message to Breeze.

Scar: I'm in Inverness. Are you here?

The likelihood was slim, but she'd stopped responding to me, so it was all I had.

No response. The message didn't show as read.

Scar: Tell me you're okay. That you're safe.

I stared out at the passing cars and busy road. I didn't think she'd be on the streets, but I found myself looking all the same.

I drove through the wide shopping streets, eyes open for working women.

I might not have known Inverness, but I knew prostitution. Ma had worked in a number of different saunas. She'd also had a list of men who would come to our flat for her services, usually during the day when I was at school, but not always. She relied on the money so couldn't afford to hide it from me completely.

A darker haze came over my mind. Memories that I tried hard to repress but that wouldn't die.

Ma with men in our flat.

The one who'd grabbed me, knife in his hand.

The one whose voice gave me nightmares.

Down the road, an older model silver BMW pulled over. A woman emerged from the shadows. She leaned down to talk to the driver through the open window, hesitated, glanced up and down the road, then climbed in.

It wasn't Breeze, nor anything like my long-dead mother. But all my muscles locked.

The car drove away, and I heaved a shuddering breath and took off after it. The single biggest problem I had with this type of work was the danger the women had to put themselves in to earn a wage. The lass I'd caught a glimpse of barely had time to check out her buyer before getting into a vehicle with him.

She could be killed. Raped and dumped somewhere.

My pulse picked up, and anger flooded me in a hot rush.

It happened more often than people knew. My mother and her friends had any number of horror stories, none of which were reported by any official channels. They weren't included in any statistics but shared between the women so they knew what car or man to avoid. What dangers there were.

Nobody gave a fuck about a brutalised prostitute, unless she was actually murdered and the police had a situation on their hands.

I tailed the BMW through the city to a more isolated stretch where low-rise warehouses sat in wide yards along a quiet road. The John pulled up in a dark corner, and I drove past, my knuckles white where I gripped the steering wheel hard.

It wasn't Breeze. It wasn't Ma. But I couldn't stop the panic in me.

I left the car farther down the road and padded back on foot. There were a couple of lorries parked outside the warehouse, so I concealed myself behind one then inched along until the BMW was in view across the open space.

Despite the darkness, I could see movement. A head bobbing up and down.

Like some kind of fucking creep, I stood frozen to the gravel, waiting for the woman to finish blowing the dirty arsehole who'd picked her up.

I had no idea what the fuck I was doing here. There would be dozens of women out there tonight, working. Some of whom might talk to me. Instead, I was playing bodyguard to a woman who hadn't asked for it.

More memories pushed at the back of my mind.

Dark, tormenting scenes. Of bruised arms and bleeding lips. The acute and unmistakable smell of the drugs my mother smoked or injected. The hatred I had for the men who came to our door.

Ones who joked about being my da.

Again, the one who reached for me without me seeing his face.

I gritted my teeth and forced myself to breathe through my nose. Back when we'd been imprisoned on Torlum, Sin had encouraged us to talk about our past. His mother had been no angel. That didn't change the fact he'd loved her. Same as I'd loved mine.

Even after all she'd let happen to me.

Abruptly, one of the BMW's doors opened, snapping me out of my tortured reminiscence. The woman half fell out, the man's hand across the car, shoving her. I straightened, eyes glued to the scene.

The man muttered something low and sneering, and the woman shuffled back, her body language wary.

If he attacked her, I'd be over there in a shot, laying into him with my fists. I'd use up the angst in me and take out my emotions on the bastard's face. Beating him to a pulp would help right now.

But instead, he tossed a few notes out to flutter at her feet, yanked the door closed, then hit the accelerator. Spitting gravel, he shot out of the car park and was gone.

The woman crouched and snatched up the cash, stuffing it into her bra. From a small bag, she fished out a bottle of water, rinsed her mouth and spat on the gravel, then walked away.

They hadn't driven far from the bright lights of the city streets, but I still returned to my car and drove past a couple of times, making sure she got back to safety.

I couldn't bring myself to talk to her. I couldn't find the words to ask if she'd heard the name Breeze. Met a lass with blonde curls to her chin. Attitude and pretty eyes.

Instead, I found a quiet place to sit in the car and get lost in my turmoil.

My plan to hunt down Breeze was fucked. Some part of me had snapped at seeing even the slightest hint of my childhood trauma.

Even more, I despised Breeze's choices.

If I knew where she was, I would do anything and everything to stop her entering into this life and drowning in its wastes.

*L*ying across the back seats of the car and waiting on morning, I sketched a new tattoo outline. A woman's face, with curls that framed her perfect features. After the meeting, I would drive home and set to work with my tattoo kit. Struan wanted more done on him, but I had the strongest compulsion to add to my own ink as well.

But business came first.

I had an eight AM appointment with McInver's lawyer, so I left the car and walked to Queensgate, finding a fancy building with a polished brass plaque outside, identifying Mr Golding's legal and estate management practice.

When I'd been little, my grandparents had used a lawyer to obtain rights over me. Ma had died, and the only other option was the foster care I'd eventually end up in anyway. I'd sat in an office like the one I stood in front of now, stating my name and not knowing what the fuck was going on.

I wouldn't be so intimidated this time.

I grasped the handle of the door, but it wouldn't budge. I rattled it, and a second later, a man scuttled down the hall beyond.

He flung the door open, the same slim, grey-haired, slightly scatty-looking Englishman I'd met at the mansion.

"So sorry," he uttered. "The office is not officially open for another hour, hence the door being locked. Come in, come in, please."

He ushered me inside.

"I'm honoured," I murmured.

"No! It is I who is the honoured one. I can't tell you how grateful I am that you called me. I was having kittens waiting. Forgive me, I say too much. This is just wonderful."

He led me up a flight of stairs and to an office.

"Take a seat. There's coffee, water, and biscuits here on the tray. Did you travel far this morning?"

I wasn't under any illusion that I could con this man. McInver had wanted Sinclair, not me. No matter that we were both his sons.

I knew if I told my brothers of this plan, Sin would have felt obliged to step in. He'd done enough for our family. It was my turn to take the reins.

The lawyer took his seat and waited expectantly for my answer, his eyes bright and his smile warm.

I took a breath. "Listen, I have no doubts over McInver being my da, but what I'm not clear about is your role and what ye want from me."

The man dipped his head. "Of course, of course. As you know, your father suffered a sudden illness, no doubt the result of the shock that struck him when his glorious home was set on fire."

I sat taller, questions at the ready.

The lawyer rattled on. "I spoke to Mr McInver's doctors yesterday, and he is still yet to wake. Most distressing. Which only adds to my utter delight in discovering you at the house. Your father spoke to me with great enthusiasm after discovering your existence. He had plans to make you his heir and instructed me in advancing those."

The crunch point. I gestured to myself. "Me, Camden?"

"Indeed. As fine a son as he could wish for. He mentioned how tall you were and how much you look like him. I can see it so clearly."

He meant Sin. I was over six foot, but my brother was a beast.

But the old fucker clearly hadn't told his lawyer my name.

Relief built inside me, with urgency to use this mistake. "Can ye tell me what the police are doing about the fire? Did they catch anyone?"

"I'm afraid I cannot discuss any concerns of a legal nature yet," the lawyer said. "There are procedures to adhere to before I can be explicit with you on confidential matters. First, I will need to prove beyond doubt that you are kin to Mr McInver. I have organised for a blood test to be taken this morning, which your father had already sanctioned. We will know the result within a few days. I assume this will be acceptable?"

The test wouldn't be a problem, unless there had been a huge mistake, but waiting days before I could get any answers piled on the frustration.

I grunted agreement. "Fine. Then what happens?"

The lawyer sighed deeply. "Your father had very specific instructions on the treatment of his heir. Once the blood test is back, I will be able to explain exactly what that entails. Rest assured, it will be all you deserve and more."

A buzz sounded in the hall outside, and he stood. "That will be them now. I'll be right back. This won't take a moment."

He left, and I slumped back in my seat.

For Burn's sake, I needed to get this information. To have the power to help him.

But in this fancy building, with an expensive lawyer urging me with smiles to jump through hoops, it also felt very much like a trap.

I left the lawyer's office and returned to my car. I'd done all I could do in that respect and now just had to wait.

I checked my phone. Lottie had messaged to say they were with her mother and all was well. Struan had also sent a text saying that Thea was trying everything to locate which police station had Burn.

I sat in my car and stared at the city streets.

I couldn't return home. Not right away. I was still buzzing with emotion. Not just from submitting to McInver's tests but also because of Breeze. I was a mess, and at the very heart of the fucked-up centre of my life was the man who'd used my mother to make me.

Without plan or conscious decision, I drove to McInver's place.

This time, I didn't skulk through the woods. I was days away from proving I was the heir to his half-burned mansion and his life of degradation. Fuck him. This time, I drove right up to the entrance.

There were no other cars in the car park, and the same police tape fluttered where it hung from the front door.

I ducked under it and stepped into the hall.

When I'd been here before, I'd been looking for bodies. Murdered Augustus, who'd vanished, presumably at the hands of McInver's guards, and Burn, who I'd pictured succumbing to smoke inhalation.

Now, I was chasing ghosts. Just like the John in the BMW last night, McInver had used women without giving a damn what happened to them. My mother had been one of them. Breeze was the last.

"Hope ye choke, ye old fucker," I muttered at the house.

Ignoring the ruined side, I wandered the corridor back to McInver's office. The place must've been built in stages, because even though one part was rubble, this half felt sturdy. The phone line in his office had still worked. I flicked a switch on the wall, and the light illuminated over my head. The power wasn't even out.

Had to be what the lawyer was panicking over. He couldn't make any decisions on the place without a family member's approval. I was his backup plan.

I found the office again and entered. On McInver's desk, a pile of letters waited, with a row of smart-looking pens, and a heavy paperweight of a stag's head sat in the corner.

The same answerphone blinked, and I pressed the play button.

A new message from the hospital requested his representative contact them. Must've been before the lawyer rang.

Idly listening, I picked up a pile of folders left on the side cabinet, finding nothing of interest.

A second message began, a sultry female voice spilling into the room. "Honoured member of the List. Please be notified of the timing of tomorrow's auction."

I stopped moving and listened.

"Bidding will start at ten AM. Be prepared to fight for our sweetest of delights. This one will be made available immediately for our winner and has no restrictions. Think Marilyn Monroe with expert training. I'm sure you won't need tempting, but this product is untouched and primed for use, with desperate need to be owned by the right buyer after the last couldn't...fulfil their claim. Log in at the usual place for pictures and more, or dial in to make your bid."

The message ended, and I half fell to the phone and stabbed at the buttons until it played again. Nausea and surety gathered. Breeze had been auctioned a day or two before we met. McInver had only stopped himself from fucking her because he wanted to save her for his heir. This was how he'd bought her. And how she was calling herself unused.

It played again, and I registered every word.

The answerphone message had been sent yesterday, and it was eleven-thirty AM now. An hour and a half after the auction started.

With frozen fingers, I dialled Breeze's number from my phone. It hit her voicemail. Didn't even ring.

Devastation swept through me, and with a howl, I snatched up the stag paperweight from the desk and tossed it at the window, shattering the glass.

She'd sold herself again, and I was too late to do anything about it.

Or was I?

Despair wasn't my way of working.

I forced myself to calm and use my fucking brain. Then I picked up the phone and dialled the number from the answerphone message.

"Hello, sir," the same sultry voice purred. "I'm so glad you called. I noticed you hadn't bid on today's auction and really didn't want you to miss out."

My pulse slowed and, finally, I could be in with some luck

10

Breeze

Flat on my back on satin sheets, I laid out, a blindfold hiding the opulent hotel room from my eyes. I was entirely naked, and my hands and legs had been tied to the four corners of the bed.

In line with my buyer's request, I was completely shaved, silky smooth and bare from the eyelashes down.

Between my spread legs, a vibrator had been left.

Prepared and ready for the member of the List, whoever he was.

Vanessa had brought me here, but if the choice of venue was unusual, paid up for several days, too, she didn't say. Instead, she bundled my clothes into my bag and hid it in a drawer, then secured me in place. Before she left, I'd asked a single question: What happened if nobody came? My greater concern—what happened if they left me in a state?—wouldn't have been answered. She'd informed me that I was naïve to think that exclusive hotels were haughty. They knew full well what people with expensive tastes liked to do and were discreet if they found situations in their rooms.

Still, I had the feeling if I screamed, no one would run to help.

My skin crawled. I hated this. But it was the only way to get into the system that had absorbed my sister.

For her, I'd withstand anything.

A click came, and the hotel room door opened. Or I assumed so as I couldn't see. I hitched a breath, cooler air sliding over my body. Then the door closed and a lock engaged.

He was here.

A long pause followed while he looked me over. His gaze no doubt travelling over my breasts. Between my legs. At the vibrator that was waiting to be plunged into me. Would he do that before using his dick? Surely not. He'd want to make me bleed himself first.

Fresh bitterness flooded my mouth. Whoever this sick bastard was took pleasure in this. Commanding young women. Treating us like property. Whatever he did to me, I'd withstand. Vanessa had warned me to say yes to everything. The worst-case scenario was his displeasure. Being thrown out without answers.

Sensing the man moving closer, I held perfectly still.

For what felt like minutes, he said nothing. Did nothing. Yet I picked up the urgency of his breathing. He was wound up, same as me, so much it felt like anger radiating from him.

Finally, he spoke. "Anything?"

One word, so briefly spoken. I strained to detect anything other than a deep, Scottish accent. Maybe younger than expected? I couldn't be sure.

Almost desperately, I needed more words from him.

I hadn't cared at all before this moment, yet something surged in me.

"You've paid for that right," I whispered back. "What would you like to do?"

"Mark your skin," he snapped back.

I froze with my lips open, pulling the words apart. His voice was familiar. Painfully so. My mind was playing tricks on me.

It couldn't be who I thought it was. And he was waiting on my answer.

"Mark me however you want. I'm yours."

This had to be a kink thing. Hitting me with some kind of whip. Maybe drawing on me. I had no idea.

I sensed the man moving around the room, preparing something. Then his presence came closer again.

Buzzing filled the air.

The vibrator. My pulse sped.

A hand landed at the apex of my thighs. I jumped, unable to stop my reaction. His fingers spread my pussy lips, and a cool piece of material swiped me. I swallowed back a rush of emotion. This was exactly what I'd been expecting. To be played with. Fucked. It was weird to be cleaned first, but whatever. I could handle it.

Then something scratched at my skin, buzzing right on the inside of my left lower lip.

It stung. I stifled a gasp of pain.

My buyer kept up the action, drawing in a tightly controlled pattern.

In a rush, I realised what he was doing. Not the vibrator. Not a sex toy at all.

The bastard was tattooing my pussy.

Outrage filled me. I had to be wrong. Surely no permanent damage was allowed.

He worked quickly, ignoring how I'd stiffened. The scratching stopped, and he moved, then revealed my other lip to repeat the action.

This was fucked up. Wrong. And yet I couldn't bring myself to tell him to stop. I'd given him permission, and I was seeing it through, paralysed with mixed-up emotions.

The ache ebbed and flowed, never so much I couldn't stand it, but having a strange effect on me.

Once the shock eased, it... God. It made me wet. I was dripping from it, turned on by the pain.

This was so screwed up. So unexpected.

After another minute, the buzzing ceased.

Gaping silence filled the air. The man gently pressed at my pussy, I guessed cleaning up his work. Drying me, too. Then he moved away from the bed.

At the start of this, I'd expected some kind of sex act. But nothing about this had felt sexy on the buyer's side. His hands hadn't lingered on me for any second longer than it had taken to complete his task.

The feeling of overwhelm I was trying to hold back rolled through me, and I closed my eyes despite the blindfold. There was only one person I knew who did tattoos. One person who hated the game I was in. The actions I had to take.

Impossible.

It couldn't be him.

I opened my mouth to speak, but he beat me to it.

"No lotions. Keep it dry for a few days. It'll heal fast," he gritted out.

Too briefly, his hand touched mine, lightly gripping my fingers before sliding down to release one restraint.

The hotel room door clicked as if he'd unlocked it, then it slammed.

"Scar?" I croaked.

No reply came.

"Scar!" I yelled.

Tears welled, and I let them soak the blindfold and roll down my face.

He'd found out about my auction, bought me, then... What? Punished me? Punished himself? Fuck! It was too much. I'd lost my opportunity to question a buyer who might know about Summer. Yet for some reason, that wasn't the source of my tears. It was a whole other feeling I couldn't understand.

With a hand free, I could have released myself from the constraints. Looked at the stinging site of his work to see what he'd drawn. But the most I did was tear away the blindfold and stare in anger at the room.

All I could think about were the tiny signs Scar had given of his feelings.

How I'd let him mark me but he'd done it so gently. How he'd turned me on while trying to do the opposite.

It gave me a wake-up call of just how bad it could've been at the hands of someone who wanted my pain.

He'd left me in safety in the room, then walked away.
As long as I waited, he didn't come back.

11

Lottie

Forgiveness was a choice, only possible when old wounds had healed or when they needed to be patched over for sanity's sake. We'd been back on Torlum for three days now, and I desperately wanted to leave. Despite the fact I'd grown up here, and fallen for Sin here, the beautiful island only held unhappiness for me.

Every day I'd lived here had been under the shadow of my father's abuse, my mother's tolerance of his anger, and how he lashed out with his fists. Sin had been imprisoned here, and my father had been a party to that, too.

It was too raw. There was too much still unanswered. Every hour that passed on this land felt like we were barrelling towards an attack.

The need to forgive felt more of a burden than a decision.

My wounds were fresh. Sin's, too. My ability to move on meant not being exposed to it over and again, and that was the problem.

Moving Ma across the island to Thea's grandmother's echoing Victorian house had been relatively easy. If people had seen us, they'd minded their own business.

I'd scrubbed and cleaned every surface. Tidied away the clutter my mother found offensive. Made up beds, did laundry, and kept her off her feet for the sake of her baby.

Every second, I'd itched to leave.

We would have gone yesterday, but a storm had pinned us down, rattling hail against the windows, summer meaning nothing to the Hebridean weather.

In the low afternoon light, it was finally lifting.

Sin had left on a mission he'd asked me to remain home for. I hated being apart from him. Feared what he was going to do.

Him being away from me scared me more than anything else.

"Lottie," my mother called.

I set down a box I'd carried upstairs and ran back down. In the kitchen, my mother sat at the table, one hand to her stomach and her eyes rounded and full of emotion. A wounded look she'd worn since our return.

"Are ye okay? How are ye feeling?" I asked.

"Much better now you're here." She patted the chair to her left.

I took the one opposite, earning a small disapproving scowl.

"Tomorrow, I want ye to come to church with me," she announced, then smoothed over her hair, worn in the same plaits as I always chose.

"Sorry, Ma. We'll be leaving today."

Several times now, my mother had asked me to stay, or said things that included me in her immediate plans. I couldn't do it. The guilt tore at me, but it wasn't happening.

It might not have been her who'd laid her fists into me,

but she hadn't stopped it. She'd never told me it was wrong or let me know it wasn't my fault. She'd sided with him, and above that, contributed in her own way to my misery with her constant criticism of me.

I loved her, but whatever relationship we could salvage now Da was gone, it would be on my terms.

Ma sighed. "It would be so much easier if ye just stayed. Less upheaval."

"What do ye mean?"

She tipped her head at the door. "That man you've brought back with ye..."

"Sin, my boyfriend."

She wrinkled her nose. "Is he?"

"Yes."

My mother gentled her gaze. "I know how it is with a first love. Ye think the world of the boy and assume nothing's going to go wrong."

"But—"

She held up a hand. "It won't last. These things never do. I'm sorry, sweetheart, he isn't going to stick around."

I blinked, confused. "I don't understand."

My mother gave an indulgent smile. "That's because you're so young. It's my fault for keeping ye too close, the naïvety never left ye. Once that man gets tired of your company, he'll drop the relationship faster than either of us can blink, and then what will happen? That's what I mean by saving the upheaval. You're better off staying here with me."

A sick feeling swirled in my belly. "Why would he get tired of me?"

She gestured up and down my body. "Well, ye caught his attention, but you're not the sort of girl who can keep it."

My history of hurt from this woman deadened the hit.

She meant because of my weight.

It had always been like this. I'd never been allowed to simply exist. Ma picked holes in every aspect of my appearance, and it didn't matter what I said to her.

Even in the grief of losing her lover and escaping her abuser, she hadn't changed.

At least the guilt I'd been feeling could lift. I eased up from the table and set my expression to neutral. "Like I said, we'll be leaving today."

"You're needed here to help with the baby. Don't be silly."

"I'll be back when I can."

"You're being fanciful. Seeing things that aren't there," she continued. "Did he tell ye he loves ye? It's a trap. It doesn't mean anything. Trust me, because I know better, and I wasn't a girl still carrying her puppy fat. I held down a marriage. That isn't easy."

And I was done. I snatched my coat from the hook by the kitchen door and fled the house. The feelings I was trying to suppress burned me.

Halfway up the rain-soaked path, Sin stopped in his footsteps. "What's wrong?"

No matter how much I hated my mother's words, they hit too close to home. Worse now I had my huge, too handsome lover in front of me. I'd never had great self-esteem. What if she was right, and I was naïve? What if the lust I saw in him and the love I felt all vanished and went away when he got bored of me?

It would destroy me.

The crush that had sprung to life within me on the cold, dark beach at the first sight of him surfing with his brothers had turned into full-blown adoration. I knew him.

Understood him. He'd gone out today, and not for a second hadn't I trusted in his actions.

But maybe I was projecting everything I felt onto what I saw in him.

"Nothing," I muttered and moved past him.

Sin caught me with a big hand around my biceps. He tipped up my chin and examined my features, his dark hair damp from whatever he'd been doing out in the storm.

He made a grumbling sound, then tucked me into his side, and we exited the garden to the road that wound through the island's only village.

"There's one last thing we need to do before we go," he said, his tone careful. "And on the way, you'll talk."

"I don't want to."

"Aye, but ye will."

I shot him a look of frustration. He tilted his head at me from his lofty height, an invitation that brooked no refusal.

Annoyance mixed with my upset. It took a long moment before I realised we were strolling in broad daylight past the houses of the villagers who'd once imprisoned him.

I halted. "We should cross the moor. It isn't safe here."

"And I told ye and the rest of our family that I'm sick of running. I willnae live in fear. This afternoon, I met with the islanders who backed your father on the night we escaped."

Some people were born leaders. Sinclair was one. He'd been imprisoned yet made sure of his and his brothers' safety. He'd enabled their escape and had come back with a plan to keep them free.

I stared in awe. "God. What happened?"

"It took some persuading to get them out of their houses. But I made it easy for them. I said I knew that they'd been lied to about us. Told we were criminals in need of rehabilitation and that they'd looked the other way in the belief that they were helping us. I put all the blame on your father and Augustus Stewart."

We started walking again, and I gazed at each house as we passed. "And none on them. They got off easy."

He rolled his shoulders as if removing a burden. "I implied that should they act against us again, despite now knowing the truth, I'd be forced to take action. One fucker even asked how, and whether I'd reveal each individual's involvement to the authorities."

I couldn't imagine Sin volunteering anything to the police. "What did ye say?"

He gave me a wolfish grin. "That I'd more likely return for them myself to take my own revenge. After that, they were falling over themselves to apologise and make amends."

I gave a short, surprised laugh. He made it seem so easy. I was no good with confrontations.

Then I wanted to laugh at myself. I was so bad at them that I let my mother manipulate me into feeling awful despite every other piece of information I had being the opposite to what she'd claimed.

We ambled on, the rain ceasing and a warmish sun breaking through the cloud layer. At the tiny harbour, with fishermen coming and going, I stopped the man I loved.

"Ma told me that your interest in me is temporary. Probably based on the fact I let ye have sex with me. She says you'll lose interest and I'm better off staying here with her."

Something dangerous flashed in Sin's eyes. He folded his arms. "How seriously did ye take her words?"

I never wanted to lie to him. "For a moment, it made

sense. I've never really been sure why ye like me." My voice wobbled, but I pushed on. "I'm short and chubby, not especially pretty. I'm not clever or strong. Proof being how easily that hurt me."

His expression revealed nothing.

Abruptly, he grabbed my hand, turned, and turned me back in the direction of the Victorian.

We marched up the path. Outside the kitchen door, he stopped me.

With deadly certainty, he held my gaze. "Repeat after me. Sinclair Stone is in love with me."

My breath caught, and I closed my eyes.

But he wasn't allowing it. He squeezed me and made me look at him again. "Say the words."

I mumbled it, earning a nod.

"Now for more. I'm beautiful inside and out. Caring, kind, so smart, and he doesn't deserve me."

"Stop," I weakly protested.

"Say it, Violet."

I did, my voice stronger this time.

"One day, he'll be my husband, and he'll be lucky to have me—"

My mouth fell open, and I whipped up my hand to press it to his lips.

Sin had always been highly touch-sensitive, rarely enjoying it until we'd collided in our hot-burning relationship. Now I knew he needed it. Needed *me*.

He kept his gaze locked on mine. For a moment, entirely in shock, I just breathed.

Then I pulled my hand back and repeated what he'd said, adding my own words. "I'll make the best wife and give more than I take. I'll give him children we'll both love.

We'll protect them with our lives and never let anyone hurt them."

"We'll be happy," he finished. "We already are."

I nodded, entirely captivated by him. Sin was rough and ready, scarily big and intimidating. And he was mine.

I turned to the door. My mother was standing there, watching us. The single-pane glass must have meant she'd heard everything.

I reached to open it, and she snapped her mouth closed, stepping away. Passing her, I grabbed my rucksack and Sin's from where we'd left them in the hall, then stood before her once more.

"I won't live with ye," I said, trying to be calm. "I'll visit, when I can, and I'll be there for the birth, if ye ask. I'll be sure to make sure my baby sister knows she's perfect exactly how she is. But my life isn't here anymore. Maybe it never was. I'm going back to my family with the man who loves me for all the reasons ye chose not to."

I walked away.

As we exited the gate, Ma called after me, "I'll be waiting when ye come back. Just know, ye won't get the big bedroom. Your aunt is coming tomorrow. I knew you'd be ungrateful and leave me. After all I did for ye!"

I didn't turn around to dignify her with a reply.

"I can't believe I just did that."

Sin huffed a laugh. "Get used to it. I want ye to claim me, loudly and to anyone who'll listen. That shite is hot as fuck."

Warmth spread through me, displacing the cold from my mother's treatment. I grasped Sin's hand and picked up the pace.

"How hot?"

"Like if ye don't take me somewhere private, I'm going to spread your legs on the road and fuck ye here where anyone can see."

A thrill zipped down my spine. I moved faster.

Along the cliffs that lined the white sand beach, a trail led up to a hidden cave. Thea and I had played there as children. She'd once hidden Struan there, too. It had a soft, sandy floor and was safe from prying eyes.

Sin let me draw him along the track and under the cave's lip. He was so huge in the space, but neither of us hesitated, acting on the sense of urgency that had been gathering for days.

Ma was a light sleeper. I hadn't felt comfortable having sex in the room next to hers.

Now, I needed Sin more than ever.

I'd barely stripped my jacket to make a lining for the floor, when Sin's hands were in my loose-necked tunic dress, yanking aside my bra cups to expose my breasts. He groaned and dropped his face to nuzzle then kiss my cleavage, drawing his tongue across my skin until he found my nipple. I dug my fingers into his short hair, moaning at how good his mouth felt after days of nothing.

Pawing at his clothes, I rid him of his long-sleeved shirt, another pang of lust hitting me at the sight of his broad chest. His bulging muscles, and the tattoo that I'd been branded with, too.

He took the opportunity to half tear my dress over my head, then unclip my bra.

He feasted his gaze on me. "If I die, and the last sight I have is of your body, my afterlife will be spent jerking off over ye."

I giggled which turned into a rushed intake of breath

as he sucked my nipple, running a finger and thumb over the other to tease it into a peak.

"I meant every word I said," he said between licks and sucks. "You're the best thing that ever happened to me. I'm sorry I didn't do a good enough job of convincing ye of the fact. I'll do better."

"No," I started to protest, but he held up a hushing finger, then shifted lower to kiss my belly.

No longer was I self-conscious of him seeing my curves. It was all too evident how I affected him.

He travelled his lips down my body.

"Before I knew ye properly, when we'd only exchanged a few words, I was obsessed with your body. First, your pretty face with those big, innocent eyes. Your tits as a fast second. I dreamed of fucking them so often it was unreal. Then sliding into your tight cunt always came up hard behind."

He entwined his fingers into the sides of my underwear—the last item I had on as my sandals had fallen away.

"Lift," he ordered, removing the knickers when I obeyed.

Sin picked up my leg and wrapped it around his shoulder, laying a hot kiss on my thigh. He repeated the same with the other, his gaze locked on the centre of me.

"I wanted ye for myself. Pretty quickly, that image moved on to wanting to put a baby in ye."

He blew on the core of me, and I shivered, hopelessly gone for his words.

Since we'd started sleeping together, never once had we used protection. In a few days, I'd have an idea of whether those actions had consequences.

My deepest hope was of seeing a positive result on a pregnancy test. I so badly wanted to carry his baby. He wanted it, too.

We'd certainly put in the effort.

"I want everything with ye," was all the reply I could give.

"Good." He grinned then inched forward to lick me between my legs. "Fuck. You're soaked, and ye taste incredible."

With his thumbs, he held me open for his tongue, lapping at me before settling to suck on my clit. I arched into his intimate touch then moaned loud.

I'd never get enough of this man. Every time he touched me, I went to pieces. When he slid a finger inside me, I nearly came from that thick intrusion alone. Then he added another, crooking them at the right angle to hit a spot inside that sent sparks through my body.

I said his name, and he sucked harder, keeping up the slow pace of his fingers in and out of my body, sliding in the arousal only he could cause.

Pretty soon, my breathing turned heavy, and I was barrelling towards release, gripping his hair before sliding both hands to my breasts. I thumbed my nipples, and Sin swore against my flesh.

He sank back to give me one hard suck, and I splintered, the pleasure overwhelming. Everything he did turned me on, but being the focus of his attention like that never failed to make me succumb in minutes.

I gasped his name and spasmed around his fingers, gripping his head to slow him down.

Sin growled and surged up my body, displacing my legs from his shoulders. They fell open around him, and he snapped to undo his jeans, freeing his huge cock.

I could only lie there, breathing after I'd forgotten to

for a minute, and reeling in sheer desire.

He lifted my heel to his shoulder, lined up, then thrust inside me.

We both gave up sounds of pleasure.

He filled me in ways I could never imagine. So thick, it always took a moment for my body to adjust. He could barely wait, starting a slow, torturous rolling series of thrusts that sent me delirious. The determination on his face. The devotion and need etched into his brow.

The feeling was unbeatable, the driving need only growing. We had only just begun, and I knew we'd get better at this, at knowing each other and learning ourselves, too.

But this basic meeting of our bodies couldn't be matched.

"Love how ye take me," he growled out. "Ye were made for me. Mine."

"Yours," I agreed.

Then all words were lost. He worked himself in and out of my body, getting harder with each thrust.

Pretty quickly, I was keening his name, right on the brink of a second orgasm.

One thing for sure would push me over the edge.

I tightened around him, and Sin slowed and dropped his forehead to mine.

Inside me, he came, that final act my catalyst.

My climax matched his, startling me into silence. My hearing gone for a beat, too.

He dropped down to the cradle of my body. I wrapped my arms and legs around him, and we clutched one another, slowing, rocking. Breathing together.

"I love ye." I nestled a kiss into his hair.

Sin turned and fitted his mouth to mine. He delivered a long, meaningful kiss. "I'm in love with ye in ways I never thought possible. You're my whole world."

He grazed a hand down my body, taking a lazy squeeze of my breast, then to the place we were still joined.

He was still hard, but he pressed a finger in my entrance, stretched around his dick. I let out a gasp as he forced the finger inside, then added another. Two digits, bracing his thick cock.

I was already so full, but the sensation was strangely pleasurable.

Then he slid them over that spot inside me, slippery with his cum and mine, giving just enough space to play.

"I want ye to come again. If you're not already pregnant, I want my cum as deep inside ye as it can be so it'll make ye so."

I could only answer with a whimper and let him toy with me. He worked his hips in shallow jerks, his fingers making minute movements as well.

He'd already made me come twice in the space of minutes. Surely I couldn't again.

But that constant pressure, the too-full sensation gave way to fresh heat. I took my hands back to my nipples, pulling on them lightly, and using my thumbs to extend them. My gaze, though, I kept on Sin.

He stared right back at me, every part of him devoted to my pleasure.

The third orgasm struck me in a silent, satisfying wave. I broke eye contact and gasped, doing exactly what he wanted. Taking in his cum for my body to use.

Sin kissed me again as soon as I'd regained my breath. Then he grinned, lifted to sitting, and slapped my bare backside. "I reckon that time did it."

Too satisfied for anything other than a smile, I dragged him back for another kiss. "If it didn't, I can't wait to try some more."

We dressed and left the cave. I had sand in my plaited hair, but nothing could bother me now.

"Back to the boat?" I asked.

Sin scrubbed his fingers over his dark hair. "There's one thing left to do before that. Scar asked me to check out the hostel."

"Your prison keeper's grave." I grimaced. "Let's do this thing."

We set off across the moor to the site of their imprisonment.

When we neared, Sin wrinkled his lip. "There was one person I didn't see when I'd talked to the islanders. Jenkins. He used to torment Burn. Keep was going to sell my brother to the old pervert. She threatened that for Cassie, too. In a way, I'm glad he's gone. I don't think I could have made a deal with that dirty fucker."

"I didn't know him that well, but now I think of it, it was probably my mother keeping me away from him. At least she did that."

Perched on the moor ahead, the dilapidated white hostel building waited. For some reason, I'd expected to find a pile of burned timbers and blackened stones. The closer we got, the more I could see how the men had trashed it before they left. Windows were broken, and rubbish had been strewn around. Clearly no one had been out here.

"I'll check the grave, then we can go." Sin stared for a moment then strode to the building.

I followed, unwilling to leave him alone with his demons.

But I was a few paces behind. Too slow to see what he did as he rounded the corner.

The shock on his face, however, spoke volumes.

12

Camden

Balling up a sheet of paper, I tossed it across the cabin's living room. It missed the bin. I scowled in frustration, stormed over, snatched up the offending item, and slammed it in.

Then I kicked the metal bin for good measure. It clattered across the floorboards and hit the wall.

Struan poked his head out of the kitchen. "The fuck was that?"

"Nothing," I grouched, returning to my seat.

All afternoon, I'd been refining and reworking my sketch of a woman's face I planned to tattoo on my upper arm. Every attempt looked like Breeze.

I couldn't avoid her. After what I'd done to the lass, I'd never hear from her again.

Since I'd miraculously won the auction, my outrageous bid not only accepted with McInver's bank details presumably saved, but bringing an end to the sale, I'd been acting under a kind of haze made of panic and concern, and my only excuse was I'd wanted to stop her. Make sure she couldn't do it again.

But I'd overstepped the line by so much, it might as well have not been there.

"Bullshit. You've been messed up for days. Talk to me." Struan joined me, sinking into the seat opposite. With colour in his cheeks and ease to his movements, his recovery seemed good.

Which gave him headspace to have far too fucking much awareness of me.

I didn't even know how to ask for advice.

My oldest brother watched me. He tapped his fingers on his knee. "Okay, twenty questions then. Is it about a girl?"

I rolled my gaze his way. "Course it is."

He pulled a 'well, duh' expression. "Does her name start with a B?"

I lifted and made to walk away. He'd never met Breeze. People had been gossiping.

He grabbed my arm and yanked me back down to sitting. "Jesus. Okay, no names. Remember I grew up an only child and have no clue how to do this big brother shite, but I'm trying."

"We all grew up as only children," I grumbled, but this time gave him my full attention.

"I was thinking about what ye told us when we were surfing," he said. "How seeing... I mean, your experience at McInver's house, how that kicked off your sexual side. Is that what's bothering ye?"

I shrugged. "Other than walking around half the time with a boner I can't get rid of, no."

"That, I can advise on. I never had a da, but one of the teachers in school gave me a tip. Hold your breath and flex a muscle. Don't know why, but it works."

"What the hell kind of school did ye go to?"

Struan snorted a laugh. "Fuck off."

"Seriously, that teacher had issues. Talk about over-stepping."

"Jesus. Now ye put it like that, maybe he did. But it still worked, so hear that part and never mention the rest of it again."

We swapped a grin, and some small part of my tension eased.

"Then there's the other method," my brother added. "The one I learned all by myself. Having sex with a lass. It beats jerking off a thousand times over."

"I wouldn't know."

"Wouldn't know the fact? Or wouldn't know what to do? Because I can talk ye through that as well."

I groaned. "I know how sex works."

"No, you've watched porn on Burn's phone. Not the same thing." He sat forward with his elbows on his knees, warming to the theme. "For example, women don't roll around and moan and scream. Not unless ye really know what you're doing, which nobody does at the start. Porn is pretty one-sided and aimed at the pervert watching. Real sex is both partners working to give each other pleasure. That takes time and trust."

I squinted at him, something clicking. "You've been thinking about this."

"Aye. I'm suddenly in a relationship for the first time in

my life. Gotta make it work."

There wasn't much about discovering my sexuality that didn't bother me. The fact I'd been turned on by seeing Breeze restrained to a bed. How I only had to conjure the image to be uncomfortably aroused. How when I touched her, tattooed her, I was pretty sure she'd found that a turn-on, too.

If we'd been in a different situation, and she'd been bared to me and waiting for me to give her pleasure, I wouldn't know what to do. And how had that suddenly become top of my list of concerns?

"How do ye make a woman come?" I blurted.

My big, bad brother appeared entirely unfazed. "Ask her to show ye what she does to herself. Then copy it until ye can do it better."

"Is that possible?"

"No solo wank is better than having someone else in control."

For a moment, our conversation stalled. If he was picturing Thea, I didn't want to know. But sure as fuck, a pretty-eyed little thief was on my mind.

My brother came back to the conversation. "Let me ask ye something. Do ye think your early life experiences made ye not interested in sex?"

"Like my mother screwing guys in front of me?"

"Fuck. That happened?"

I raised an eyebrow. "She had one punter who would leave her bedroom door open and pay her more if she called my name while he was drilling her. The first time, my reaction was real. After that, she told me it got rid of him quicker, so if I didn't mind, she'd keep doing it."

"That's messed up. Did she ever let them touch ye?"

I locked my jaw. "No."

Not that guy anyway. I forced myself to keep talking, get my attention off how my fucking scarred face hurt with remembered pain. "I see your point. It could've repressed something. But the rest of ye didn't have this problem."

"My ma never used our home, still, I didn't get away unscathed. I have my own issues."

"Like what?"

"I never wanted to get to know a lass. Fuck intimacy. But Thea made me her boyfriend, and I'm slowly working the rest out, because it's the best feeling to have that. You'll be able to do the same and overcome your bullshit."

"What if the only person I want to have sex with is the one who'll tear me limb from limb if she sees me again?" And why the hell had I just confessed that?

Struan arched a dark eyebrow. "For real? After she stole our car? What did ye do?"

My damn cheeks flamed. "Sharing time is over. I'm not revealing that to anyone, but just assume I went to the dark side for a minute. It was consensual, I think, but now I'm shutting up."

His gaze travelled over my heated cheeks, and my older brother grinned big. "I've pissed Thea off more times than I can count. If you're genuinely sorry and are willing to learn from it and make it better, a decent grovel might save your skin."

I watched him for a moment, then nodded. If I ever saw Breeze again, the least I owed her was an apology. Even if that couldn't make things right.

Fuck. I'd never want to let her go again.

His phone rang in his pocket. He extracted it and frowned. "Sin. Finally."

He answered it, and I checked my own screen, staring at the missed call from my brother. He'd tried me first, but I hadn't heard it.

But also, a message from the lawyer had come in.

Golding: Apologies for the delay. The DNA test result has finally been returned. I am thrilled to confirm that you are indeed the son of Mr McInver. It would be my honour to meet with you tomorrow at the mansion—

I closed it down, my heart pounding.

Struan put our brother on loudspeaker.

"Keep's grave is empty," Sin snapped.

I gaped at the phone. "Empty like someone dug her up?"

Wind buffeted the other end of the line, and I pictured them outside the hostel, a scene from a horror movie in front of them.

"Got to be. The earth has been hacked into, and there's drag marks."

Struan gagged. "Did she claw her way out? Wouldn't put it past the demon woman."

"That is nasty," I spat. "She was worm food. Could it have been an animal?"

Sin made a noise of disagreement. "If there was a creature here big enough to pull that woman from under the earth, that's some kind of beast. But no, there are no bones, no pieces, no shredded flesh. Violet and I looked all around. We're heading back to the boat now."

I was already on my feet and snatching up the car keys. "On my way to get ye."

"Thanks, brother. I won't be happy until we're well away from this fucked-up place."

That made all of us.

A couple of hours later, I had retrieved Sin and Lottie and was driving us home. Lottie talked about her mother, but we agreed to hold the rest of the conversation until we reached the cabin.

Once we were back, Thea had returned from a shopping run with Max's partner, and she and Struan had made dinner.

"Eat first," Thea said, hugging a pale Lottie. "Gross stuff after."

We wolfed back hot dogs, cleared away the dishes, then sat around the table as a family. It hurt that we were missing Burn and Cassie still; everything we did had to be agreed on as a group.

Sin filled us in on meeting the islanders. When he got to the part about Jenkins being absent, Struan, Thea, and I exchanged glances.

Of all the residents of Torlum, he was the one who made my skin crawl. Lottie's dad had been the ringleader, keeping us locked up, but Jenkins had repeatedly come by the hostel. Tried to buy Burn and Cassie. No guesses to what he would have done with them if Keep had let him. When we'd fled the place, he grabbed Burn while everyone had been distracted. Our brother had escaped and made it to the helicopter just in time. As we'd taken off, he'd told us to look down to witness Jenkins' house burning.

Shock filled me. "I knew it was too much to hope that he died in Burn's fire."

Sin scrubbed his face, his expression beyond troubled. "Unless we're missing something, I can't imagine any other scenario than Jenkins dug up Keep's body and has stored it somewhere. I made myself visible on the island. He didn't challenge me. His house is a shell with nobody in it. The cops didn't appear. We walked away unopposed."

"What's his end goal?" Struan muttered.

I didn't like the conclusions I was reaching. "It can only be to use her against us. We need to decide what we do now. We talked about building a life here. Do we abandon that and run again?"

Sin watched me for a moment. "What do ye think?"

"That he might have a body, but he doesn't have any proof. No gun or knife with my fingerprints. I killed her, but I hadn't planned it. I'd only lashed out to redirect her Taser so it hit her and not one of us."

"What happened to the Taser?" Thea asked.

"I smashed it to pieces and threw it into the sea."

She chewed her lip. "There's a ton of evidence at the hostel, of her and all of you."

"Which also implicates the people who kept us there," I argued. "We worked on their smallholdings. Used equipment. I'm pretty sure the islanders would get in the way of any investigation, based on the conversation Sin had with them where they were only interested in saving their skins."

As macabre as Sin and Lottie's discovery had been, it didn't change anything.

"Let Jenkins rot with the dead body he stole. We keep our eyes open but continue with the plans we made," I concluded.

Sin dipped his head. "Agreed."

The others echoed his sentiments, talking shite about Jenkins.

Through the cabin's windows was nothing but black night. I had the urge to head out and check our boundaries, watch the road and be sure no one had followed us home. I stood from the table.

"Burn's probably at greatest risk of all of us," Lottie said quietly. "He's in a jail cell somewhere, unaware of any of this. If Jenkins is talking to the police, they already have Burn in custody. Easy to pin another crime on him."

God, she was right. I opened my mouth to tell them about the meeting I'd had with the lawyer. It was all the more urgent now to find Burn and free him.

The cabin's front door rattled, someone thumping on it.

Everyone jumped to their feet. I stormed across the room and peered through the spyhole. Then in shock, I threw the door open.

Standing on the other side, in a pretty summer dress, with a bag over her shoulder and her lips pressed flat in emotion, waited my blonde bombshell by the name of Breeze.

13

Breeze

From the entryway of the brightly lit cabin, Scar stared at me open-mouthed. Behind him, his family was halfway to the door, including a couple of faces I didn't recognise. Three of the five had seen me naked. Wasn't that a trip.

I pulled my focus back to the man I'd come to see. Definitely to yell at.

"Come in," he finally managed.

I held my ground, my arms folded. "Does everybody know?"

A pretty woman with long, dark hair pressed Lottie's elbow. "Is that Breeze?" she stage-whispered.

Lottie nodded, raising a hand to give me a small wave.

I guessed the stranger to be Thea, whose clothes I'd borrowed, and the man with her to be the other brother. But I wasn't ready to make friends.

Scar slowly shook his head. "Nobody knows."

"What don't we know?" Sin asked.

I didn't offer an answer, and Scar seemed stuck on staring at me.

The brother who had to be Struan pointed between us. "He did something to her which really pissed her off, but he won't give details."

Sin lifted his chin. "What happened to the car ye stole, Breeze?"

There was no hostility in his tone, but I stiffened even further, out of my comfort zone and with a sudden urge to run.

Why had I come here? After waiting in the hotel room so long, it had felt like my only option. Right now, I was worried about my sanity.

His brother's question sparked Scar to life. He twisted around to frown at them all, then stepped outside, closing the door behind him.

Leaving the two of us alone in the dark summer evening.

I backed up a couple of steps, and he put his hands out as if to placate me.

"I waited for you to come back," I said, hating the way my voice trembled.

"I'm sorry," Scar uttered at the same second.

I shut my mouth, and he pressed his advantage.

"I've been thinking about ye endlessly. I can't stop picturing what I did—"

"What you did? You tattooed your name on me," I hissed.

Once I'd gotten over the shock of what happened in

the hotel room, I'd unchained myself, rubbing my limbs from where they'd gone stiff. Then I'd drawn the curtains and clicked on a lamp.

Only then had I finally examined myself.

On the inside of my swollen, sensitive lower lips, in purple ink, he'd tattooed CAM on the left and DEN on the right as I looked down my body.

Branded his name into my most intimate flesh.

He watched me. "Is it healing?"

"Yes, I followed your kind instructions," I snapped. "Your name is healing beautifully on my pussy."

He pressed his lips together, and outrage flooded me. I stalked up to him and prodded his chest with my finger. "Is this funny?"

Scar towered over me, and he didn't budge, even though I was in his personal space. His gaze locked on to mine, and something stirred deep in my belly. He'd apologised, but there was something else in his gaze. Pride?

I glared back in confusion. "Explain to me why you're sorry."

"For scaring ye. For if it hurt."

But not for the act itself.

My anger warred with other, darker emotions in me. "But you're not sorry for actually doing it," I concluded. Then I pushed it further. "You like the thought of it."

He didn't answer, but his gaze sank down my body.

Such an asshole. Such an infuriating, hot jerk.

"You're imagining it now," I taunted, low. "Those letters against my silky smooth pink skin. Your name, *right there.*

Camden."

None of this was going the way I'd planned. I'd meant to yell at him then demand we talk about the realisation I'd had before the auction. Not tease him.

Definitely not get turned on by it.

His focus snapped back to mine, the eye contact startling. In his blue-eyed gaze, desire burned.

He inched closer, tilting his head. "Yes, Breeze. I'll confess it. Whatever my regrets, it is the hottest fucking image in the world to know my name is there. Or maybe it's the memory of ye getting wet with it, or perhaps that time ye sucked my dick. All are contenders."

My hostility melted. From wanting to tear into him, I was now squarely in the zone of wanting to tear his clothes from his oversized frame.

A smirk curved his lips. "Did ye come here to tell me off?"

Before I could reply, he added another thought.

"Because I'm seriously fucking happy to see ye."

He had to be magnetic. That was the only reason I felt a pull towards him. Happy, too. I could live in this feeling. The rising attraction. The promise of pleasure. I'd never felt it before him, and this taste wasn't enough.

No.

Had to remember my irritation. I controlled my hormones and said what I'd come here to say. "Your brother, the one who's missing, recognised me."

His expression morphed from heated to one of concern. "I asked about that. Ye didn't know him."

"I don't. Never met him. But it occurred to me he might have mistaken me for my sister."

Scar's frown deepened. "How? Are ye that similar?"

"Not unless you'd only ever seen a photo of our faces." I drew an imaginary oval in the air over mine. "Summer is taller than me. Curvy. Our body shapes aren't that alike. But our faces, especially when we were younger, are really similar. That's why it didn't occur to me straight away."

"Then you're thinking Burn met her online?"

"It's possible."

Something passed over Scar's gaze, and his brief expression of relief died. He led me to a small table outside the cabin's big window.

He gestured for me to sit, but I stayed on my feet. Relaxing around him was not an option. Likewise, he remained on his feet, too, resting his backside on the table.

"I didn't know Burn until recently, and I don't know any of his friends. He never mentioned anyone called Summer. But there's something else. Burn—Jamieson, I mean—is severely dyslexic. I can't imagine him easily chatting by text."

Damn. The hope that had driven me guttered.

My inspiration hit a dead end. I'd been so sure.

Then, in the dark recesses of my mind, a memory surfaced. "Hold up. Summer used to record voice messages for someone." I concentrated, fixing onto that image of her in my mind speaking quietly into her phone. I snapped my gaze up to Scar's. "She used to disappear out of the room to chat with someone, and she'd use headphones to hear the replies."

"Are ye sure?"

I nodded, my certainty growing. "She never told me who, but this started a long time ago. We were maybe fourteen or fifteen. Or even younger. I assumed it was a friend from school, but what if it was him?"

"It's a long shot but possible." Scar stood and held his hand out for me. "Let's go inside and ask Sin. He knew Burn when they were young."

I wrinkled my nose, hesitating to take his hand. "Your family hates me."

He huffed a short laugh. "For the car? Ye did us a favour. Come inside and I'll tell ye how."

I ignored his hand and stalked ahead, and we went into the cabin. His family were either sitting on the sofas or pottering around the dining table. Lottie spun around then skipped over.

She hugged me. "I'm so glad you're okay. I've been worried about ye." Then she pointed to the other woman. "That's Thea, as I'm sure you've already guessed. Then Struan is over there."

I gave them short nods, too conscious of how these people saw me.

"Good to see you again," I managed to Lottie.

She beamed in a way I definitely didn't deserve.

Scar tugged me to sit on the sofa. The others settled around us.

"I apologise about the car," I said before anyone else spoke. "I panicked and had to get away. But then the police took it."

"Where was this?" Sin asked.

"In Edinburgh. I'd parked it outside my mum's block

of flats. Not a good area. When I came back, the police were watching it."

They all swapped looks.

"Like I said, ye did us a favour," Scar offered. "The car was stolen, and the previous owner died under, how do I put this, suspicious circumstances."

I pulled a face, adding up what wasn't being said. "Do the cops know that one of you killed the owner? Because my fingerprints are on that car."

Scar choked on a laugh. "No, at least we don't think so. Have ye ever been fingerprinted?"

"Never."

"Then there's no way they'll connect ye to her death, so don't worry." He swapped his gaze to the others. "Breeze has been searching for her sister and thinks she and Burn knew each other. There's a possible connection that we're trying to unpick. Sin, did ye ever know Burn to have a girlfriend?"

The huge man shook his head.

"Did he ever mention the name Summer to any of you?" I added.

More negative shakes.

Sin had glanced away and was staring into the middle distance, his thumb and finger stroking his chin. He was similar enough to Scar to be familiar, but when I looked at him, I only imagined him hurting people.

"I mostly only knew Burn from seeing him around," he said slowly. "But you've stirred a memory. When he first arrived at the hostel, he seemed upset about not being able to talk to someone. I assumed it was a girl. When we finally managed to get a phone, he was very secretive about recording a message then made a show of deleting an account. It seemed to be something final. He was miserable for months."

I switched my gaze to Scar. "What hostel?"

He closed his eyes briefly. "Long story. Tell ye later."

"Have you found your brother, yet?" I asked, though with little hope. He wasn't here, which must've meant he was still missing.

"No, I can't see that changing anytime soon," Struan griped.

Another dead end for me.

My hunt for Summer was a roller coaster. Every time I got a clue, I'd hit another snag. Her phone wouldn't start up, despite me borrowing a charger at the hotel. Now this.

I wished beyond belief that outside McInver's, when Burn had spotted me and seen my sister, I'd stopped and spoken to him. He had answers, I was certain.

But there was no way of reaching him.

"Actually," Scar said, summoning the attention of the whole room. "There's something I need to tell ye. Last week, I went to McInver's lawyer to try to get information from him. He demanded I take a DNA test before he'd talk to me."

"Fuck that," Struan said.

Scar held his gaze. "I did it. He's confirmed I'm McInver's son and will meet me tomorrow so I can officially become his heir."

Shock rippled through them all.

"I know what you're going to say. But this is the only

way we can get to Burn."

"By stepping up for an abusive bastard? How the hell is that even going to work?" Struan bit out. "McInver wanted Sin."

"And that abusive bastard father of ours is in a coma," Scar replied. "He doesn't even know this is happening, and none of it is to help him. The lawyer was desperate for someone to have authority. I'll have that. I can talk to the police and find our brother. I know there are risks. I know everything you're going to say. But I've done it, and it's on my shoulders, like all the other decisions I make on behalf of my family. Be as pissed off with me as ye want, it's done."

Struan swore, anger in his expression. Lottie appeared concerned, Thea considering it all.

Sin held his gaze, something of approval in his regard. "We can't lose ye, too," he said.

The man at my side stood. "Ye won't. You'll trust that I've got this and let me step up. I'm going to McInver's tonight. I want to be ready." He peered at me. "Coming?"

I jumped to my feet, glad to be leaving. In a minute, we were out of the house and in a different car, speeding away towards an unknown fate.

Somehow, I was along for the ride.

14

Breeze

We left the estate Scar's family lived on, passing two castles, a loch, then through giant stone gateposts. Nothing about this man made sense, including where he lived.

"How did ye get out here?" he asked, his gaze on the dark and deserted road.

"A train, then a taxi, followed by a long walk. I didn't want the driver to know where I was going so I had him drop me off at that village." I gestured to the cluster of streets that sat alongside the open water. It was only a few minutes' drive from the gateposts, but had taken me an hour to hike.

"Ye remembered where I was."

"When I left here, I memorised the location."

"Why?"

"I want to see McInver," I stated, derailing the conversation with the first thing that came to mind. "I wish he would wake up."

Scar frowned then took out his phone, holding it

against the steering wheel to press a number. It rang, and he passed it to me. "His lawyer sent me this number. For all ye want the old man to wake, if he does, I'm fucked. Now put it on loudspeaker and we'll find out the latest."

I did, and a gentle Englishman's voice answered.

"Heathcote Hospital, Julian speaking."

"Julian, my name is Camden McInver. You're treating my father."

"Yes, sir. Thank you for the call. I was informed by your father's lawyer to expect you to make contact. Would you like to see him?"

We swapped a look of shock.

Scar cleared his throat. "Is he awake?

"No, I'm sorry to say there's been no change in his condition. Let me take you to his bedside. I'll switch to a video call, and you can talk to him for as long as you like. I believe it can be soothing for the patient."

The call ended, and a video request came in.

"Shall I accept?" I asked.

"Why not? At least we'll get to see him and be sure."

I pressed the button.

Julian's face appeared onscreen. If he was surprised to see me first before I panned to McInver's son, he didn't say. "Good evening, miss, and you, sir. I'll take you in now."

On the phone's screen, a wide hallway passed by, then we were taken into a private, luxury suite. Nothing like any hospital I'd ever seen apart from the medical kit around the bed.

A bed with a wizened old man in it.

"Here we are," Julian stated. "I'll leave you in privacy. Go ahead and talk to your relative for as long as you like. Just end the call when you're done, and I'll collect the phone later."

I muted the line and stared. "I don't know what's weirder, a hospital that is more like a hotel or staff who clearly handle video call visits more than in-person ones."

Scar peered across at the screen. "Jeez. He seems dead already." He swung his gaze back to the road. "Talk to him if ye like. Tell him from me that he's a despicable piece of shite. I have nothing to say to him beyond that."

I held in a laugh and watched the screen. There, the old man appeared harmless. Not rich or powerful. Nothing like the cruel, scary person who'd appeared by the bed when I was chained up and whispered evil things.

Tubes pierced his pallid, wrinkled skin. Blankets weighed down his bony limbs.

He couldn't provide me with the information I needed. Perhaps not ever if this was how his life was going to end.

"What the hell is wrong with you?" I whispered to him. But I kept the phone muted. Who knew who listened in. "You hate and you hurt, and the world is a worse place for you being in it. Whatever happened to make you this way was yours to correct, not to repeat. I hope one day you figure that out."

Then I hung up.

"Who was the woman you killed?" I said to Scar, needing to keep talking.

In all the times we'd met or spoken before, when he'd rescued me, in our text chat, or in the hotel room, I'd resisted asking questions. I didn't want to know him or for him to know me.

Suddenly, that changed.

Anger still haunted me, but I was stuck on the realisation I'd had lying on that bed with my pussy throbbing from his tattoo.

He'd cared enough about me, in a twisted way, to stop me from doing what I was doing.

I might have been following my sister's trail, but I couldn't pretend she was the only reason I was here.

Scar let out a sigh. "I'm not even going to ask why ye assume it was me when my older brothers are meaner and scarier, but to understand what happened, there's a whole long story that comes before it."

"Involving McInver and the hostel your brother mentioned?"

He inclined his head and went quiet for a long moment. Then he started speaking. "Sin, Struan, Burn, and I are all McInver's sons, but none of us knew that, or each other, pretty much, until the past year or so. One by one, we were kidnapped and taken to an island to be hidden away so others could claim McInver's money."

I goggled at him. "Kidnapped. By who?"

"Two men who are both now dead. Thea's da was one of them. He's also Lottie's da, but she only just found that out. His business partner's wife is a distant relative of McInver's, and the business partner planned to have his son inherit, which is why we needed to be out of the way. We didn't know who our father was, and McInver had never claimed us, so coupled with the fact we were mostly delinquents, it was easy for them to disappear us and convince the islanders we were there for criminal rehab."

"A whole conspiracy wrapped around snatching McInver's cash."

He grunted agreement. "Aye, and check us out now. I'm driving there to claim it, though the last thing I want is that man's money. But I still need to do this to find out exactly where Burn is being kept, and also because it could help us claim back Cassie, our little sister. She was with us for a while but got snatched back into foster care."

"They kidnapped her, too?"

He dipped his head, his dark hair falling into his eyes and concealing them from me. "It wasn't long after she showed up at the hostel that it all came to a head. Ye asked about the woman I killed. We never knew her name, but we called her Keep. She was our prison keeper and managed us using ankle trackers and her Taser to give us a shock if we stepped out of line. One night, an islander came to her and asked to buy Cassie or Burn. Ye can imagine what for. It turned into a fight, and I twisted her Taser on her. She pressed the button, shocked herself, and dropped dead from an instant heart attack."

I had no words.

In my whole life, I hadn't met anyone with a truly charmed existence. All the kids I knew from school had issues, poverty and all kinds of abuse being common. But this took the biscuit.

"To think, when we met, I thought you were a rich boy," I said.

"Because ye saw me as McInver's son. I understood. I'm not as bad as ye think."

"You're still a jerk."

"Aye, but you're in a car with me, so that feeling isn't too deep."

I ignored the tease in his tone, and he continued his story.

"After we escaped our prison, we went to the mansion for answers. None of us were interested in getting to know the old man, but there are some mysteries that had to be solved. Sin needed to know what happened to his mother. I have my own demons."

My gut tightened as his words formed a picture, added to by his brothers' reaction to what we were doing tonight. "Are you in danger?"

His gaze sought mine for a brief moment before he turned back to the road. "I don't know. Half the time, it feels like we're still being hunted, and dead bodies are about to pop up, the other half is the fact that we are mostly innocent. Until someone tries to act against us, we're trying to just live."

For a long while, neither of us spoke. It was hard to imagine everything that he and his family had been through, and I couldn't easily make sense of any of it, but I knew for certain that I'd had so much wrong about him.

My perspective of him shifted, just a little, but every inch I gave up only enabled my need for him to grow.

A need that confused me and had the potential to humiliate me.

Outside the cabin, he'd gazed at me with want. Said he'd been attracted to me, but his actions were different to any man I'd known before.

"What happened in that hotel room?" I burst out. "Or any of the other times you've had access to my naked body and did nothing?"

"What do ye mean?"

"You never copped a feel."

His mouth opened. "Are ye asking why I didnae assault ye?"

"I mean..."

"What the hell kind of men do ye know who'd do that?"

"Bad ones. Or maybe just average ones. Men have always taken grabs at me. In bars, at school, in supermarkets. Even my neighbour cornered me in the stairwell last month after he'd come back drunk. From a young age, I've always known it's safer to assume they're all dangerous."

"What's that neighbour's name?"

"Nunya."

"Nunya?"

"None of ya business. My point is, I don't know many men who'd give up the chance of a quick grope."

"Because ye only know arseholes. If this is a twisted way of asking if I'm attracted to ye, then fuck yeah. If it matters, you're the only woman I've ever been attracted to. But in no way is that ever going to make me into a pervert who touches a lass without her permission."

It was my turn to stare with my mouth open.

"What?" he said, driving us on through the dark.

"Give me a minute for my brain to tick over. I'm having to reform my views on guys. Or maybe just on you some more." I worked that through in my mind, creating a new category of Decent Man in my head. "I turn you on, though," I added.

"Ye do."

"A lot?"

"Constantly."

"And that thing about me being the only one, are you mainly into guys then?"

"Not at all."

"So why am I so special?"

He didn't answer.

It took until we were rolling into McInver's grounds again before my pulse rate normalised.

We exited the car in an empty car park, the half-ruined mansion a silhouette. Goosebumps broke out over my skin. I drew Summer's light-knit cardigan closer around my corn-flower-blue dress.

"I expected worse."

Scar led me up the steps, ducking under police tape so we could enter the house.

"Low voices until we're sure no one else is here," he said. "It's been empty on my other visits, aside from when I met the lawyer, but I'll need to check that we're safe."

The smell of burning hung in the air of the entryway, grit crunching on the marble underfoot. I hadn't seen much of the place when I'd been brought here. I'd been confined to one room, hidden in another, then dragged down to the great hall. Now, the doors to the hall drooped open, the night sky visible through the roof beyond. Rubble piled where I guessed other rooms had stood.

What a difference to the home of a vicious pervert. I couldn't stop a grin from spreading. His powerbase had gone.

It took a moment to realise Scar was staring at me.

He angled to get a better view of my face. "There was me thinking it might be hard for ye to come back here. Bad memories and all. You're standing there smiling."

"Something wrong with that?"

"Not at all. I like it."

There was an undercurrent to his tone I wanted to explore.

To understand how far that like went and how much the tension between us could grow. Which was insane considering our history.

He advanced to stick his head in the hall, then returned to me, and we took the corridor that led to the left. On silent feet, we padded along, occasionally glancing into rooms and keeping quiet. Likewise, no other sound came from within the vast house. Perhaps I should have been worried about the place collapsing, but both Scar and the lawyer had been in here, and it was still standing.

We reached a room, and he paused us. "McInver's office. We were on the phone here when I got caught."

I wrinkled my nose. "Before I ran."

He rested a shoulder on the wall, only the faint light through the corridor's windows showing me his brooding expression. "Ye came back."

"I did."

He studied me for a moment longer. "Ye could have called."

"I... I didn't..."

"I mean ye could have called me with your theory on how Burn knew Summer. Instead, ye came to me."

Heat crawled under my skin. "Do you need a reason?"

His gaze dropped to my lips, and I moistened them, a weight descending over me and time slowing. He was going to kiss me. I wanted his mouth on mine.

From in the office, a phone rang.

Neither of us moved, locked in our draw.

I'd kissed boys before, but never anything more, at least not voluntarily. I'd never longed for them, hadn't felt a sense of urgency like this or suffered an unending battle of attraction and frustration.

A beep followed, and a voice played out in the depths of the office. "Mr McInver, just a quick confirmation that your payment has been received in full. We wish you every happiness with your purchase."

It was Vanessa from Baby Girl.

How Scar found me and won the auction had been a mystery, but it happened, and other events had taken over. I'd been content to wait for an answer.

The reason was all too obvious now. He'd used McInver's access to buy me.

I didn't care. I'd been pissed off that he'd prevented my discovering another member of the List, but... My thoughts reached another conclusion. Scar was a member of it now. At least temporarily, he'd taken over from his dad.

His expression of hunger had dropped at the answerphone message and now sank into a frown, like he'd realised the same thing.

He'd bought me.

"Come on," he grumped and stomped on down the hall. This time, without waiting on me.

I skittered after him.

He opened door after door, continuing his check of the place. Marching on, he came to the end of the corridor and tried the exterior exit.

"Locked," he muttered.

"Wait up," I said, half out of breath from his pace.

But already, he'd headed to a smaller door to the right of the exit, leading into the interior of the house. It opened outwards, and pitch-black stairs led down.

I peered into the gloom. "Horror movie says nope."

Scar illuminated his phone's torch, not needed until now because the corridor's wide windows had let in enough moonlight.

The light bleached the stone stairway. Anything could be down there. Intruders. Animals. McInver's first wife turned pet monster.

Scar proceeded down it.

"Are you crazy?" I hissed.

"Just taking a look," he replied and kept moving.

The stairs turned, and he vanished, the area of his light bobbing.

I peered down the corridor, the creeps taking full hold of me. Scar had gone down there because he was driven by angst over what he'd done. If he got killed because of stressing out over me, I'd kill him again myself.

Something creaked, and a tap followed, I guessed the

sounds of him exploring.

"What's down there?" I whispered.

His light stopped moving. No reply came.

"Scar?" I called a little louder.

The cellar plunged into darkness.

Oh hell, no.

Panic struck me. I scrabbled in my bag to find my phone. It was somewhere at the bottom, loose amongst all the junk I carried. God, why did I have all this crap?

Finally, my fingers curled around it, and I whipped it out and stabbed at the screen to get the torch to work.

Nothing happened. It was Summer's phone. I groaned and tossed it in the side pocket, starting my frantic search again.

Suddenly, from beyond the curve of the stairs, came a bloodcurdling yell.

It resounded, echoing down the hall.

"Ahh!" I shrieked, staggering back. In my haste, I tripped over my own feet, landing on my ass.

Not for a second did I tear my gaze from the open cellar doorway.

My pulse sped. Scenarios crashed together in my mind. Someone had grabbed him. Someone hiding down there had hurt him. I needed a weapon.

A figure stormed the stairs, and I sprang up, ready to fight, my bag swinging in my hand.

Scar strolled up the last few steps, his shoulders shaking with laughter. "Going to hit me with that?"

My jaw dropped, and I tossed the bag down. "Fucking

hell. I thought you were hurt. You are no longer in the Decent Man category I invented just for you and right back to being a jerk."

He closed in on me, something in his right hand. A dusty-looking bottle.

"Ye called me Scar instead of Camden."

"That's what everyone calls you."

"You're not everyone." He got closer still, walking me backwards until he'd crowded me against the wall. Then he bent over me, placing the bottle down on the windowsill at my back. "I introduced myself with my real name the first time we met, upstairs in this godforsaken place, when I tried to rescue ye."

I pressed my fingers to my chest over my speeding heart, and my other hand to his t-shirt. His heart thumped just as fast as mine.

The magnetic, compelling, velvety sense of him surrounded me, and I liked all too much the cautious, yet determined gleam in his eye.

I parted my lips and tilted up my chin. "Yes, Camden. How could I forget? You tattooed it on me for anyone to see."

His breath ghosted over me.

Yet he didn't move, seeming caught on indecision or something else.

Fuck it. I pushed up on my toes and pressed my lips to his.

Everything apart from that familiar bloom of heat was forgotten.

My kiss was slow, giving him a chance to stop me. Instead, he gave a deep sound of surprise then angled his head to better meet my lips.

A thrill rushed through me. At his warm, hard body, so big against me. I couldn't stop my moan when he opened his mouth and slid his tongue over mine. I'd wondered how he'd taste. Addictive was my answer. Sexy, powerful man.

His echoing groan had him squeezing me tighter. He ran both arms around my back to bring me to him. Every one of my senses tuned in to him.

I clutched on to his arms, so turned on. My nipples pebbled, and I needed more. Everything.

Except despite all of this, a question wailed in my mind.

Why hadn't he kissed me?

I'd been the one to close the distance.

My conclusion hurt, and it drained the passion from the moment.

Breaking our kiss, I moved away, stooping to grab the bottle from the windowsill. Then I turned and stalked down the corridor, leaving a no doubt confused Scotsman in my wake.

15

Camden

The quiet of the empty house stretched around me. Breeze's footsteps had disappeared into the dark, but I hadn't pursued her.

Not yet.

Holding myself together while she'd kissed me had taken everything I had. An internal battle raged.

Images flashed through my mind, things I wanted to do to Breeze. It built on how I was angry at her for the choices she'd made, but also fucking delighted that she'd come to me. I was out of control and spiralling.

I'd paid for her at an auction, for fuck's sake.

In McInver's house, it was all too present how much I was like him.

I breathed through my nose, my hands clenched into fists. Then in my head, Struan's advice returned. He told me to talk to her. To ask.

Something had to give or I'd explode.

Breaking the tight hold on myself, I strode down the

corridor, following her flight. At the wide-open entrance foyer, I paused.

A clunk came from up the stairs.

In a patch of light from a high-up window, Breeze sat near the top of the marble steps. She took a swig from the antique bottle of champagne then brought her attention to me.

The moonlight silvered her curls. I'd seen her like this before, the night of the fire when I'd brought her back to the cabin. Then, she'd been terrified. Now, she was a fucking goddess.

"Why did ye walk away?" I asked.

I suspected an answer but needed to hear it from her.

"I'm not yours."

"Never said ye were."

"What I mean is, you don't own me. I'm guessing that being the heir somehow enabled you to access McInver's money to pay for me at the auction." She took another deep swig of the wine. "That contract is over."

I moved to the base of the stairs then climbed a couple of steps.

"I know that was on your mind," she continued. "I felt it in the way you kissed me. You were holding back."

"True," I confirmed.

"But there's more to it. You judge me. Which is fucking offensive." Breeze watched my every move, my slow prowl up the stairs. "I know you hate what I did, or what I was prepared to do, but I would sell myself a thousand times over for those I love. I'd endure anything. Women are strong in that respect. It's men who put the price on things like virginity and ownership."

"I don't judge ye for that, but I won't lie and say I approve. It makes me so angry to think of ye in danger." I advanced until I was just a couple of steps below her.

Every inch I got closer to her, the need within me grew.

Heated my blood.

Left me harder than ever.

"So much you branded your name on me for any man to see and take as a warning."

At least in that, I was innocent. "No."

"What do you mean, no? That's exactly what you did."

"Ye want a proper apology for the tattoo. You're right. I'm sorry. But tell me which way I wrote the letters. From whose perspective do they read?"

She glanced down at her body. Sheer desire shot through me.

"For me, looking down on them," she slowly concluded.

"Exactly. Nothing to do with anyone else. Now, how do I make it up to ye?"

Breeze's scowl remained, but she beckoned me. Then she rested back on her elbows, still holding the champagne but reclining on the steps.

She'd kicked her sandals off. I knelt by her bare feet.

Purposefully, she moved them either side of me. I shifted into the gap where her dress rode up her legs.

"Tell me how to make it up to ye," I repeated, my voice deep and rough.

"Kiss it better."

All my reason was lost.

The towering need crested, taking control.

I placed my hands on her knees, earning a short gasp from the woman, then drove my fingers higher, pressing into her soft skin and drawing up the material of her dress.

Several times, I'd seen Breeze naked. No matter how sexy she was, without her consent, it had been wrong. Now, I let myself feel every wave of attraction. Absorb the image of her spread out for me. At this rate, I was going to fucking come at the sight of her underwear alone.

I lowered my head and pressed a kiss to the inside of her knee, then another to her inner thigh.

I pushed her skirt to her waist, revealing her little black pair of boy shorts. Sexiest fucking thing I'd ever seen.

"Take them off," she ordered.

Didn't need to tell me twice.

Twisting my fingers into the sides of the underwear, I drew them down her long, slim legs. Then she was bared to me, and a pulse of painful lust burst through my veins.

From my position, I had a perfect view, including of how wet she was, glistening in the moonlight. But the tattoo itself was half concealed.

The image of her pussy had been imprinted in my mind when I worked on her, and if it had swollen or been sore, that wasn't obvious now.

"I want to touch ye."

"Open me up. Find your marks."

I slid my fingers into her most delicate flesh, parting them in a V and fully displaying the ink. The purple letters stood out, bold capitals, still slightly raised, but healing exactly as she'd said.

My breathing stuttered, and I couldn't take my gaze off her.

"So fucking beautiful," I muttered.

Then I ducked to kiss right on her pussy.

Breeze moaned and dug her fingers into my hair.

I kissed her again, this time trailing my tongue over each of the letters, mapping them, then up the centre of her to her clit. Her taste imprinted on my soul. "Tell me what ye like."

"More. Keep going."

This had to be good for her.

I took her fingers and brought them to her core. "Show me where to touch and how."

"You won't hurt me. Even if you do, I don't care."

"I mean I've never done this before. Teach me. I want to make it good."

She paused, and I lifted my gaze to hers. It was all too apparent how my words had turned her on.

Then her hand moved, and I glanced back down to watch her put two fingers to drive a circle over her clit. As she worked herself, she couldn't avoid touching the closest letters of the tattoo. Fucking hell, that was hot.

"Do that with your mouth. You claimed my pussy, now get to know her."

I flattened my tongue and copied her actions, alternating with sucking. She urged me on, and every time I felt the ridge of the letters, fresh need built in me.

Breeze arched into me, her breathing coming faster. I guided her hand back to her centre again and to her entrance. She showed me by touch, and we both slid a finger inside her tight, hot body.

My dick pulsed, and I groaned.

"Deeper," she urged. "Press where I'm pressing."

She withdrew, and I doubled down on what she'd asked me to do. My fingers and then my tongue in her cunt. My devotion hers.

Breeze moaned again, sending sparks of pleasure through me.

"Sit up," she ordered abruptly.

I obeyed, dizzy with lust.

"Take off your shirt."

I ripped it from my body and tossed it.

"Kiss me."

From the cradle of her hips, I leaned over her body and laid my lips on hers. This time, I didn't hold back. I kissed her like she was all I needed to live.

I had no experience, no technique, nothing to follow but the beating pulse of my desire.

This was so different from our earlier brief kiss.

We moved together, fitting perfectly. I wanted to devour her.

But first, I needed to make her come.

Pulling back, I kissed her cheek, then her jawline, and settled myself between her legs again, wasting no time in getting reacquainted with her beautiful pussy.

This time, I pushed two fingers inside her and focused

on sucking her clit, then alternating with swoops of my tongue. This I could do for days. Each sound of pleasure she gave up showed me what she liked.

I was a quick learner.

Pretty soon, she was winding small circles with her hips and panting. Then she took a breathy moan, and her pussy clamped down on my fingers.

"God, I'm coming," she groaned.

Pleasure lurched in me. I kept the pace until she collapsed down, then slowed, working her through it, relieved for her but the need in me only more painful.

Breeze guided my head away to stop me, and I rose, instantly hooked on her blissed-out expression.

"Open your jeans," she commanded.

I hesitated, because this had all been about her, no matter how I felt.

More, I'd resisted the flashes of how I wanted this to go so I could focus on her pleasure. The twisted ideas in my mind.

"Switch places. Let me work out what you like." She went to sit up.

I held her thigh. "No. This was enough."

"I want to reciprocate."

"Ye don't have to."

"Why refuse me?" Propped up on her elbows, she tilted her head. Then curiosity brightened her eyes. "Okay, how about you show me what you like. I'll hold still and watch."

Without knowing she was delivering into my twisted fantasy, she stretched out and took hold of the banister.

With her other hand, she grabbed the lip of a higher step. Then she extended her legs so she was spread out before me.

My heart thumped. My dick hardened.

"Do your worst. I'll stay exactly like this," she added.

I couldn't admit the extent of what I wanted. Constraints around her wrists and ankles, stopping her from getting away from me. It was fucked up. This was still a huge turn-on. It was enough.

As my answer, I opened my jeans and finally released my heavy, too-hard cock. Instant relief came as I fisted my length.

Breeze stared wide-eyed at me, her focus on where I jacked myself off. Her pink tongue darted out to wet her lips. "I kept remembering that you had a pretty dick. Couldn't get it out of my head. But damn, the size of it."

I swept my thumb through my precum, groaning at how good it felt. How I liked her words.

I alternated staring at her perfect face then down to the core of her. Then I spread her pussy lips with my fingers again, revealing my name.

I probably should have tried to last. Make a better impression. But the sight of the tattoo only drove me on. I sucked in a breath and moved faster, gripping myself harder, imagining plunging into her.

Pressure built up, and my balls tightened. I was so hard I was going insane. Almost seeing stars.

Then Breeze spoke. "When you tattooed me, it made me so wet I wanted you to make me come on that hotel room bed."

Like I was smashing through a barrier, my orgasm shattered me. I groaned loud, a shout of pleasure that echoed in the cavernous entrance hall. My cum spilled over Breeze's pussy, landing in pulses. For several dizzying seconds, I could barely breathe, staring at the perfect sight before my vision failed and I hung my head.

Finally, I caught my breath, and I trailed my fingers through the mess, then rubbed my cum into her pussy lips, pressing down on my tattooed name.

"God," she uttered on an erotic-as-fuck moan.

I wanted to thrust my cum inside her, some instinct driving me that was as hard to resist as the thousand others I had when it came to this lass.

Breeze didn't break her hold on the steps and the banister. Instead, she let me touch her until my breathing had returned to normal.

Whatever normal was. What we'd done had changed me. I wasn't sure how yet, but everything was different.

I wanted more from her. For her to take it all from me.

Her tied up so it wasn't just a game.

I'd never admit that.

I wanted her truths, too. The thoughts mixed up in my head to create a dizzying, alarming new idea.

The people I cared about left me. My mother, my grandparents, gone. Burn and Cassie taken. My family in constant danger.

Breeze had already once run off and put her life at risk. If I chained her to a bed, she couldn't do it again.

And I was the most fucked-up person in the world for finding that hot.

16

Breeze

Of all the ways I expected to remember this man, forever associating him with a throbbing pussy was a surprise. Maybe if I told him, he'd get a kick out of the fact. I'd watched his every reaction when he'd seen the tattoo. How delicious his response, how turned on he'd got, and how much I'd liked him rubbing his cum into it.

I loved the ache.

Felt alive after weeks of worry and stress.

It gave me a connection to him unlike anything I'd felt before. It was tentative, and new, and freaked me the hell out.

Then there was the other side of it. My reaction to how my tattooed skin hurt. Instead of wanting him to stop, I'd found myself needing more of the pain. No, I worked it through, not the pain itself, exactly, but him touching me.

Confusing as hell.

We'd cleaned up and dressed quietly, and even after what we'd done, he'd given me privacy. So respectful. My anger for him hadn't vanished, but my orgasm had quietened it.

Side by side, we explored the next floor of the mansion.

There was a clear division in the building. The right-hand side beyond the great hall had burned down completely, and the hall itself was half ruined, but everything to the left was sturdy. The first suite of rooms we checked out included a formal living room, complete with high-backed fussy sofas, and a couple of empty offices. Nothing of interest, so we carried on.

From the ancient, hopefully priceless champagne I'd drunk, I had a slight buzz going and the world felt lighter. "Do you really own all this now?"

He shrugged. "Like we saw, McInver isn't dead, but it looks like I already have some rights. The lawyer will tell me the extent of it tomorrow."

"What did your brother mean about McInver wanting Sin and not you? If you're both his sons, what does it matter?"

"McInver rejected me because of this." He tapped his scarred face. "He implied to Sin that he knew why it happened."

"You don't?"

"I remember the event, but I never knew who did it. I was just a kid."

Pretty quickly, I'd become used to the ridge that ran down the side of Camden's face. It was part of him, in the same way his unruly black hair was, or his dark-blue eyes. It added to his beauty. Gave him a dangerous edge that I'd only seen hints of in his character.

Yet someone had hurt him badly when they'd inflicted it.

I knew bad people. My mother's boyfriend took pride in having connections into Edinburgh's lowlife. He and his buddies shared exploits about the shit they'd pulled like they were swapping family news.

It incensed me that someone had exacted that level of injury on a child.

"McInver is an asshole. The person who hurt you, whoever they are, needs to die."

Camden gave me his cute, upside-down smile. "What do ye care?"

"I don't. I don't even like you."

He grinned bigger then opened an opulent gold-and-white door. Inside, a big bed dominated one side, its four posters and draped material making it even more fancy.

I blinked at it. "McInver's bedroom?"

He scanned the room. "No personal possessions, and it doesn't look well used. I vote guest room for important people he wanted to impress."

It hadn't been my room. I'd been elsewhere in the building, away from the more public zone. Hopefully in the bit that had been destroyed.

We carried on down the hall, passing a bathroom which I ducked into to complete my clean-up.

When I emerged, Camden was in the doorway of the room opposite. "Ye like reading, am I right?"

"Yeah, why?"

"Check this out."

I followed him in, taking a second for my eyes to adjust to the gloom. Unlike the other rooms, this one had the windows covered. That couldn't conceal the tall shelves lined with books. Gold letters gleamed on cracked spines. More bookcases sectioned up the room, holding thousands of volumes.

"A library," I breathed.

"Wait for it."

He flipped a switch, and lamps sprang to life on tables, spreading a gentle glow across the dark oak and soft furnishings.

I let out a laugh. "Oh my God. The house still has power?"

"Yep. I think this is part of why the lawyer wants to see me. He can't do anything to this place without authority. McInver started the paperwork for appointing his heir. As far as the lawyer's concerned, any heir will do."

I wandered into the room, eyes wide at the array of pretty tomes. I'd wanted clues about my sister but had given up the idea that that would be in writing somewhere. Instead, I let myself indulge in the beautiful library.

The shelves near the entrance housed rows of identical leatherbound editions, the titles unfamiliar to me but sounding old and important. The midsection, with a wide table, contained tall encyclopaedias and maps. I moved on in a kind of dream state, discovering a section of novels with authors I recognised like Austen and Hardy. This was something else. It could have all been burned, but somehow it survived.

"Do ye work?" Camden said out of the blue.

I turned to see him leaning on the heavy oak table by the maps.

"I was at college until I graduated this spring, but I worked evenings and weekends as a promotions girl at events since I was fourteen. I haven't taken any shifts since I've been looking for my sister."

"Promotions?"

"Everything from walking up and down the middle of a department store in fancy dress offering coupons to shoppers, to long Saturdays in the rain standing outside a beer festival, ushering drinkers inside with a fake German accent. The pay was good, and they always had work going."

He snorted amusement. "What did ye do at college?"

"That's not so interesting."

"Why?"

"Because girls like me get offered a limited choice of courses, and because the government paid for it all, I had to choose from within those."

He tilted his head, impossibly handsome under the warm library light.

I sighed. "Childcare, hair and beauty, or catering. Basically lining us up for entry-level jobs or living on benefits. Guess which I chose."

"I can't call it. None of those suit ye."

He was right. None had. "I chose catering. Summer picked hair and beauty. Neither of us enjoyed what we were learning, but mine came with modules on business studies, so it wasn't all bad."

"What would ye do if ye had a choice?"

I exhaled, his question skimming the edge of my nerves. I'd never told anyone this, apart from Summer. "I always wanted to study English literature. It was my highest grade at school, and I loved it, picking apart books and finding themes. But there's no job at the end of that, so the government wouldn't fund a degree in it, so my education is over."

"Librarian sounds like a good career."

"Doesn't it?"

Camden rounded the table and dropped onto a dark leather sofa, resting an arm on the ornate rolled back. He gestured with his chin to the shelves. "I'm in no rush to move on. Take your time. Look around."

Oh, the temptation.

If I started opening books, I wouldn't want to stop. I could spend days in this room, learning what was here and making a reading list.

His offer set off a longing deep inside me.

It was too much, and I couldn't indulge.

Instead, I drifted over to where he reclined, dropped my bag to the floor, and knelt on the leather sofa. Camden had one leg up on the seat, and his arms spread across the low back. He held his position, letting me come to him.

I crawled up his body until I was straddling him. Gently, I placed a finger on his cheek and pushed his face to the side. Then I dropped a kiss on the top end of his scar at his temple, another on his one cheek, and one more on the curve of his jaw where the ridge disappeared.

His hands landed on my waist and slipped down to cup my hips. He turned to catch my lips with his, and we kissed like this was a normal, natural thing we could do.

It was all too easy kissing this man.

He was a drug, the only one I'd ever indulge in, and though I needed the distraction, I couldn't afford to get addicted.

In a minute, the kiss went from exploratory to heated. He slid his hands back to my ass, and I put mine on his chest, using the purchase to grind on his lap. A prickle of pain resounded from the site of my tattoo. I repeated the action, breaking our kiss on a short gasp at how good it felt.

Camden kissed my cheek. "I don't want to hurt ye."

My heart thudded. I knew what he was saying. We'd only just done stuff, and he was worried about me. "What if I like it?"

He stopped to look at me. "Being hurt?"

"The tattoo pain definitely did something to me. What? You liked how I spread out for you. Tie me up, if you want."

Instantly, his gaze shuttered. "I'm not into that."

Under me, his dick pulsed.

"Are you sure? Your body says otherwise."

I ground down on him. Camden groaned and closed his eyes.

This was better than talking. In the beautiful library, surrounded by books, I could lose myself with this man.

I didn't want to like him, or have him get to know me or be under my skin any more than the tattoo he'd drawn. All our chat would do is make me want to be his friend, and that wasn't happening.

"I want to try more things," I stated instead. "For some

reason, my pussy is really interested in you, despite everything you did to her. We have time to kill before morning, so either play with me or sit and watch me read. Your choice."

Something registered in his gaze, a battle I didn't understand. He didn't answer, but his fingers dug harder into my hips.

I climbed off him then stooped to pick up my bag.

I hadn't joked about carrying around a lot of junk. When I'd left the hotel room, I'd taken the things Vanessa had brought. The constraints. The toy.

I pulled out the leather wrist and ankle cuffs, each with a length of fine woven rope on them.

Camden let out a hard breath and grabbed my biceps to pull me back to him for a kiss.

Excitement buzzed over my nervous system. "I was right. You'd like me to be constrained."

"I don't want to want that."

"But it turns you on anyway." I took in the corners of the sofa, the ironwork which made up the frame. Perfect for tying someone to.

"Technically, these belong to you anyway," I said. "You paid for me and for these. I'm not going to push you into anything, but we aren't a couple. This isn't a date. Whatever we get up to is tonight only, and I want to indulge."

He stood in a fluid motion, placing me back on the couch to stand over me.

"I was in McInver's office when I heard about your auction." He took the leather restraints from me and put them down on the sofa. "I thought I was too late. I was desperate and ready to gamble everything. I rang the number back, and the organiser was over-fucking-joyed to hear from a McInver. She'd wondered why I hadn't bid. I told her to mind her own business. To place a higher bid again using my regular payment method until I owned the girl she was selling. It worked. She said there was another eager buyer but still snapped to obey me, just based on the number I was calling from. It made me realise two things. First, that I'd do whatever it took to win ye. And second, that McInver holds more power with them than just a regular buyer."

I stared at him, stuck on the third implication of his discoveries. That I'd been luckier than I could imagine. An eager buyer sounded terrifying. I knelt up on the sofa, reached for my hem, and stripped my summer dress.

"You saved me. That doesn't mean I feel like I owe you anything, in case you're worried. But it is a massive turn-on. There aren't many people who'd stand up for me."

His hungry gaze sank over my body, down my collar-bone to where my boobs overspilled my bra, then skimmed my waist. I took hold of his shirt and tugged at it.

He peeled it off, revealing solid shoulders rounded with muscle, and leading to a tight waist. His inkwork. The outlines he was working on.

I had a thing for his strong arms.

Feasting my eyes on him was no hardship. "Jeans next," I ordered.

As he removed them to leave him just in his boxers, I picked up two leather cuffs and fixed them around my wrists.

I perched on the edge of the sofa and gestured at the back. "Loop the ropes through the ironwork and tie my arms back."

Urgency claimed me.

The reminder of the auction was messing with my head. The only thing of any value I had was my virginity. I didn't want it anymore. Didn't want to have the capacity to put myself in danger. I needed it gone.

More, I wanted to be as close to Camden as we could get. The strength of feeling was only getting bigger.

He took hold of the rope, extending my arm out. "Can I take your bra off first?"

I nodded, more than spellbound by him.

Camden knelt in front of me. He reached back to unfasten the clasp, then slid the bra down my arms to cast it aside. He leaned in, but I pressed against his chest.

"Tie me up first."

Holding my gaze, he tied off the rope to the back of the sofa, one side then the other. He swore, then swore again. "Ye have no idea how beautiful ye are."

"Liking it now, huh? Cuff my ankles and tie them to the sofa legs."

He looked me over, assessing me, then peered around the room. Camden moved away and collected deep cushions from two other sofas elsewhere in the room, then put them behind my back so I could recline, still with my ass at the edge of the seat, but in a better position now.

Working this thing out as we went along.

He fastened my ankles so I was completely tied up.

With my arms pulled back and my legs spread, I was completely vulnerable. He could do anything. Yet I trusted him. "I'm at your mercy. What are you going to do about it?"

"Use my position of power to make ye scream."

I moaned softly, and he knelt in front of me once more. In this position, we were face to face, and he started with a kiss. A seductive, hard kiss when he slipped his tongue into my mouth and showed me how this was going to go. He wanted to dominate me. I wanted to let him.

He kept an even pace, skimming his hands up my sides to hold my shoulders. Then he drifted his thumbs around my rib cage to my breasts.

I closed my eyes, sitting forward from the cushion because I wanted his mouth to keep going down my body.

He slowed the kiss. "Do ye want to be blindfolded?"

"The one from the hotel is in my bag."

I kept my eyes closed, hearing his actions rather than seeing them. The blindfold eased into place over my eyes, and blackness stole my sight. Instantly, my senses were heightened.

"All good?" Camden asked, low.

"Really good," I mumbled back.

Without warning, his hot mouth landed on my breast, startling me into a short cry. He sucked hard in one place then curled his tongue around my nipple and sucked again. Then he lightly bit on me.

The sensation almost overwhelmed me. It felt so good. I'd already been wet for him, but he was going to soak me. "More," I commanded.

He switched sides and bit my other nipple, soothing it with his tongue straight after. Then he sucked on my plump skin, moving from place to place, his actions delivering delicious pinpricks of pain.

Exciting me more than I could have imagined.

As he worked, he moulded and shaped me, playing with my tits in a way no one had before. He grazed one hand down over my belly, sending sparks fluttering, and into my underwear.

"These need to go. Got another pair?"

"Yes," I stuttered.

He wrenched them, tearing the offending material away. Instantly, he cupped me between the legs.

"Fuck," he drawled. "You're soaking. So gorgeous, naked and waiting on me."

In my position of being tied up, I couldn't relieve the throbbing at the juncture of my thighs, and the jolt of lust shot through me at his touch. I needed him to move his hand.

Anything to help ease the ache.

Camden made a sound of interest. "There's something else in that bag of tricks of yours. Can I use it?"

It took me a second to realise what he meant. The vibrator.

I nodded, and the toy buzzed a second later.

Not being able to see was both strange and freeing. I pictured him holding the pink, ridged device. His expression of need. I had no idea what he was going to do with it first, and that was a fucking thrill.

He drew the device between my tits, circling them, then glancing over my nipples.

I arched forwards to meet it, needing more. "Press it harder."

He obeyed, dragging over my skin until I was gasping.

Rustling came. "Took off my boxers," his gruff explanation followed. "I need to be closer to ye."

"Please," was the only reply I could manage.

Two fingers landed under my jaw, tipping my face up. "Open," he said.

I opened my mouth, breathing shallow. Then his dick pressed against my lips. I'd done this once already, plus on the dark stairwell, I thought I'd got a good look, but he felt bigger than my memories supplied.

I widened and angled to let him glide in.

Instinct had me flattening my tongue. His unique taste flooded my mouth, and I breathed through my nose as he slid in and out.

I pictured myself like this, spread out for him on the leather couch and sucking his dick.

"So perfect," he uttered. Then he pulled out of my mouth, a line of saliva clinging to my chin that he brushed away with his thumb.

Camden grabbed the cushions behind me, pulling them away so I had nothing supporting my back.

I listened to hear what he was doing. The sofa shifted, and he eased his big body behind mine, positioning me on his lap.

I sighed, tipping my head back and letting myself enjoy every inch of his hot, hard body beneath me. He banded an arm underneath my breasts and picked me up to settle me better. His hard dick was now directly under me. I wriggled to move over it.

He groaned and took hold of my thighs to guide the

action. Then the vibrator buzzed to life where he held it against my leg. Without warning, he shifted it directly to my clit. I jolted and moaned.

"Hard or soft?" he rasped in my ear.

"Hard."

He obeyed, and the tip pressed against my soaking core, centring on my clit, but over and over pushing into the tattoo. The pain mixed with the tendrils of pleasure, so I tipped my head back, entirely captivated.

Camden was so much bigger than me. I could sense how he was staring down our bodies. How hard he was under me. How much this turned him on.

His other hand was splayed across my chest, holding me in place. He brought it up to grip the base of my throat.

"Ye should see how gorgeous ye look on me. Your body is incredible."

He palmed my pussy, splaying his fingers wide and revealing the tattoo. His dick pulsed, and he growled a desperate sound of lust.

Strong fingers twisted into my wealth of curls, and he yanked my head to expose my throat. I gasped, spasming between my legs, an orgasm building.

I badly wanted him to slip inside me. I was so exposed to his every touch, so deliciously turned on by him and willing to do anything.

"Fuck me," I demanded.

"No."

"Why not?"

He didn't answer, his grip on my hair tightening.

"Please," I tried. "I need more."

"If and when I fuck ye, it won't be like this. I want ye to see every second of it. But either way, you'll scream my name."

My body took over. The light pain at my scalp, the vibrator at my aching pussy, and the dominance in our positions drove me over the edge. Without any more actions, I came. Arching my back, I gasped out then collapsed onto him in blissful happiness.

A moment later, he thrust between my folds then jerked, coming, too, and growling his pleasure under me. Wet landed on my thighs, and his hand went straight to it, rubbing it into my core. On the tattoo then lower.

This time, he hadn't even penetrated me as we'd worked out how to play. Now, he pressed a finger into me, then two, taking his cum inside.

I moaned again. Why the hell was that so erotic?

It didn't matter. We'd only just started, and I already needed more.

17

Breeze

With his chin on his arm resting on the back of the sofa, Camden watched me. After our mind-blowing sex session, we'd only left the library to clean up, then we'd hidden away in here once more. Our cosy, safe refuge.

I liked browsing the shelves, knowing his gaze was glued to my every move.

"Are ye on the pill?" he asked.

I pulled down a musty-smelling book, examined it, then set it back in its home. "Yep. You've reminded me I need to take one."

I left the shelves and returned to the sofa to pick up my bag. The restraints and toy had been hidden away once again, but my cheeks burned as my fingers brushed over them in hunt for the foil pill packet. I couldn't find it, so I started taking things out.

"I have a question," I said, sorting through my posses-sions. Had to get my mind off sex. "What happened to the guy who got his head blown off downstairs?"

Camden shrugged. "At a guess, McInver's guards disposed of the body. We know they left and were never seen again, because the police wanted to speak to them but couldn't. I've been all over this place, and all over the grounds outside, and I've seen no sign of a corpse or a hastily dug grave. My guess is they threw him in the back of a car and dumped him somewhere." He gestured to the growing pile of items between us. "Why do ye have two phones?"

"One is Summer's. I found it in her room a few days ago. It won't charge, though, so I haven't been able to activate it."

He picked the phone up and turned it over, puzzling at it. "It's a waterproof one in a pretty solid case. Can't imagine it breaking easily."

"It's frustrating." I set down my hairbrush followed by some clips. "If I could get into that, who knows what I could find out."

"Ye must miss her so much."

I'd been fine until that second. Riding the energy of possibility. Distracted by how Camden and I had crashed into each other. Maybe it was the calm way he asked, but emotion bubbled up inside me. "She's all I have, apart from my mum. My best friend. We've always been there for each other, until one day, she was just gone." My words spilled out. "There was no warning. She didn't message me to say she was going anywhere, everything was normal. But for some reason, she chose to put herself up for sale and then she vanished."

His jaw ticked. "An auction."

"Yes. Exactly the same as I did."

"That's why. Ye were trying to follow her." His gaze held

mine, and understanding poured from him. But there was more, too. Absolute determination. "It won't happen again."

"Is that an order or a question? Funnily enough, my tattooed pussy is a bit of a blocker, thanks to you."

"I said I was sorry. I did it because I care."

I stopped moving. "Why? Why do you care about me?"

He didn't answer immediately, and I leaned in.

"I don't get it. We barely know each other, or at least we didn't until now. I'm nothing to you. You have your own problems yet you keep showing up to save me."

Camden graced me with that same smile I was growing obsessed with. The sides of his mouth tugging downwards and the softness in his expression compelling. "Has nobody ever cared about ye before, besides your kin?"

A burst of warmth shifted the cold inside me. "No. I'm not that special."

He got up from the sofa, clearly enjoying himself. I stood, too, sweeping my possessions back into the bag. The pills could wait.

But just as I finished, Camden lurched dramatically and dropped to lie flat on his back at my feet.

"Ohmigod. Are you okay?" I stooped beside him, my heart speeding.

"That was just me falling for ye."

He cracked up, and I sat back on my haunches and scowled at him.

Then Camden rolled up, palmed my cheek, and pressed his lips to mine. I kissed him back, forgetting everything. I liked this playful version of him. This peaceful moment we'd found and our hideaway together.

I really liked his fall, even if I knew I needed to lock the feelings down.

"Come on," he said, drawing us both to our feet.

"What are we doing?"

"We're going to look for another charger for that phone. In case the one ye tried was bust. There's bound to be somewhere the guards used to keep their shite."

A quick hunt around the library yielded nothing, but downstairs, at the very end of the corridor to the left of the great hall, we discovered a tiny office.

Camden started sliding out drawers and searching through boxes. "Bingo. Here. Try this."

He extracted a charger complete with plug. I connected it to the wall socket.

Still the phone didn't start up.

We waited for a minute to see if that made a difference, but nothing.

"Last thing to try. We'll return upstairs in case the circuit has gone down here," he offered. "The lights on this floor don't work. I figured the phone line itself carries a charge which is how that worked."

My heart told me this was a loss, but I nodded, and we trudged back to the library.

Sliding down a bookcase to park myself next to the plugs, I tried again.

Immediately, a symbol appeared on Summer's phone screen.

I yelped and held it up. "It's doing something."

Camden scooted over to sit next to me. "Shite. So it is."

It felt like forever, but after a minute, her lock screen appeared. I entered her passcode, and finally, I was staring at my sister's last actions before making her auction choice.

First, I opened her call list, but it was empty. Next, her messages. A thread to me and Mum sat on its lonesome. "Why aren't there any others?" I said.

"Deleted?" he guessed.

"Must be." I searched through every application she used. Everything with a messenger function. All were the same. If she'd chatted to people within them, she'd hidden the evidence.

Exasperated, I held the device in front of me. "This doesn't make any sense. I'm the only person who could get into her phone. Why hide this from me?"

Camden didn't answer, but he didn't need to. The pieces slid together by themselves. Summer had got herself into something she didn't want me to know about. She didn't want me to follow her. It was the only explanation.

It brought me back into my right mind. I'd allowed myself to get distracted this evening, playing with Camden. He could be useful to me in finding Summer, but he could also get in my way.

He already had once. I needed to nip the attraction in the bud and back away.

"What about web calls?" Camden asked.

"Like dialled from within an app? No one does that unless by accident, do they?" Cooling myself to him, I searched through each, hunting for a record.

Then I found something.

"God. You're right. Look. She called this account. It was a long time ago, but who the hell is @fucksurfing?" I clicked on the account, but it was empty of content, apparently unused.

With my heart in my throat, I pressed the phone symbol to call it.

Whoever this person was, they knew my sister, and I didn't know them.

Did they have her? Was she with them now?

The call connected.

Camden's phone rang.

With his expression stunned, he pulled it from his pocket, my sister's name onscreen.

18

Camden

"This is Burn's, not mine." I held it up, the call still ringing.

Breeze swallowed and hit the button to end it. Confusion held her expression. "Explain that to me?"

"When our sister was taken, we smuggled mine into her bag. Burn had taken off and climbed a cliff to get away from the police, leaving all his stuff behind. He's really on the run, as in has an outstanding arrest warrant. He couldn't afford to be caught. I've been using it since then."

"Is there anything on there from her? Any chat?"

"No." I showed her the empty account. I already knew this phone. "We had this on the island when we were prisoners, but Burn kept it in the end when we got new ones. None of us used it to message anyone, apart from Struan and Thea, plus that time Sin told us about earlier. When Burn recorded a final message. It isn't here now. He deleted it."

The light in Breeze's eyes had gone.

She doubted me. I hated that.

I jammed my fingers into my hair. "Listen, I don't lie. I'm not hiding anything. I never heard of your sister before, but this confirms for certain there's a connection between her and my brother."

Slowly, Breeze nodded. "I believe you. Then the @ fucksurfing account is his."

"Must be. He loves surfing, though. He got us all into it. I guess the name is a joke."

The easiness between us had gone. Breeze's attention drifted to the tattoo on my arm, the brand we all shared. A circle with a surfer carving the sea in front of an island.

I looked like a liar. Like I was the owner of the account and somehow playing her.

I couldn't think of anything to say to prove myself.

Instead, I climbed to my feet, then gestured to the sofa. "It's late. The lawyer will be here tomorrow. The first priority I have is finding out what he knows about my brother. Rest until then. Lock the library door behind me."

"What will you do?" Her voice came out small.

Not sleep, that was for sure. "I'll keep watch."

I strode from the room and waited outside until I heard the lock engage. It was the same as the first night she'd stayed at the cabin. Except our positions had flipped. She'd been the one wanting me closer then. Now, all I wanted was to fall asleep holding her.

Her trust had been shaken, but I'd get it back.

I'd make it happen, one way or another.

Breeze was mine, and I planned to keep her. She just

didn't know it yet.

*M*orning saw me awake and pacing. At eight on the dot, a silver Mercedes pulled up to the mansion, and the lawyer climbed out.

"Mr Golding," I greeted him.

"Mr Marshall. So good to see you, sir."

It was strange hearing someone use my surname. No one had in years, but I'd had to give it over for the identification process.

"I'll be using McInver from now on," I stated, my skin crawling.

"Of course! How wonderful." The slight-framed lawyer clutched a briefcase and gestured to the house. "Are you staying here?"

"I did last night." I jerked my head at the entrance and led him inside.

In McInver's office, complete with smashed window, I sat behind the desk like I owned the place.

It was a power move, but that was why I'd taken this course of action, to get the power back from people fucking with my family.

Golding perched in the seat opposite and brought a stack of papers from his briefcase as well as a tablet. "We have much to discuss. As you are aware, your father made provisions for an heir that were at an advanced stage. It only needed you to put yourself forward and take the DNA test proving your right for me to bring the process to a conclusion."

"Meaning?"

"Sign this and you are the heir with all relevant rights."

He handed over the tablet with a stylus. I scanned it, reading nothing I could make sense of, then scrawled my name at the bottom.

Fuck it. Whatever the consequences, I'd do this for Burn, and for Breeze.

Golding wilted as if a weight had been lifted from his shoulders. "Now that's out of the way, I have a long list of issues and urgent business I need you to make decisions on. Insurance companies require a response, several investments have matured, I have fielded numerous and demanding messages from your father's associates, but—"

I held up a hand. "Can I give ye the role to make appropriate decisions on all that?"

"Why," he hesitated, "yes. Though your father would not like—"

"My father's still unconscious," I interrupted. "You're his right-hand man. I can't think of anyone better for the job."

Golding sat a little taller. "Would it please you if I only brought the most urgent or personal things to your attention?"

"Aye, that will be perfect."

He dipped his head. "I'll get to work right away. You won't regret putting your trust in me. Now, there are matters of the assets you might find of immediate comfort."

He handed an envelope over.

"A credit card in your name. No limit, of course. If you follow me, I can supply the code to the garage so you can avail yourself of the transport options."

He led the way out of the office, and I tried to hide my shock at being given a card with no limit. I'd never had money. Never had enough to live on growing up.

Just like that, I could spend what I wanted.

There was a separate building across the car park from the mansion. I'd assumed it held cars but hadn't been able to get inside.

I was halfway down the corridor, following Golding as he chatted about an investment portfolio, when I finally re-engaged my brain.

"There's one matter I want handled immediately."

"Consider it done."

"The investigation into the person who burned down my father's house. I understand they've arrested the culprit."

"Quite so, though between you and me, I believe the individual has not yet been charged so officially, he doesn't exist."

We'd reached the marble entranceway. I drew to a halt, and Golding waited on me, his expression expectant.

"Arrange for me to meet him."

The lawyer did his now familiar little rapid blink and nod where he worked to understand me. Presumably, this was how he'd operated with my father. "You wish to progress the case and see the man punished. Such devastation." He gestured to the ruined great hall through the open doors, daylight not sparing the rocky and dusty floor. "With your permission, I will have a team of contractors start repairs on the mansion today. All that's happened so far is the surveyor had it made safe, the structure secured, and services to the destroyed wing switched off. It was fortunate the main building was so much older and able to stand alone. I know an excellent firm who will quote for the restoration."

"The prisoner," I prompted again.

"Yes, sir. However, I rather think you will be better suited to make the request. The chief of police is a very close friend of your father's. In fact, he mentioned coming by to meet you."

McInver was tight with the chief of police? That was an interesting turn-up.

"I'd prefer it if ye asked."

"Naturally. A moment, please." Golding took out his phone and made a call.

Footsteps came from the floor above, and I twisted to see Breeze hovering at the top of the grand staircase. She hesitated, but I gestured for her to come down.

By the time she was at my side, the lawyer was off the phone. He turned back around, his eyes widening slightly at the sight of the lass.

He brought his now rigid smile back to me. "The meeting is arranged at your convenience. The chief is keen to make your acquaintance. I have sent his contact details to your phone."

On cue, my phone buzzed in my pocket.

My heart pounded. I could see Burn. Maybe even talk to him.

Golding moved closer to me, dropping his voice. "I'd

like you to know that your purchase," he subtly tipped his head at Breeze, "was settled the moment I realised an order had been made. I apologise for the slight delay. It was only due to the formalities we've cleared up today not quite being in place. It won't happen again."

A purchase?

An order?

Golding watched my lass. "In fact, that's the other thing I needed to talk about that I'd mentioned in my office. The specific acts your father insisted on. He desired you to use the provision of young ladies to your advantage. Excuse my language, but 'fuck them freely and frequently' were his exact words. I see in that, you're just as he would have wished you to be."

Throughout the whole conversation, I'd been acting the part I'd needed to play. I'd told no lies, but I'd skirted the issue of who I was to McInver, what my thoughts were on the man, and my objectives in becoming his heir.

But I could not accept an insult to the woman I cared about.

Instant anger primed my muscles. I advanced on the lawyer. The man edged away, his eyes wide. His back hit a pillar in the wall.

"Let me make one thing clear. Breeze is not a possession to be bought or traded. Ye will not disrespect her."

He nodded vigorously. "What I mean to say is your father would commend this. Your lady of the night will receive her fee more promptly in future."

My anger spiked. Until this second, I hadn't considered myself vicious. I might have killed, but I could control my temper.

That was entirely lost.

I snapped out a hand and grabbed the lawyer by the throat. "She's not a prostitute. Apologise to her, now."

Golding shot his frantic gaze to Breeze. "P-p-please accept my apologies, miss. Entirely my mistake."

"Camden, it's okay." Breeze touched my shoulder, her tone gentle.

I liked her using my name.

But I was furious.

"He's going purple. Let him go."

The red mist cleared.

I dropped my grip and backed up.

Golding dropped into a bow, one hand at his neck. "Thank you, sir, for the correction. So l-l-like your father! If that's all for now, I will speak to you tomorrow. Goodbye, miss. My sincere regrets for the unfortunate slip."

The lawyer fled. His engine roared, and gravel crunched as he sped away.

I held my gaze up, not trusting myself to speak.

With every slip like this, I felt more like McInver. Violent and controlling. I hated it.

Breeze's fingers curled into mine. "You didn't need to defend me like that."

"Yes, I did. But ye must think I'm a monster."

I brought my heavy gaze to her, and she held up her other hand to pause me.

"It was kind of beautiful what you did."

"Beautiful?"

"Your lawyer dismissed me as nothing. You could've let that go. It didn't matter, and his opinion meant nothing." She swallowed, and her eyes shone. "Actually, it did matter. It hurt to hear myself described that way, even if it was true in the sense of the things I've done. But you just stood there and risked it all to defend me."

My heart hurt. I already knew she had no one who stood up for her. Breeze deserved to have someone in her corner. Everything she'd done was to help others. I couldn't let that slide without answer.

"Fuck him," was all the answer I could manage.

A small smile graced her lips. "Fuck him," she agreed.

My phone buzzed again, and I took it out to find a message from the lawyer on the screen.

Golding: In my haste to attend to your duties, I forgot to pass on the code to the garage. It is 456123.

Above that was a message confirming the police station in Inverness where they were holding Burn.

I held it up to show Breeze. "I'm going to take a car and go there now. I'll do everything I can to see my brother and ask what he knows about your sister. Can ye drive Thea's car back to the cabin and wait for me there?"

With concern in her eyes, Breeze agreed then released me. I set out to infiltrate the murky world of my father's police chief friend and the station illegally holding my brother.

19

Burn

Grinding metal announced one of my pet cops on their way to make their checks and ignore my requests. I'd lost track of the days now. No fresh air, no phone call, no let-up from the miserable four walls of my cell.

Beaten but not broken.

The flame in me low but still burning.

"Yay, the entertainment's arrived," I cheered at the peephole sliding aside.

The door opened. "Stand up, Jamieson."

"Not my name," I grumbled but hauled myself to my feet.

The cop, the big male one, manhandled me to face the wall. "Hands behind your back."

He clipped cuffs around my wrists.

"Kinky fucker. What's the occasion?"

"You're being taken to meet a visitor."

My breathing stalled. I jerked my head around. "Who?"

Not my family. Fuck no. If they found me, they'd be smarter than this. They wouldn't blow my single line of defence.

The cop, who I'd nicknamed Detective Dickhead, curled his lip in an unpleasant smile. "Wait and see, pretty boy. If ye survive it."

On that ominous note, he pushed me in front of him, out of the tiny cell, down the grey hall, and out of another door.

Here, he paused and checked the way ahead, almost as if he needed to be sure the coast was clear.

I'd been stuck in one place for so long, my head rushed with the change. Adrenaline, which had dried up almost completely, eked into my veins.

Detective Dickhead shoved me on and we stopped outside a room, no cameras in the corners of the hall, as I'd expected. But someone was waiting for me. A big dude. I could only see an arm through the open door.

The cop led me inside. The visitor brought a slow, dangerous glare to me. My heart nearly gave out.

My brother.

Camden snapped at the cop. "Leave us."

To my surprise, the guy obeyed and closed the door, locking us in.

I wanted to leap at him. Bury my fucking face against him and have him hug me, though I couldn't hug him back. I missed my family so much it hurt, and he was right here.

Emotion rippled over Camden's gaze, but he made a tiny slashing gesture with his hand. I locked myself down, though I'd barely moved.

His eyes darted up and to the side, drawing my attention to the room around us.

The fuck did that mean?

I caught on slower than I should. We were being watched? Still couldn't see any cameras. Maybe they were listening in.

I gave a small chin lift to show I understood.

Camden, in a long-sleeved top covering the branding tattoo we shared, fixed his angry gaze on me. "You're the man who set fire to my father's house."

Holy shite, he was acting.

I was in a fucking movie or something.

I sneered and pulled my best punk attitude out of the bag. "Fuck your accusations. Ye can't prove it, and neither can they. All this time, I've been here, and no one has charged me. Is that what this is? Yet another attempt at getting a confession I won't give?"

"No. A warning. If ye think you'll get charged then get your day in court, you're dreaming. I will do whatever it takes to be the one to administer justice. Do ye understand me?"

Several things made sense at once. I wasn't the sharpest tool, but even this, I got. He'd said my father instead of McInver. They didn't know we were related. He was trying to find a way to free me by fronting for our evil father, because the alternative was worse than I thought.

Hot emotion blazed in me, and I could only nod. "Good luck with that, arsewipe."

Camden's lips twitched, but he poured all kinds of meaning into the fierce eye contact he kept with me.

I loved my family so fucking much. This was killing me.

"I know all about ye," he taunted. "About your past. I bet I could find someone to ID ye. Maybe a lass saw ye at the house. Maybe ye were a friend of her sister's."

Where the hell was he going with this?

Oh fuck. He meant Summer.

It wasn't her I'd recognised?

"I don't know any sister," I blurted.

Camden shrugged. "I don't know. A man like ye might've fucked around with any number of sisters. Probably vanished one or two, as well."

"Vanished?" My gut crunched.

I hated the fact we couldn't talk freely. If he was implying that Summer was missing, my fucking heart was going to tear in two.

He didn't say another word, waiting on me.

I couldn't talk in code anymore. Fuck it.

Lurching, I shoulder-barged into him.

Camden grabbed me, and I rocked us like it was a tussle.

"Summer's gone?" I breathed.

"Missing completely," he whispered back. "Her sister and I are trying to find her. Tell me where to look."

My mind raced.

"Go to the Church of St Andrew. She hung out there. Now punch me in the face and throw me against that chair."

Camden's expression cracked. For a second, he banded

his arms around me in the hug I badly needed. Then he gave a yell and pushed me away.

Not hard enough.

Guess I'd have to do it myself, then.

I bounced off him, yelped like I'd been battered, and dropped into the gap between the fixed table and the metal chair, smacking into both for good measure.

It felt good, like I was alive again.

The cop came running. My brother was guided away with mutters of apology to him for my violence. I got a sneer and a fast walk back to my cell.

Didn't matter that I'd cut my face on the table or that my blood dripped to the floor. My family were trying everything they could to help me.

A pang of desperation cut through my joy. Summer was in trouble. I needed to get free so I could find her.

20

Breeze

Sunlight bathed Camden's family's cabin, just a short walk across from where I'd parked the car. Insecurity grabbed hold of me, pinning me down in my seat. Yesterday, I'd rocked up here, full of anger and ready to be intimidated by no one.

Something had changed.

I didn't know how to relate to these people. Not without Camden here.

Yet I was right outside and just sitting here, like a weirdo.

The door opened, and Lottie emerged. She waved, then came over and gestured for me to lower the window. "I saw ye pull up."

"Camden's found Burn. He's gone to see him."

She rested on the doorframe, her fair hair twisted in a pretty braid. "We know. He sent a text to Sin. Everyone's on edge waiting for news. Are ye okay?"

I wasn't expecting the question. "I...don't know."

She gave me a soft smile. "Join the club. Literally. Come inside and pace the lounge like the rest of us. No one will be mean to ye, I promise, and I'll make lunch."

My belly rumbled audibly. She giggled.

I climbed out, and Lottie stepped aside.

"I have something to confess. Remember when we came here after the fire, ye borrowed Struan's phone? I gave it back to him, but he came up to me in shock because he'd found a website open." Her eyes sparkled. "It had loads of dick pics on it. He wondered if I'd been looking up some sketchy stuff."

The amusement in her tone died. "I read your message to your sister. Nobody else saw it. I logged out of the account and deleted the history. I didn't mean to pry."

Her manner was so gentle and kind. "Camden told me he'd seen the pictures. I forgot about the rest. Thank you for logging it out."

"I'm so sorry about Summer. If ye want to talk about it, I'm all ears. If not, I know Camden will be there for ye. He's the best."

I wished I could talk. My sister had been my rock, and I badly wanted to explain the loss. But I didn't trust easily and never had. Camden was the only other person I'd even started to share myself with.

Him, I didn't seem able to stop crashing into.

I managed a quiet thanks, and we went inside.

At the dinner table, Camden's brothers sat talking in low voices. Both gave me a short acknowledgement before going back to their conversation.

We entered the kitchen where Thea sipped something

from a steaming cup.

"Hello, again," I said. "I owe you some clothes."

Thea waved away the offer. "Really, you don't. All of us lost our possessions and had to replace them, so the clothes were new. I'm not missing them."

In quick order, Lottie went through the breakfast options and refused me when I said I'd make something myself. She got on with cooking eggs on toast while I made small talk with Thea.

Once it was ready, she led me to the table and shooed the guys away.

Getting food in my belly didn't settle my anxious state as I'd hoped. Instead, I felt worse. Camden meeting with Burn was my last option for finding Summer. I had nothing else to try. Nowhere else to look.

I didn't realise that I was moping until Lottie made a soft sound and hurried over to take the seat next to me.

She held my hand. "It's okay. You're among friends."

"It just hit me that I might never see Summer again," I blabbed.

"God. Of course ye will. You're so strong. If she's anything like ye, she's a fighter."

"She's braver than me."

"See? She's got this. Wherever she is, she's missing ye, too. She'll come back."

"We get it." Thea took the seat opposite. "We're all missing Cassie, the boys' sister. And I'd fall apart if Lottie was missing."

"I'd tear the fucking world apart to find her," came a

deeper rumble from the living room. Sin scowled from the window seat.

Camden's protecting me from the lawyer's casual slight was clearly a family quality.

"Tell us about her," Thea prompted. "Your names are so cute. Summer Breeze. Are you close in age?"

Slowly, I gave over pieces of information. Small things that revealed little but felt huge to say. The women listened, the men did, too. Almost like they cared.

I peered between them all, seeing something I'd missed before. The circular edge of a tattoo peeked out from under the short sleeve of Lottie's tunic. Thea's on her arm. Sin's bold against his biceps. They all had the same ink as Camden. They were so tight-knit they'd declared that with a brand.

For a hot moment, I envied that.

A message landed on my phone at the same moment as one did on Sin's.

"He's on his way back," the big man said. "He's seen him."

Mine read the same but had a fast follow-up that hurt my heart.

Scar: Burn gave me a clue about Summer. Tell you every-thing soon.

All I could do now was wait.

Like Lottie suggested, I paced the room until he returned. I reread the text, changing his name on my phone to his real one.

Sin threw the front door open at the first sound of the engine, and a moment later, Camden strode in. I wanted to go to him, but too many people stared on.

His blue eyes trained on me for a long moment, and I nodded so he could talk first to his family. This was important. They cared about their brother and needed him free.

Camden was theirs. Not mine.

"I saw him. He looked pale but strong, so they are obviously feeding him, and presumably not beating him up. He's been held there, but no charges have been made yet."

"What the fuck's up with that?" Sin asked.

"Not sure. Whatever reason they're keeping him off the books can't be good. We talked a little," Camden continued. "But I had to be careful in case they were listening in. It was the conversation with the police chief that gave me more information. He was waiting at the door to the station when I pulled up in McInver's ride, and the guy knew the car. Commented on it."

"What car?" Sin asked, unaware that he was killing me with the questions. "I don't remember seeing any at the mansion."

Camden thumbed back towards the door. "There's a garage in an outbuilding. Four vehicles in it. I took a Rolls-Royce Black Badge."

Struan went to the window and peered out. He gave a low whistle.

"The police chief jogged down to the car and shook my hand. Said how great it was to finally meet McInver's heir. I asked if he'd heard of me, and he said McInver played his cards close to his chest, but he knew the old man wouldn't leave anything to chance when it came to ensuring his legacy and interests, emphasis on the last point."

"What does that mean?" Lottie asked. "Legacy, like ye were made on purpose?"

The three men swapped a look.

"Who knows," Camden went on. "He hesitated before he took me inside and seemed to be testing me out, talking about bullshit things. I got short with him and demanded I see the man who tried to burn down my house. I took ownership of it and told him I wanted to enact justice myself. The guy full-on smirked at me and said, 'Like father like son'. First, he implied that they were being ultra-cautious with the investigation, presumably because McInver has them in his pocket and isn't conscious to tell them what to do. Then he said I could have five minutes with the prisoner and not to do anything permanent. Any decisions beyond that, I could discuss with him at a house party he invited me to. Then I got to see Burn. He knows we're pulling for him. It was the best I could do."

Questions flew his way, but Camden held up a hand. "Hold those thoughts. This next bit needs to be in private. Breeze, come with me."

My heart gave an uneven thump, but I jogged upstairs after Camden. In the bedroom I'd slept in what felt like forever ago, he closed the door.

The quiet of the room was interrupted by my pulse, loud in my ears.

"They were friends. He didn't know about ye."

I pressed my fingertips to my mouth. "Just like I never knew about him. She kept us both secret."

Warmth shone in Camden's eyes. "Because you're both important to her. I told him she's missing and asked where to look. He said the church of St Andrews. Does that mean anything to ye?"

Nothing came to mind.

Frustrated, I racked my brain. "We never went to church. No one I know did. I can't even... Oh, wait." I took my phone from my pocket and brought up the map function, searching on the tower block my sister and mother lived in. Then I dragged the map out to reveal the local streets.

"There! That's the name of the church by where she lives," I said slowly, and I raised my phone to show him the building. "I don't get the connection, but I need to go there."

"We'll go together."

"It's in Edinburgh. Hours away."

He shrugged like the distance meant nothing. Like leaving his family's drama was no big deal.

I could say no. Do this alone like I did everything else.

"Thank you," I managed instead.

We returned downstairs. Once again, Camden commanded the room. He'd given me what I'd needed, and we had a plan.

I had no idea why, but the simple act of offering me his help made me emotional.

"Breeze and I have somewhere to go in search of her sister. Does anyone have any questions for me before we leave? I'll be back later, probably in the wee small hours."

"Ye know that car out there is worth half a million?" Struan held up his phone, showing the Rolls-Royce on-screen.

Camden gave a short laugh. "I'll be sure to add a dent

or two."

His brother smirked with him.

"The police chief is crooked, right?" Sin asked more soberly.

"That's the conclusion I'm working with. He and McInver seem tight. Considering the shite Daddy Dearest got up to, and the money involved, why wouldn't he have the police in his pocket?"

Sin nodded slowly. "Which means, as heir, ye do, too."

Camden's eyes flashed with a dark light, and he curled his lip. "Exactly. If it means I can use that to get Burn back, I'll push it to the extreme. All of it. McInver's money, his connections, and every dark corner of his murky world. Wrap your thoughts around that, and later, we'll decide how to bust out our brother."

To the tune of his family discussing prison raid options, we left the cabin.

One thought resounded in my mind. Like I'd said last night on the way to the mansion, the first time I met him, I'd thought him a spoiled, cruel, rich boy who was just like his dad.

I'd been so far from the truth.

Except now, that was exactly who Camden needed to become.

21

Camden

We rolled away from the cabin in the outrageously luxurious car. Sleek in design, with a chunky grille on the front, the Rolls-Royce hood ornament, and butter-soft leather seats, it had taken me a minute to work out how to drive the thing. Still, I'd chosen it over the other cars, because fuck the old man. This was clearly his pride and joy, and I wanted to abuse everything he held dear.

Breeze tucked herself in her seat, her gaze all over the fancy features. "Say what you like about your dad, but he has good taste." She gave a startled laugh. "I just realised what I said. He picked me, after all."

"Not commenting on that, no matter how tempting." I hid my smile and kept my eyes on the road.

Ahead, Gordain's castle loomed, and I slowed then beeped the horn as I recognised the man himself outside.

He narrowed his gaze at the car then strode over, his expression incredulous. "I'm not even going to ask."

"Better that ye don't. But it isn't stolen. Not technically."

"Good to know."

I grinned at him. "Gordain, this is Breeze."

"Pleasure to meet ye." He exchanged a polite smile with my lass, then came back to me. "I've been meaning to talk to ye. Your brother's been down to see me about work. He declined to give me any more information on what the hell ye guys are into, but I've drawn my own conclusions based on other rumours that've come my way."

"What kind of rumours?"

"The kind that follow money. A contractor suddenly given the green light to work on a ruined house. An assurance that a son and heir has been found who can sign off on the bills." He made a show of pointing out the car.

Finally, he was asking.

"The rumours are true," I confirmed. "But temporary and for good reasons."

Gordain watched me for a moment before speaking. "All right, temporary heir to a fortune. My brother-in-law, James, was raised by an arsehole of a relative. He had to unshackle himself from the man to take on his inheritance—a mansion and estate down in England. His son, Sebastian, runs it now. James didn't want to navigate that world, but Seb is better at it. He knows something of corrupt officials and how money changes hands at the top. He was even in prison once so has a handle on both sides of it."

"Looks like we'd have things in common." I sat tall in my seat, realising the reach of my actions.

Gordain inclined his head. "In several ways. They're due a visit. Seb used to pull shifts at my heli school before he and his wife had their kids. I'll have him and his da take ye out for a ride." He put meaning behind his next words. "They're the best kind of people. Sincere and honest. You'll like them."

"I'll take their advice seriously."

The older man tapped the bonnet and walked away.

I drove on, aware of Breeze's gaze on me. "It's a long drive to Edinburgh. Want to hear the story of how we met Gordain?"

"You read my mind. I was just about to say how that tattooed, castle-living, helicopter-owning man reminds me of you. He has the same all-knowing quiet competence thing going on that you do."

I choked on that but got into the story of how Gordain and his mountain rescue crew extracted us from Torlum.

A couple of hours later, we crossed the Queensferry bridge, then drove out to Leith. Breeze directed me with quiet instructions, but the more we moved into her territory, the more she shrank in on herself. This was no pleasant homecoming for her.

Pretty terraced streets passed by, people going about their business, heading home as it grew dark. A café closed its doors, the corner it sat on giving way to a rougher neighbourhood. Homes with boarded-up windows. Broken streets.

We found the church—a Victorian grey stone building with a blue sign naming it as St Andrew's—but stayed in the car.

"This will be on bricks if we leave it out here." Breeze gestured at the dash.

She wasn't wrong. Throughout the drive, people had

gawked at the Rolls-Royce. It was the wrong choice for this journey. Our aim was to get information simply by asking, not impressing.

I shrugged and climbed out of the car, jogging around to her side. "If that happens, so be it. Fuck McInver. We'll get the train home."

She stepped out, too. "I am home," she mumbled.

It wasn't convincing.

We'd left the Cairngorms mid-afternoon, and it was early evening now. Still, the church door was open on our approach.

"Hello?" Breeze called into the dim interior.

No reply came.

My only experiences of church had been on school trips as a kid, either for harvest festival or at Christmas. The scent had never left me, though. Old books, woodwormy pews, and some kind of incense burning.

The stone floor led us down an aisle to a pulpit in front of a stained-glass window.

"Ever been to a wedding?" I asked.

Breeze drifted her gaze down a tall tapestry of Christ on the cross, hung from the airy rafters, and brought it to me. "No. My mum and her boyfriend never bothered, thankfully, and I don't have any aunts or uncles."

"Me neither. I'm wondering what it would be like to be in a ceremony where ye tell a roomful of people that you're in love and the vicar gives ye permission to kiss."

Pink spots appeared on her cheeks.

Before she could answer, I ducked and kissed her.

Chastely, but with meaning. Her warm lips melted into mine, and she came with me when I pulled away.

Then she remembered herself. "Stop it!"

"Why? Seems like God likes the idea, and we're in His house."

"Unless you're planning to propose, I'm pretty sure that's against His guidance."

"Then marry me."

She shoved my chest. "Idiot."

I didn't budge, kind of stuck on the idea.

A door creaked.

"You're too early for narcotics anonymous," a voice came from the side.

We spun around to find the source. A woman of maybe thirty came out of a side room. Plain clothes, not a vicar or clergy.

Breeze stepped to her. "Hey. We're not here for a meeting, we're looking for information on someone." She took a steadying breath. "Do you know Summer?"

The older woman darted her gaze to me as if I was dangerous. She locked her jaw. "Don't know that name."

"Lie," I murmured behind Breeze's head, for her ears only.

Breeze gave a tiny nod and stepped closer again. "I'm her sister. This is important. Summer's missing."

The woman did a double take. "Missing?"

"Yes. For weeks now. She came here, we know that. All I want is to find her, which means talking to everyone who could've seen her."

"Yeah, like I said, I never heard of her. No good bringing your heavies around here."

I put up my hands. "Just the boyfriend. I'm worried about her, too."

To mark my point, and liking the boyfriend thing way more than reasonable, I put my arm around Breeze, bringing her back against my body. She resisted for a second then rested against me, slight but powerful under my touch.

I settled my expression to soft and gentle, where really, I wanted to shake the information out of this stranger.

"We haven't heard from her and are really worried," Breeze added. "It's not like her to go missing. Maybe the name rings a bell and there's a friend of hers you can send us to? Maybe there was something she came here for specifically? I miss her so much."

"Fine. Maybe I do know her. She came to meetings here sometimes," the woman answered, her shoulders still up around her ears.

"What kind of meetings?" Breeze pressed.

"A group rented out the community space and shouted about how unfair the world was and bringing down the rich."

Breeze stiffened under my hold. "Who runs it?"

"They stopped coming here six months ago when the group organiser went to prison for shoplifting. Sorry, that's all I know."

She went to walk past, but I blocked her.

"His name?"

"Whose?"

"The man who went to prison."

"Woman. They were all female. The whole meeting was. Her name was Prudence. No idea of her surname."

But Breeze did. I could see some kind of recognition in her wide eyes.

I stepped aside, and the woman fled back through the door, leaving us alone.

We exited the church more slowly.

"Who's Prudence?" I asked.

"No one important." Outside, Breeze's scowl grew. "It's the fucking group Summer joined."

"Why, what were they?"

She turned her pale, alarmed face to me. "Wannabe vigilantes. Camden, I know what my sister is doing."

22

Breeze

Of all the things she could've done. Hurt welled in my chest.

Gentle hands turned me, and Camden tipped up my chin. "Talk to me."

I started walking. Somehow, Camden's fancy-ass car was where we left it, but I kept on going.

"There's a lot you don't know about me, but one of the things my sister and I shared was a hatred for men who use women for sex."

He stayed right by my side. "Join the club with me and my family. There's a special place in Hell just for those men. We only exist because of the actions of one such fucker."

"Same, but my sister and I agreed we'd stay far away from that life. Which is why it never made sense that she'd sell herself."

He paused. "But it does make sense of how she knew my brother. They had a shared interest."

I swung my gaze up to his too-handsome face. "Is Burn

the vigilante type, too?"

"He has form."

"In what way?"

"Burned down the house of some dirty old bastard, so I'm told."

Damn. Summer would love that. "It adds up how they met. Burn told you about the church."

"Meaning he knew about Summer's activities there. And that they were dangerous. It was the first thing he thought of when I said she was missing," he concluded.

I'd led us to the entrance to my mother's block of flats. Two guys lurked by the stairwell, eyeing us. Another strolled inside, a can of rough cider in his hand. There was another conversation I needed to have, and it wouldn't be pleasant.

I stopped Camden. "I don't suppose you'd stay here and wait for me?"

"And let you go in there alone? No."

I'd never wanted this, to let anyone see the dirty underside of my life, but I had no choice. I entered the block, and he stuck close to my heels.

"Who lives here?"

"My mum. My sister does, too, in her own place." I pulled a face, hesitating to peer up at him. "If Jack talks shit to you, or to me, that's normal. He's mostly harmless, so I just ignore him."

Whatever Camden's thoughts, he kept them to himself. We climbed the dark stairs and found our way to my mother's front door. I pressed the bell and glowered into the camera.

"What do ye want?" Jack answered.

"To speak with my mother."

"Who's that with ye?"

"None of your business."

The door swung open. Jack loomed in the frame, staring at the man at my back. He took in Camden's size, his gaze lingering on the scar down his face. "Who the fuck are ye?"

Camden curled a hand around me, holding my belly. "Your worst nightmare, if I want to be."

I held in a ripple of surprise. He played the gentleman with me, but God, him being the tough guy was hot.

"Breeze?" Mum slipped under Jack's arm. She fell on me with a hug. "Where have you been?"

"Still trying to find Summer." I kept my focus on Jack until he sniffed and walked away.

I didn't like the way he looked at Camden. Not at all.

"She's a big girl, she can take care of herself," Mum repeated her favourite refrain, a little wobbly on her feet but her expression blissful. High, again. I barely had it in me to feel surprised.

"Did you know she was involved with a group who went after sex traffickers?"

My mother's face fell. I hated myself for my words but I'd needed to say them. Her reaction was important. I'd made the leap on from why Summer would be involved with those people. Sex trafficking was far too close to home.

"She wouldn't," Mum decided. "She's smarter than that."

"She did, though."

Her features crumpled. "All I ever wanted was for you girls to live your own lives. Never to get involved in that... that long-dead past. You're worth so much more than I ever was. It doesn't matter. I don't matter."

Twin tears spilled down her cheeks. I hated myself.

"What's she done?" my mother pressed. "Where is she? Oh God, no. Not my baby girl."

Her fear was real. She didn't know. Another brick wall.

Jack returned and guided Mum inside, scowling in anger. "Was there any need for that? Keep your bullshit thoughts to yourself. Did ye at least pay her bills, since ye come here all high and mighty and upsetting her? She's been worried about that."

I locked my jaw. "Yes. The money's in her account. Hers, Jack. For her to handle."

He slammed the door in our faces.

I was done anyway.

Camden followed me outside. We trudged back to the car, and he ran his arm around my shoulders. I was too cold to feel any comfort.

"Mum knew nothing. I'm going to guess that without a leader, the group disbanded. Burn suspected my sister was missing because of her actions, so all I have is that she was bought by a man from something called the List which she deliberately targeted. I don't know the names of anyone else on it. I have no way of finding it out. Summer has been missing for weeks, and I think... What if she's...?"

My throat tightened so I couldn't finish my words.

In the twilight, Camden stared down at me.

"Forget it," I forced out. "You don't need to hear this."

"Where do ye live?" he asked.

Right. He was taking me home. I muttered my address, and we returned to the car.

In twenty minutes, we'd driven into the city.

"Was the debt for drugs?" Camden asked quietly against the purr of the engine. "Jack said she was worried about bills. That was to feed their habit, aye?"

Miserable, I didn't bother holding back information. "Yes. The second time she's got in hot water with a dealer."

"Without help, she's going to do that again. Her man is going to persuade her you're a cash cow who can bail them out for a third, fourth, and fifth time."

He was right. I knew it, and it was parting information he was giving me as he wanted to help. This time, I didn't answer.

Then we were pulling up outside my flat on Gilmore Place. Camden eyed the street, busy with takeaways, and the tall apartment blocks above them. This was Edinburgh proper, the architecture grander, the tourists closer.

I went to say goodbye and to ask him to text me when anything new happened and if he saw his brother again, but he climbed out of the car. Hesitantly, I followed.

"You'll get a ticket." I gestured to the bus stop he'd parked on.

"Ye keep worrying about that. McInver will get a ticket. We don't need to care."

True.

He locked the car, leaving it exactly where it was.

"Uh, are you coming in?"

"Aye, Breeze. I am." He gestured for me to go ahead.

Inside the narrow stairwell, I jogged up the first flight and went to start on the second, but Camden stopped.

"Which neighbour was it that cornered ye?" He scrutinised the two doors on this floor.

Shit. I hadn't made up the story, but a confrontation didn't feel like fun.

"I don't need you to fight my battles," I said instead.

"Never said ye did. But all women should have men helping out where they have problems with a guy. Having your back, not pushing in front."

I liked that way too much.

The front door opened below, and two people entered—the handsy neighbour whose name I didn't even know, and a woman with him. She giggled, and he kissed her neck, unaware that we were standing watching.

Camden sank back into the shadows.

Feeling a little bolder for having backup, I moved to the top of the stairs. I was done with being treated badly. Thoughts of Summer putting herself out there in anger at our past emboldened me.

"Hi," I said. "Remember me?"

The kissing stopped. The neighbour, a bearded, average-looking English guy, twisted to see me. "Just a girl who lives here," he murmured to the woman. "Come on, I want to get you inside."

My blood boiled at his dismissal.

"No, don't go anywhere with that man," I bit out, worried for her safety if he'd picked her up at a bar. I had to out him. "A few weeks ago, right here, he shoved me against the wall and tried to kiss me. I said no. He wouldn't back off, choosing to grope me instead."

"What the hell? You lying bitch," the neighbour snapped. He held the woman's upper arm. "Don't listen to her. She's jealous after I turned her down. I'm not seeing anyone, particularly her."

"You're the liar, and this wasn't consensual. It was a Saturday night, and I'd just come home from work. This should've been my safe space, but then you showed up."

"Yeah? Got any evidence?" He pointed to the non-existent security cameras, his ugly mouth twisted in a sneer. "Didn't think so. Bye-bye, Barbie."

"Are ye serious?" the woman asked. Her eyes rounded and fixed on me.

"Deadly. Don't go inside with him, no matter what he said to you. He isn't safe."

She hesitated for a moment longer then wrenched her arm free.

"Stop," the neighbour said. He took another grab at her and kicked the door closed so she couldn't leave.

Camden pushed off the wall and prowled down the stairs. "Let her go. Now."

The neighbour froze. "Who are you?"

Camden peered back at me. "Can't use the worst nightmare line again. Maybe just the guy who needs a wee chat with your sorry arse."

He yanked the guy aside and released the woman. She skittered into the night, waving down a cab. The man tried to follow, but Camden held him.

"Now, ye need to learn how to treat women." He switched his gaze to me. "Want to watch? Or ye can go on up. I'll follow in a minute."

"Watch what? What are you going to do?" the other man bleated.

"I'm naw repeating myself."

"I'll watch," I decided. His dark side didn't scare me like it probably should.

Camden jerked the guy ahead of him. "Open your door."

My neighbour whimpered but fished out his key and opened his door.

Inside the flat, Camden tossed him to the floor. "First, what's your name?"

"P-Paul."

"All right, Paul the Perv, you're going to apologise."

"Sorry," the douchebag spluttered.

"For..." Camden prompted.

"The hallway thing. I thought she was into it."

"Talk to her, not me, you fucktard."

My indignation rose, and I rounded Camden to stare down at the man. "You thought I was into it? How?"

"You're always staring at me whenever we pass each other."

"That?" My mind was blown. "I looked at you and you thought that was an invitation to assault me?"

"Oh, come on. All I did was make a move. It was only a

kiss," the guy said, like I was being unreasonable.

"You're a fucking idiot." Camden stepped over him then hauled him to his feet, holding him out. "Breeze, take your best shot."

My neighbour laughed.

The sound infuriated me. I got in his face. "For your information, I look at everyone I pass as a safety mechanism. Women do it because we have to be aware of our surroundings. If you want to know if a woman is interested, ask her. Do you understand how wrong you got this?"

Rarely before had I challenged a man in this way. It would be foolish to without the backup I now had. Tomorrow, I'd probably regret this, but right now, it felt great.

"Yeah, whatever," he replied. "It's not like I'll touch you again."

In a reflex, I grabbed his shirt and kneed him in the balls.

My neighbour went down like a lead balloon. He groaned, lying on the floor.

Camden squinted at the jerk then lifted an eyebrow at me. "I was going to add my own hit to the party, but that was spectacular."

He stepped over my neighbour, treading on his hand. To the sound of the man's howls, he guided me out and closed the door.

I sprinted upstairs with Camden following.

At the door of my shared flat, I paused. "That was amazing. I've been scared to come back here so I didn't run into him."

Darkness still troubled his eyes. "Men are trash."

"Not all of them. I know one decent man." I held his gaze for a moment. "Okay. I don't know if anyone's home, but this is me."

In my two years of living here, I'd never brought anyone back. Except it didn't feel weird. Not just because we had a common goal, but more, I liked being around him.

I didn't want him to go.

We entered the flat directly into the kitchen, and I flipped on the lights. "There's four bedrooms, one of which was the living room, so there's not much shared space. The other people who live here are all women, and mostly they go home for the summer. I'm the only one who stays all year round. I got lucky finding it, after the last place I lived at got condemned and we all had to go in a hurry. The government paid the rent while I was studying, but I just finished college so I'm on my own from September. Which probably means I'll be homeless as I haven't worked at all."

I was nervous. Babbling.

I reached my door. "That's my room."

Camden poked his head in, taking in my chair covered in clothes. The stack of library books on my bedside table. The pictures of me and Summer on the wall. In a sneak attack, he curled his arm around my waist and spun me inside.

Against the closed door, he took my mouth in a determined kiss.

I ran both arms around his neck, instantly needing more. I sank meaning into the clinch. It was too much having him here. And not enough.

He'd learned enough about me tonight to see how I

was a hot mess with issues through the roof, and I didn't want him to leave me.

Camden tore his lips from mine. "Come home with me."

"What?"

"Pack a bag. Stay with me." He stepped back and jammed his fingers into his hair. "I know I'm not the safest person to be around, and there are any number of reasons ye could need to remain here, but I have the worst feeling..." He pressed his lips together and started again. "I want ye with me. Anything else I say is just an excuse."

My heart ached, and I brought my hand up to cover the sudden pain. I'd told myself I didn't want this, but the reality was entirely different. Sharp, insistent need tugged at me.

He wanted me.

Throughout my life, Summer and I had been problems no one had time to deal with. Mum loved us, but we got in the way of her boyfriends and habits. When she couldn't cope, social workers would pick us up and we'd be taken to foster homes for a week or two. Sometimes longer if she'd caught the attention of the police and had court dates. Nothing bad ever happened in any of the places we'd stayed, but the foster parents knew we wouldn't be there long, so at best, we were treated as guests, at worst, ignored and left to our own devices. Not that we needed them. We had each other.

I'd never let anyone else in.

But more and more, I wanted that with Camden.

This could be a huge mistake, but I wasn't sure I could stop myself.

"Listen," he continued, because I hadn't managed a word. "I can fix what happened between us. I'll change the tattoo. Make it into flowers or something. And I meant what I said about helping to find Summer. Finding her is as important to me as freeing Burn. The police chief might know something about the List. It's a good place to start."

I closed my eyes, hiding myself from him. Camden overwhelmed me at the best of times. Now, even after everything he'd seen, the whole of me in small parts, he was still offering himself.

I was in such danger with this man.

"Okay," I answered. "Until we have answers, I'll come back with you."

He gifted me that same addictive grin of his and ushered me on to pack a bag.

Together, we left Edinburgh, returning to the north.

23

Camden

Breeze tapped her phone then searched on something, the passing headlights of cars strobing across her in the passenger seat. "The women who know about the members of the List aren't allowed to talk. They have to sign a contract. I did, too."

"How did ye get to know about it in the first place?"

"Summer told Mum where she was going—a night-club which sells sex on the side. Mum used to work there. She was disappointed in my sister but said she understood. How it was easy money."

I kept my thoughts to myself about her mother. She could have prevented this, but she'd stood by and let it happen. My own mother had done the same, and my love for her was tainted by a resentment I didn't enjoy but couldn't stop. Breeze didn't need any more of my opinions.

"I know one of the dancers there," she continued. "I'm going to ask her whether the police are in on it. She probably won't tell me, but it's worth a shot."

She dialled a number and lifted her phone. "Is Divine there? It's her cousin. Thanks."

She waited a minute, then a voice came on the line. "No, it's Breeze. Quick question before anyone gets suspicious. When you worked on the kind of deals I came in for, did you ever encounter any top-ranking police? Yes or no will do."

Even across the car, I could hear the answer. "What the hell, sis? I can't, you know that."

"Just yes or no, please. I told you about my sister, Summer. She's still missing, and you can help me find her. I don't want to get you in trouble, I only need to know."

Divine made an off sound like she'd tutted or clucked her tongue. "Yes," she answered eventually.

"Then it's safe to assume they're in on it. At least the top brass. Would they ever help?"

"Oh, honey. No."

"Are they members?"

Another silence came, then Breeze pulled the phone from her ear and peered at the screen. "Damn. She hung up on me."

"Good to know the extent of it," I said.

"Right? That police chief is either being paid off by Mc-Inver, or he is on a par with him and uses women, too."

I drummed my fingers on the steering wheel. "I'll find that out when I go to his house."

Breeze took in a long breath. "What if he's got Summer?"

"Then I'll find a way to free her."

"God, it's all adding up to one big picture. All these rich guys doing whatever they please to whoever they like. The cops turning a blind eye. You and your brothers and sister getting kidnapped because of that money. Me and my sister only existing..."

She swallowed. "When you met my mum, what did you think of her? Besides assuming she'll keep coming to me for drug money."

"I shouldn't have said that."

"Maybe, but I appreciated the concern. Answer the question."

"That you look just like her."

"And that she's young, correct? Mum was fourteen when she fell pregnant with me, and fifteen with Summer."

"Jesus."

"Exactly. A year before that, she was trafficked to the UK from Eastern Europe and sold for sex. We didn't know any of this until we were maybe ten and eleven and had just returned from a month living in foster care. Mum worked hard to clean herself up and got help. Part of her therapy was no more secrets."

My heart broke. "That must've been hard to hear."

"Harder to live through. Her buyer used her for six months then passed her on to a brothel. She thinks her mother sold her in the first place, because she'd been sent on an errand, not grabbed from the street in the small town she grew up in. Our dad fell in love with her, but he was no better than any other brothel user, and eventually, he abandoned her, too." She lifted a shoulder. "Except by then, she was mid-teens with two babies."

"Please tell me someone helped her."

"Thankfully, they did. She was taken in by a charity. They sorted out her legal status so she could live and work here, and got her benefits and a place to stay. She tried so hard to be a good mum but she was a child herself and a traumatised one. It messed her up so badly. Her confession to us was the last time she really made an effort to fix her broken mind. Now Summer is gone, she's fallen back into drugs. When I find my sister, I want to take Mum away from that flat and do whatever it takes to get her clean."

She scrubbed at her eyes. "I've never told anyone that. Not the social workers, not any schoolfriend. Everyone judges her, but they've no idea what she went through."

I felt those words.

I'd judged her, too. Considering the shitshow of my upbringing, that made me a prize arsehole.

"I'm sorry for what happened to her and ye. I see why Summer did what she did. She wants to fix what happened to your mother."

"I think so. But I can't imagine it's a battle anyone can win."

Her words settled around me like a challenge.

All my life, I'd believed the same. I could never win against the forces that acted against me. The men who'd bought my mother. How they'd used her. I'd wallowed in anger at the impact it had on me, too.

But what the hell was I doing if it wasn't rising to that battle?

We'd crossed the Queensferry bridge again, but I took an abrupt turning, some deeply held instinct changing our course to the A985.

"Short detour."

"Where are we going?" Breeze asked.

"Stirling." I clenched my jaw, adrenaline tightening my muscles. "Back to where I was born."

Breeze had shared her most deeply held secrets with me. I didn't know where I was with her. How much she'd forgiven me. I knew she wanted me enough to come with me tonight.

Maybe I was doing this to deepen our connection.

Maybe I was chasing my own demons.

We crossed the river again at Kincardine. Like some kind of twisted tour guide, I took us east into Falkirk first. Breeze watched me until I directed her to the sight that appeared in many of my childhood memories of coming home. In the dark, the huge horse head statues of the Kelpies glowed in a pretty welcome.

It only felt threatening now.

"I've never seen them," she said softly.

"It's the only nice thing you'll see tonight," I grumbled back.

"Is this your way of showing me your dark underbelly?"

I only grunted agreement and got us back on track for the town I'd been stolen from before my imprisonment on Torlum and since never wanted to return to. Like in Edinburgh, McInver's Rolls-Royce Black Badge drew stares. I cruised straight along Drip Road and pulled up in the shadow of a social housing block.

"Here," I finally told Breeze.

"Is this where you lived?"

I killed the engine and twisted to face her, picking up her hand to bring to my scar. I traced her finger down the gnarled length. "Ye asked about this. Here's where it happened."

Her expression crinkled with emotion, and her fingers curved to cup my face. She waited, her touch so soft.

The pressure was getting to me, memories crowding. I climbed from the car, and Breeze followed.

Hopping the fence, I crossed to the housing block's front door, shared between several flats. "It happened when I was seven. Ma used to run her business from here, which is my polite way of saying she fucked guys in our home for money. It was the middle of the night, and the man tied me up so I didn't fight back. He was behind me, so it's Ma's face and reactions that stuck with me."

Breeze pressed her fingers to her mouth and carefully stepped over to join me. She looked up at the windows of the white three-storey building. "Which?"

We were standing right outside it, the ground floor one ours. I pointed it out, and she peered through the glass.

"It's empty."

"So?"

Breeze moved to the intercom and hit the top button. It crackled like someone had picked up.

"Delivery for number one," Breeze chirped.

"Wrong buzzer, dumbass," a man groused back.

But the door popped open all the same. Breeze grabbed

my hand and towed me inside. At the first door, she raised an eyebrow, then barged it with her shoulder.

The cheap lock gave instantly, opening up the flat I hadn't been in for so long. If I thought the memories outside bad, now, they came thick and fast.

Closing us in, Breeze led me to the dark, bare living room. "I can't imagine what you went through, but if you'll talk, I want to hear all of it." She kissed my jaw, pushing up on her toes to reach my cheek next.

Then she moved back to give me space.

Words came in a rush.

"I don't know who the man was or why he did it, but his attack ended with my injury. He broke in, or maybe Ma let him in, then he grabbed me from my bed. Tied my arms behind me and trussed up my legs as well. He bullied my mother then slid his blade down my face. It touched bone. I blacked out. After, my mother waited till morning then took me to a friend's house where a community nurse was visiting. They ordered her to take me to hospital, and she eventually sent me in with her friend, the next day or later. I guess she didn't want to face the awkward questions of how it happened."

Breeze clapped her hands to her mouth but didn't interrupt.

"The docs stitched me up, and I remember conversations about treatments I might need in future to help improve the appearance. Injections, surgery, some kind of freezing therapy."

"Let me guess, you didn't get any of those."

I shook my head. Ma had decided it wasn't worth her

while.

"The doctors at the hospital alerted social services, but they still let me go home. After that, we were living rough, sleeping on sofas of Ma's friends or even outdoors during the summer, presumably to avoid trouble. The bandage on my face got grubby."

While my mother either slept or had been passed out, I'd peeled it off myself in a stranger's bathroom, horrified at what lay underneath. It had been much worse then, red and raised.

I knew now that the term was hypertrophic scarring, but as a boy, I'd thought my life was over. I'd hated it. Hated how everyone could see that I was different.

Even then, I knew it would never go away.

"How old were you?"

"Seven. A couple of years on, my mother died. Grand-parents had miraculously been discovered, and they took me in for a time until my grandfather unexpectedly passed away, and my chronically ill grandmother quickly followed. My years with them were my salvation. They'd signed me up for school and applied for funding so I could take extra-curricular courses, like computing and art. I used to draw all over my arms and up my neck, creeping it around to my face."

Realisation dawned. I'd always hated my skin and now was in the process of changing it with my tattoo gun. Fuck, the sketch I'd been doing for new ink was of the most beautiful woman I'd ever met. What better to ink permanently on the shell I hated.

Breeze, the woman in question, stood in the middle of the living room where I'd been slashed. She didn't gaze around, she didn't examine the place at all. Her full attention was on me as she gave me the time to air my story.

I stared at the lass in amazement. "How come you're not disgusted by it? Why is it when ye look at me, ye don't stare at the scar?"

"You see your scar as your defining feature. I see all of you." She moved into my space and ran her hands over my biceps, squeezing them. "I see the strength you have, not just in these muscular arms but deep within you. I see your quiet confidence. The way you handle situations. The way you love your family." She wrapped both arms around my neck and landed another thought-stealing kiss on me. "That tattoo you put on me was because of the life your mother led, right?"

"I couldn't bear that for ye."

"You hardly knew me, but see how much you cared? I get it now. I understand what drove you on." Fierce determination came over her. "There's this smile you do that I've only ever seen directed at me. It's like a flash of amusement, but humble at the same time, and so beautiful it brings me to my knees. I'm glad you've told me what happened to you, because I get the chance to stand here and tell you I'm so sorry for how you suffered. It was wrong that you were hurt. It was wrong that you were hidden. It was wrong that you didn't get the medical treatment you deserved. I won't pass any judgement because I know how much you love your mum. I only want to set the record straight."

I kissed her, bringing my hands to her face to hold her steady. I'd thought my first sight of Breeze had been my sexual awakening, but I'd been wrong. It was so much more than that. In a short space of time, I'd gone from wanting her desperately to needing her completely.

I didn't know shite about love, but I knew a lot about my heart.

I was falling in love with Breeze.

However she felt about me, forevermore, I'd protect her. Wouldn't try to stop the devotion she inspired in me.

Our kiss got harder, feverish. It was dark in the room, with bare but clean floorboards beneath our feet, no curtains and only faint streetlight to outline us.

Breeze tore her lips from mine. "I realised something else, too. You've been worried about how much you're like your father. You're scared to tie me up because he did. That's my fault. I teased and used it against you, but that was unfair. What if your need comes from the story you just told me? You were constrained when you were cut. You need that control to feel fully alive. To have the freedom to feel attracted, needed." Her eyes flashed with certainty and deep desire. "Let go with me. I'm here to catch your fall."

Fucking hell. She could be right. I was ready to find out.

24

Breeze

I backed away from Camden and scooped up my bag from the floor. From inside, I took the light leather cuffs with the coiled rope, then I scanned the room. A rail ran around the centre of the window. Perfect.

In quick actions driven by my nerves, I stripped my dress, fastened the cuffs to my wrists, then clipped the link on the end of each rope to the centre of the rail. I sat on the bare floorboards with my arms extended directly above my head.

The whole time, Camden watched me.

His gaze trailed over my bare shoulders, lingered on my tits, then sank lower.

"If you want to tie up my legs, you'll need to do that part," I told him.

My voice had a thick quality to it. I needed him. I was already wet from imagining this.

He palmed the hard ridge of his cock which strained against his jeans, checked the door, then moved to two feet in front of me, throwing off his shirt.

"You're so fucking beautiful," he said.

I kept my mouth shut, needing him to run this.

I wanted it to be cathartic, so he could cleanse this place of its horrors. I also needed it to be complete. Me and him, fully joined.

Camden knelt so our faces were the same height, then prowled to me, taking my mouth in a blistering kiss. As he drove me wild, he twisted his fingers into my underwear and yanked them down my legs in a purposeful draw.

I didn't stop my moan.

He'd barely touched me, and I was dripping. There was something about the combination of being at his mercy while at the same time knowing he got crazy at the sight of my pussy. His name tattooed there. It had my nipples hard and poking through the soft material of my bra.

With that slow steadiness I loved about him, Camden ran his hands under my ass and lifted me.

Suspended by my wrists from the rail, I gasped, peering back to make sure it held as I strangled his neck with my legs. But I'd taken my attention off the man in front of me right at the second he brought my pussy to his mouth.

With a groan, he licked me, his tongue lingering over each letter of his name before plunging inside me. There was nothing I could do but drop my head back and revel in his touch. In the strength it took to hold me up to his clever tongue.

He shifted his grip so all of my weight was on one of his hands, then used the other to hold me open. With a mutter of curse words, he speared me with his tongue then sucked on my clit so hard I yelped. I didn't care if anyone could hear us, or even see us through the windows. They could barge into the room right now, and I wouldn't tell him to stop.

Camden slid a thick finger inside me, curling it to my G-spot in the way I'd shown him. His lips pressed to my belly, my hips, then back to the centre of me. I was dizzy with lust, it was happening so fast and he wasn't slowing.

Before when we'd done this, I'd been blindfolded. Now, between gasps, I raised my head to watch him tongue-fuck me.

Camden took everything seriously. Working my body, he had down to an art. Concern etched onto his brow, and I trusted him to make this good for both of us because that's what he did. Took on a task and excelled.

Abruptly, he turned me, positioning me with my feet on the floor, head down, ass out and him still between my legs. I hung from the ropes, peering back to watch him admire me then bury his face once more.

In this pose, I was even more open to him. Somehow, it was hotter as I couldn't see everything, only feel as he licked and sucked. My huge, bare-chested man, solid, serious, and wild about pleasuring me.

The first spasm of my orgasm caught.

My brain sputtered out.

Goddd, he was good.

"You're going to make me come," I managed.

Camden lightly bit on my ass cheek, breathing hard. "I want to fuck ye when that happens. Can I?"

"Yes. Please," I said without hesitation.

He carefully turned me again so I sat on the board,

arms extended, and jumped up to shed his remaining clothes. Completely naked, he knelt between my thighs.

"I don't have a condom." He stroked his dick, precum leaking and gleaming at the end.

I gave a stressed laugh. "And I never found my pill packet. I don't care. I'll work that out later."

"I don't care either. I'll pull out, but—"

"No but. Just keep going."

We were crazy. Both of us virgins, our future hopeless, but nothing was stopping this.

Camden took hold of my hips once more and raised me so the blunt end of his dick was at my entrance. He leaned forward to kiss me, at the same time thrusting inside.

I uttered a sound somewhere between a yelp and moan, echoed by the groan he made. Camden set his forehead on mine and closed his eyes. He withdrew and thrust again, holding me by the hips so I was positioned exactly where he wanted.

"I never knew," he half whispered.

I could only whimper agreement.

It felt so good. Too good to have not been doing this every time we'd been together. Camden laid another fast kiss on me then brushed over my clit, adding an electric jolt to his incredible glide in and out. His dick pulsed inside me, thickening impossibly further.

He cupped my breasts, grounding himself on my body, before losing himself in a slowly building rhythm as he worked out angles and speed.

Mindless, I could only receive. Feel.

This had been beyond hot before, and the connection built on that and gave it weight. Meaning. I wanted to hold him, to run my fingers into his hair and drag him down for a kiss. But I needed my hands freed, and I didn't know if that would still work for him.

Camden had spilled his soul. He needed this to bring something good into that awful darkness. It had to be his way.

I closed my eyes and succumbed.

Then I was moving.

Still deep inside me, Camden lifted me so my legs went around him and reached out to detach my constraints. The ropes fell away from my wrist cuffs, and I whimpered, throwing my arms around him.

"I know, I know," he whispered and kissed me, carrying me across the room. In a stark, small kitchen beyond the living room, he set me on the counter and continued kissing me, slowly withdrawing his hips.

"Look," he demanded, gesturing down to the place we were joined.

I watched his length disappear inside me, spreading my flesh, the CAMDEN tattoo surrounding.

"Tell me if I hurt ye," he urged. "I need this to be good."

"It doesn't hurt. It's perfect. I just need you close," I said against his lips.

He nodded and picked up the pace, fucking me like he was drawn to me. Like this bonded us, united us, made everything okay.

We kissed, the intimacy so much it was almost overwhelming.

The coiled heat of my orgasm bloomed again, concentrating on a different place in me, higher, where he hit a spot over and over.

I clutched him and focused on that feeling. Like he knew, Camden kept his pace exact, his arms shaking, banded around me. It was too intense, all-encompassing how badly I needed him like this.

His powerful muscles tightened, the same need driving him. Between us, we made desperate sounds, our hands clutching each other, our skin sweaty. Desire rushed. The chemistry we generated enough to start fires.

We abandoned our kiss to breathe against each other's lips, both focused intently on the pleasure blazing between us.

Every thrust drove me higher and sent sparks flying.

I rocked my hips to meet his moves, then suddenly, my climax struck. My moan this time was silent. I gaped against Camden's cheek, holding him so hard while shocks blinded me. As if I'd charged him up, he slammed into me, pounding for a wild minute with skin slapping until he growled a masculine sound of deep satisfaction, pulled out, and came on me and over his fist.

Fresh shocks rippled through me. I tugged his hair to bring his mouth back to mine.

We kissed as our skin cooled and reality settled back in.

"That was..." he said.

"Everything," I concluded.

Camden smiled that perfect, brilliant smile and kissed me again. "Agreed."

He reached to turn on the tap at the sink, rinsing his cum off his hand. I watched, my mind up to no good.

"This is weird," I confessed. "I didn't want you to stop. I wanted you to finish in me. I can't believe I said that out loud."

He stalled out, the information doing something to him. "Fuck. Okay. Next time."

On that promise, we got ourselves together and left the small flat, now refreshed with better memories.

"It helped, coming back." Camden hauled the door closed behind us, checking out the car which still waited on the road. It was like the thing was cursed; no one went near it. "I'd demonised this place in my head. It felt like I could never go home, and at least now I'm sure I don't ever want to. I don't live here anymore, and that's fine. Thank you for listening, and for everything else."

Hand in hand, we returned to the Rolls-Royce.

"I remember what the man said," Camden continued, pausing outside the car, "when he'd grabbed me and was facing off with my mother. 'Choose, little whore,' he told her. 'Your face or the kid's.' Obviously, she picked mine because her face earned her money, but isn't that fucked up?"

Ice filled my veins, stark against the lightness of how he faced his trauma. "Awful," I forced out my answer.

But his words...

Choose, little whore.

In a heartbeat, I knew who'd cut Camden's face.

And just as quickly, I was sure I couldn't say a word.

25

Camden

We arrived back at the cabin in the thick of night. From Stirling, we'd bought food from a takeaway I used to love, then I said goodbye to the city probably forever. Breeze offered to drive, but I told her to sleep, and minutes later, her eyes had closed, giving me a couple of hours to deal with the weird place my head was at.

The beating of my demons.

The sex.

Killing the Rolls-Royce's engine, I jogged around the car to collect Breeze in my arms. She curled into me, still asleep and so pretty my heart ached.

Inside the cabin, Struan lifted his head from the sofa. His dark eyes took us in, me carrying my lass, and his mouth quirked. "Everything good?"

"Very."

We both knew he meant the conversation we'd had.

I'd been convinced she hated me, while at the same time borderline insane over wanting her. Struan had been right. The constant overstimulation had calmed. I wanted her just as badly, to try more things with her. To sleep buried inside her. But my body was now under control.

"Good to know," my brother said. "Thea likes her. Lottie does, too." He stretched out his arms and gave up a huge yawn. "After ye left, we had a long conversation about jailbreaks."

My phone buzzed, interrupting him.

We were all here, aside from Burn. Who else had my number?

Breeze stirred, and I set her down on the sofa and extracted my phone from my pocket.

Scar, the screen read.

"What is it?" Breeze asked, her voice groggy.

There was only one person who could be dialling from *my* number. The missing heart of our family. Our six-year-old sister.

"Cassie," I breathed. "It's our girl."

"Cassie's calling, wake up," Struan bellowed up the stairs.

I swiped to answer the call, my hand shaking.

Doors opened, and footsteps drummed. The three of us huddled around the phone and I put it on loudspeaker.

"Hello?" her little voice came.

"Cassie, it's Camden. Struan's here, too. Are ye okay?"

Sin, Lottie, and Thea half fell down the stairs, their eyes wide and their focus on the phone.

"I didn't know there was a phone," she whispered. "I just found it. I called Burn."

I swallowed a lump in my throat. "We're really glad to hear your voice. Can ye tell us where ye are and who you're with?"

Noise came from her end of the line, a thud followed by a distant shout. "I'm in a house with a mum and dad. They have one big girl and lots of dogs, but the dogs live outside in cages."

Another shout came. Sin grabbed my arm and pulled the phone towards Lottie.

"It's me, sweetheart. Can ye tell us who's shouting?" Lottie asked.

Cassie took a sharp breath then sobbed. "Oh my God, Lottie. Can ye come get me? I don't like it here. I want to come home."

"We miss ye so much. We're doing everything we can to find your house. I promise you'll be back with us soon."

"Burn told me that if I was ever scared, to remember who my big brothers were. He said you'd protect me. Where is he? Burn? Are ye there?"

"He's not here right now, but all of the rest of us are," I promised.

A door slammed down the phone line, and she sobbed again. "I don't know my address. I don't know anything."

It was a stroke of luck I'd never put a passcode on that phone, or this call could never have happened.

"Are ye still in Scotland?" I pressed.

"Yes. There's a neighbour on one side who keeps hors-es. She was arguing with the da here about his dogs scaring them and she's Scottish."

"Is it a farm? Are there other animals?" I continued.

"I don't know!"

"It's okay." My heart broke at the fear in her voice. "Everything's going to be all right. Just tell us what you've seen outside."

"There's a line of those big windmills right by the house. I can see them from my bedroom. They make a thudding sound."

A wind farm. I raised my gaze to my brothers.

Lottie took over again. "Is there water near the house? A river or a loch?"

"There's a river. And a little road."

"Does the house have an upstairs?"

But Cassie went deadly silent. Something clicked on her end of the call. Breeze reached out and hit mute on my phone, her eyes rounded in fear.

A man's voice sounded on the line, muttering something indistinct.

"I didn't do anything," Cassie squeaked, her voice high. Afraid.

"And I told ye to stay in your bed and sleep. Ye defied me again," his voice came through louder. He sounded older. Maybe drunk.

"I will. I—"

"No, ye were spying on me. Poking that little nose into my business. Ye need to learn a lesson."

All six of us stood rigid, even Breeze who'd never met the girl we all loved.

The call disconnected, and my phone darkened.

Lottie cried out, turning her face into Sin's broad chest.

He enclosed her in his arms.

"That man sounds like my da," she said around her tears. "I know that fear. I know what it is to wake in the night and have that anger directed at ye."

"She's not safe there," Sin replied, his stern expression now savage, furious. "Did we get enough information to find her?"

"A pair of houses on a plot of land big enough for one to have horses," Thea summarised. "Dog cages. Wind turbines close by. A river and road. Everyone get searching on your phone. There can't be that many wind farms. We'll make a hit list then start searching tomorrow."

"But she's in danger now," Lottie said.

"We have to believe she'll be okay. Foster carers are paid, right? He won't hurt her or he'll lose money if she's taken away," Thea replied.

"Hurt comes in many different ways. She was ripped away from us, and the only salvation, the single thing that kept me going, was imagining her somewhere lovely with a caring family who wanted her there. That was traumatising." Lottie scrubbed her face. "We're getting her out, one way or another."

"Aye. We tried to do this the social worker's way. Fuck that idea," Sin agreed.

"Are we serious about this?" Struan asked. "We're going to grab her? I'm down, but there's consequences."

The energy that had come over us all simmered.

"She's six. She needs to go to school and not be on the run," I stated the obvious. "All this we discussed before. We know what's good for her—"

"Don't say it isn't us. Not against what we just heard," Lottie pleaded.

"I'm not. We'll get her out. But what if there is another way?" I replied.

Everyone looked at me.

From the case that held my phone, I pulled out McInver's credit card. Until now, I hadn't spent a penny of the money. Breeze had bought our dinner. The car had been fuelled up.

This had been one huge bone of contention between me and my family, but I'd done it anyway, and now I could justify it.

"We said fuck his money, but what's the odds her foster family would accept ten grand to hand her over and pretend she's still with them?"

Everyone stared at me.

"There's other cars in his garage. We'll take them. Take his cash. Hunt down Cassie and get her out in a way where we won't have the cops chasing us for abduction." I focused on my brothers, the objectors to my actions. "I hate McInver as much as ye, but here's the thing, if he dies, all his shite is mine. By law. Which makes it ours. Using it doesn't make me like him or forgive what he's done. It's repurposing it for the sake of those I love."

Breeze had given me the ability to see past my obsession with not being like my da. Who cared if we had anything in common? I was my own man, and my life belonged to me.

"Right on," Struan said after a long pause. "Screw him. We'll take what we want and bring our sister home."

An hour later, we'd pored over maps on our sister hunt. Thea had been right—wind farms weren't that plentiful, but there was still a long list of places that fitted the bill.

We divided up the areas and constructed a plan for the morning.

Then we took to our beds.

Breeze came with me to the room she'd first stayed in after the fire, no hesitation or question over where she'd sleep. Behind closed doors, under soft lamplight, I pulled her into my arms and took her mouth with mine.

Tomorrow evening, I could have the answers she'd been waiting for. My invitation from the police chief gave me the access that could help us find her sister, and I'd work as hard at that as I had with my own.

But what then? Would she walk away? I couldn't tell, and it was driving me insane.

Breeze returned my kiss, tugging me closer, and leading me to the big bed.

I pushed her down on it but stayed standing. "Don't move."

From the chest of drawers, I collected my tattoo kit. Then I plugged in the gun and prepped the ink.

"What are you doing?" Breeze asked.

Righting a wrong. Giving her choices. I shrugged then knelt on the rug by her feet. "I didn't expect ye. I had no idea how to handle the mindfuck being around ye brought, and that turned into me hurting ye. After an evening of working through the bullshit problems that men cause, I'm ashamed of what I did. How I laid my hands on ye. Pierced your skin with a needle and put my fucking name on ye like you're property."

Breeze listened, some emotion churning in her eyes.

I held up the tattoo gun and flicked the button to start it. "I need to fix what I did. I'm going to change your tattoo."

The lass I wished could be mine leaned forward and cupped my cheek. She kissed me, her blonde curls falling forward in a curtain, cutting off the world. At the same time, she took the tattoo gun and flipped the button to silence it.

"No," she said.

"I have to—"

She set the tattoo gun on the bed, then dragged me onto her until we both rolled back on the mattress. Breeze's lips coaxed mine into a kiss that stole every bit of my attention. It wasn't just her taste, or her body under mine, but the sense of bone-deep connection that drove me to heights I couldn't comprehend.

"I have to make it right," I tried again. "If ye don't want me to change the name, then how can that work?"

I stared down at her.

Breeze stroked her fingertips up my neck and into my hair, the light scratch of her nails sending trails of sparks. "Leave that to me."

She yanked on my shirt, and between kisses, I threw it aside and scrabbled to rid myself of my jeans. Breeze stripped her dress but let me remove her bra. I took two handfuls of her perfect tits, my dick so hard in my boxers I was going insane.

But Breeze pushed me back to the pillows, then straddled me. She'd worked beside me this evening with quiet determination. Now, a devilish need shone in her expression.

"Hold the headboard."

I obeyed, grabbing the wood.

"Tell me how to use the gun."

With her sitting directly on my rock-hard dick, I could barely think, let alone speak. But I forced out the words. "It's ready to go. The needle is a fine liner. Wipe over the skin to clean it with one of those wee packets. Press lightly with the needle and keep it moving. Are ye tattooing yourself or me?"

"You."

"Draw whatever the fuck ye want."

She could ink me anywhere. I'd carry her mark with pride. Didn't matter what it looked like.

She nodded but didn't pick up the tattoo gun. Instead, she stripped her underwear, leaving her fully naked. Then she pulled down my boxers and cast them aside, settling back over me with her bare pussy on my dick.

Nothing could have prepared me for this. Her beautiful, bare body astride mine. Her tits high and tight. Her waist swooping in from her hourglass figure.

My dick pulsed, leaking for her. We'd had sex already this evening, but I wanted more. Everything.

"Keep those hands where they are," Breeze instructed.

"I like ye taking control," I admitted.

"Tell me that in a minute." She glided up and down my length, wet and hot. Then she rose, fitted the end of my cock to her entrance, and sank down.

Open-mouthed, I groaned at how good it felt. At the

sight of her impaled on me. Breeze rested her palms on my chest, working me in quick slides before she was fully seated.

I pulsed inside her, and she shivered.

The whole time, her gaze held mine. "Ready?" she asked.

I was losing my mind. "Are ye seriously going to tattoo me while ye fuck me? Think I died and went to heaven."

Breeze snickered a laugh but picked up the little cleaning cloth.

I braced myself for where it would land, breathing hard as she lifted off my dick then slammed down again.

Then the little minx inched back until she was just riding the tip. She swiped the cleaning cloth across the base of my dick.

Holy fuck. I tightened my grip on the headboard, alarmed.

"No sudden movements," Breeze instructed.

"Are ye fucking kidding me?"

She bit her lip and took up the tattoo gun, her hips making slow, teasing circles. She flipped the switch then brought her gaze to mine again.

I knew exactly what she intended to do. Her revenge, or maybe her making us even. I didn't care. I couldn't open my lips to protest, even though this was going to hurt like a motherfucker.

Breeze adjusted her position, fucking me a couple more times before settling still and bringing the needle to the base of my cock. She pierced my skin, moving the needle quickly.

"Agh," I yelled.

"Want me to stop?"

"Fuck no."

Each time she pulled the needle away to swipe over the skin, she rotated her hips too, keeping me hard. Keeping me in her while she worked.

"You're bleeding," she muttered.

Of course I fucking was. I was engorged, and the skin at the base of my cock was thin. I didn't answer, though. She needed to finish this thing, whatever it was.

Breeze returned to her task, inking me in as much of an intimate place as I'd done to her.

The more she did, the harder I got.

Whatever she was drawing, she brought the ink down in a loop to meet where she'd started. I gave another pained howl, groaning with relief when she shut off the machine.

A thump came at the door. "Tell me to mind my own fucking business, but does anyone need help?" Struan called. Amusement played out in his tone.

"Too late," Breeze called back.

"Mind your own fucking business," I yelled at the same time.

He gave a dirty laugh, then his footsteps disappeared. Breeze grinned down at me. She picked up a cloth to clean my tattoo. It came away bloody.

"Can I use my hands now?" I asked.

She nodded slowly, stunned, as if realising what she'd done. I grabbed the cloth from her, clamped it across the small, fucking sore tattoo, then flipped us so Breeze was on her back. She gave a huff of surprise, then groaned as I fucked into her, still holding the base of my dick.

I'd lost all reason. Together, we were dangerous. Soft hearts and hard choices. For her, I'd take anything. Give anything. Bleed for her.

Breeze reached between her legs and rubbed her clit. In a minute, she spasmed around me, not letting up the pace, coming.

"Show me," I demanded.

Gasping for breath, Breeze slid her fingers to open her pussy lips around where I impaled her over and over. My name bracketed where I fucked her.

I tossed aside the cloth I held over my tattoo, finally seeing what she'd inked into my skin. The letter B.

Her initial.

In the way that I'd claimed her, she'd claimed me right back.

My climax hit in head-spinning, unending spasms. I pulsed into her. This time, I didn't pull out. I wanted my cum inside her. I wanted everything dark and dangerous with this lass.

I was in love with her, and nothing else mattered but this.

26

Breeze

Camden rolled off me, one hand to his poor, abused dick. "Stay right there," he ordered.

He jogged to the bathroom, turning on the brighter light, no doubt to inspect my handiwork.

I lay back on the soft quilt and gazed at the ceiling, a little amazed at myself. When he'd done this to me, I'd been furious. Now I'd reciprocated, it felt natural. Camden and I were destined to crash into each other and leave scars.

He returned, so gorgeous naked, and with a cloth in his hand. He handed it to me. "Think I bled on ye. I promise I'm healthy."

I held the warm, damp hand towel and watched him. Camden took up a small bag and extracted some little packets. He cleaned the site of his tattoo then taped it up, his perfect, upside-down smile in place the whole time.

I chewed my lip. "I planned to write my whole name down the centre, but that would've meant no sex."

His grin spread, and he leaned over to kiss me. "Ye like

sex with me."

It was a statement, not a question, but I nodded, not so shy about it anymore. He finished what he was doing, then joined me on the bed, taking the cloth from where I still held it. Camden eased my thighs apart and swiped over my skin, mopping away his blood.

His gaze locked on to my core, and he groaned. "You're leaking my cum. My name is covered in it."

He dipped his fingers into the wet and brought it higher to swipe over my clit. I'd already come once, but instant pleasure bloomed. I arched into his touch.

Camden gave another laugh, but darker now. More serious.

He stretched to kiss me, then pressed his lips to my chest before lazily tonguing my nipple. "Play with these," he instructed.

I palmed my tits then rolled my nipples between my fingers. He groaned, watching, then kissed my belly and went lower still. Camden moved his hand to slip two fingers inside me and at the same time sucked my clit.

I moaned softly, and he stroked and sucked me.

"Love feeling my cum inside ye," he muttered against my core. "Going to make ye come again."

We were playing with fire, but I needed every touch. I stretched to grab the headboard like he'd done, neglecting my nipples so all my focus was on his actions.

His tongue joined his fingers to slide inside me, into the slippery wet from his cum and mine. Then he returned to my clit and sucked hard.

Pretty quickly, he had me moaning.

I ached from where we'd had sex, but it only added to the sensation. Camden made a sound of half pleasure, half pain, one hand to the base of his dick.

"Every time I get hard from now on, your tattoo will be right there," he gritted out.

"Does it hurt?"

"Like a motherfucker. I love it."

I spasmed around his hand, closing in on another orgasm.

Abruptly, Camden reared over me and fucked his fist. With his gaze glued to my core, he spread me with his other hand, revealing his name tattoo, his fingers half inside me to open my channel. Then he came again, painting his cum in and on my pussy. He drove it inside me. Adding to the mess we'd already made.

God, I'd never get over his rapt expression. He made me mindless. Every touch drove me more insane for him.

Not for a second did he stop playing with me. He fucked me with his fingers, extra slick with the new cum all over me, and drove circles into my clit.

In seconds, I came, too, splintering apart and squeezing his hand. My eyes closed of their own accord, but every inch of me was on fire from his act.

I'd lost my pill packet somewhere at his mansion. I'd been home but not bothered collecting another. Now he was making me orgasm with his cum in me.

It only made me want more.

Open-mouthed, I gasped for breath, my mind so dizzy. Camden kissed me, then bundled me in a hug with my legs entwined with his.

"Shower?" he asked, hot and sweaty against me.

Yeah, a washcloth wasn't going to cut it.

I shrugged, still boneless. "In a minute."

He made a low growl and kissed along the side of my face, down my neck and back up. "Warning, if we stay like this, I'm just going to want to fuck ye again before that minute is up."

I kept my eyes closed, lost in the feel of him holding me. "Before you start getting any big ideas, I need to give you instructions on tattoo care. First, keep it clean and dry."

Camden laughed and kissed my breast.

"Second, don't rub over the surface."

He grabbed my hand and took it to my pussy, spreading my fingers into the mess. "Feel what we did. I'm addicted to that."

"I am, too," I confessed.

"Good. Because I'll be doing that to ye constantly from now on. Every chance I get."

Except how many chances did we have? Tomorrow, we'd be out hunting for Cassie. In the evening, he'd be infiltrating the List.

After that, who knew what would happen to us.

Instead of answering, I pulled him over me and lost myself in his kiss. He got hard again, fast, and groaned in the mix of pleasure and pain that I knew well.

The night continued in a way I wasn't sure it could ever go on.

*M*orning came after a night of intense, soul-defining lovemaking. I was exhausted but rejuvenated, too.

Split between Thea's car and the Rolls-Royce, we all travelled to McInver's mansion. Camden's family needed more and better vehicles to start the search for Cassie.

In the car park, Struan climbed out and gave a low whistle. "This is some dystopian shite, but I pictured worse." He gestured at the scaffolding which hadn't been here before. "Is repair work happening already?"

Camden squinted. "The lawyer said something about that. He moved fast."

None of them seemed to give a damn about the house, though. We all followed Camden to a wide and low out-building. He flipped back a panel, revealing a keypad. After he entered a code, the garage doors, designed to look like the same yellow stonework of the house, silently slid open.

Three cars waited inside, the fourth bay empty, presumably where the Rolls-Royce had sat.

Camden opened a box on the wall with another code and pulled out sets of keys. "Choose your poison. They're all fuelled up."

Struan walked straight to a dark-purple Bentley sports car. Sin to a massive, matte-black Range Rover. Camden tossed the keys, replacing the last in the box again.

Outside, they parked the cars in a line and climbed from the vehicles for one last pep talk.

"Everyone's got a destination," Sin said. "Keep in touch,

take photos in case we need them later. Scar, you're on call to handle the money side of it."

Camden nodded. "I'll message the lawyer now to ask for cash. Can't imagine a foster carer wanting a paper trail with the banks involved."

Lottie twisted her fingers together. She'd been quiet all morning, and the reason for that hurt my heart. Last night, she'd said she knew what Cassie was going through. She'd come from a home with a violent parent.

I'd lived under fear of Jack's friends but none had ever laid a hand on me. Mum would've killed them.

"What if they won't sell her?" she said softly. "That's all I've thought about all night. We find her, she runs to us, but they won't let her go at any price."

"Then we take her," Camden stated. "Either there and then if we can, or later. It's better for everyone if we do it the gentle way, but we're taking her back. Agreed?"

Everyone nodded.

"Then we spring Burn," Struan added. "Ye missed this conversation because of your mission to Edinburgh yesterday, but we're not turning our backs on Burn. If we need to run once we get Cassie, no fucking way are we leaving him behind."

"This your jailbreak plot?" Camden asked.

Struan inclined his head, his expression deadly serious. "Aye, we can't raid the police station. They'll outnumber us ten to one or more. The only way to do it is to get Burn in transit. Which means giving them a reason to move him."

"How do we do that?" I asked.

No one questioned why I was making myself part of this plan. I didn't know Burn. I'd only seen him once. But my sister cared about him. Camden did. Which made him mine to help, too.

"There's two ways we came up with," Thea said. "Probably from watching too many movies. First, an emergency at the station. Fire or flood. But that's hard to execute and get away with, especially considering our pyromaniac is the one in a holding cell. The second option would be easier. He gets sick or injured and has to go for medical treatment to a hospital."

Camden took this in, reaching out to hold my hand. "Or there's the other option. If I can persuade the police chief to release him to me, then disappear his body, we won't have anyone looking for him."

Which all pinned on his meeting with the police chief tonight.

Camden's family discussed this in low tones, making plans and decisions.

My mind had gone to a darker place. A stark realisation of what was to come.

Camden had one chance to access the list and find Summer. Things were moving too fast, and his family were too hot-headed to leave their missing siblings out in the cold. They were going to buy or steal the little girl. They were going to break Burn out of his cell. The minute that happened, for one or both, they'd be fugitives.

And if we hadn't found Summer by that moment, I'd never see her again.

Somehow, this had become a knife's edge of my family versus his.

27

Camden

We struck out on our hunt. Sin and Lottie drove south to take two wind farms near Dunblane and Kinross. Struan and Thea went farther to the southwest, skirting Glasgow to find ones nearer the coast. Beyond that, they'd split the ones between Glasgow, Edinburgh, and the borders.

Hours of driving, but no one hesitated.

Breeze and I headed north. Considering the fact I had my date with the police chief tonight, we couldn't go as far afield, so took on the mountains and the high-up sites of Dunmaglass and Stronelairg.

Google Maps gave us nothing, with no good view of nearby properties, so I had less of a sense for our chances.

Our worst fear was misinterpreting Cassie's rushed information. That the wind farms were distant specks from her window and wouldn't help in our search.

I gritted my jaw and kept on driving. Thinking like that didn't help anyone. It felt good to take action at last with a chance of success.

In the passenger seat, Breeze stayed quiet. She gave directions when needed but otherwise wasn't in the mood for chat.

A lot had happened between us in a short time. I guessed it overwhelmed her. Or maybe it was worry for her sister which had her subdued. Problem was, my energy thrummed at the opposite end of the scale.

I was burning up with heat for her. So happy to love her.

Talking about it felt dangerous. Like she'd wince and look away if I said any of what I felt. So instead, I channelled it into the hunt. Finding our way off road and into the mountains in pursuit of houses that might contain a scared six-year-old.

But our search proved fruitless.

By late afternoon, we'd trekked around both the wind farms on our list and found only a couple of industrial buildings or the occasional bothy. No family homes. Definitely no horses in the exposed, chilly locations.

I turned us back towards home. It would take an hour to get back, then I'd need to leave for tonight's meeting.

"Hey, call Lottie, will ye?" I handed my phone to Breeze.

Obediently, she placed the call and put it on hands-free as I drove. Lottie answered on the first ring.

"We're heading back," I told them. "No luck here. What about ye?"

I already knew from earlier text messages that the first place they tried had been no good.

"I think we found it," Lottie said on a breath. "We've

been staking out this house for the past hour. It's in a valley with wind turbines on a ridge right beside it. There are two cottages side by side, one of which has a kid's swing outside and a pen with German Shepherds in it. Next door has a paddock with two ponies in. Every time the dogs bark, like they did when we went to knock on the door, the horses go mad."

My heart thumped. "What happened when ye knocked?"

"No one's home. There's a car here, but it's a little runaround, parked around the side. I bet the main family one has been taken out somewhere. They're bound to come back sooner or later, and we'll be waiting."

I sucked in air, aware I'd been holding my breath.

"Fucking hell, I hope that's the right place." I put my hand over my chest. "Keep us posted."

"We will. Sin wants to talk to ye."

My brother came on the line. "Don't take any big risks tonight. Fact-finding only," he demanded in his low rumble. "With any luck, we'll all be back at the same time ye return, and we can decide what to do with whatever you've found out. This I'm going to repeat because it bears repeating. We can't lose ye, too. It's enough to tear the world apart for our two youngest. Spare me the heart attack of ye being taken as well."

"Nothing is going to happen to me," I promised.

"See ye on the other side."

We hung up, and I breathed a little easier.

Across the car, Breeze wouldn't meet my gaze. We were on a stretch of hillside heading down to a wide-open moor.

The view was glorious, but that wasn't the reason I pulled over and rolled off the road to halt the car.

"Are ye worried about me finding Summer? Or not finding her?"

"No, I'm good."

"I know today has been frustrating," I tried again, trying to work out why she was feeling off track.

"It hasn't. I want to find Cassie, too. You all love her so deeply, and each other. Your whole family has been forged in this awful circumstance. You're so close. I have this wave of desperation to get you back together again. Anyone would."

I didn't like her putting herself on the outside of this.

I caught her hand and held it flat over my heart. "Some people are easy to love."

Breeze stared at me like I was the maddening one. After a beat, her gaze lingered on my left eye, then down to my mouth and back up to my right eye. Like she was drawing a triangle on my face.

Heat kicked inside me.

She uttered a swear word and unclipped her seat belt, following suit with mine. Then she leaned over and kissed me. Not soft and gentle, but fierce and needy. Determined.

Breeze reached to tug my shirt out of the way then undid the button of my jeans. Her fingers brushed over my injured cock, and instead of stopping her, I let my brain blip out with a rush of pleasure.

She was distracting me. I knew it. My cock knew it. Guess who was going to win that battle?

Breeze freed me and ducked to enclose the head of my

cock in her hot mouth. I could've checked our surroundings. Made sure we weren't being watched by some lucky hiker, but I was a goner for this lass. She only had to kiss me and I didn't know my name.

She flattened her tongue around my dick and braced herself over my lap, taking me in as far as she could go, and as far as the position would allow. Had to love the Rolls-Royce for the luxury of space. When she came up, I lifted my arse to push my jeans down farther so I could widen my thighs.

Both of us paused to look down at the tattoo, covered with film which broke away the harder I got.

"Love seeing your initial on me almost as much as my name on ye," I confessed.

Breeze shivered and returned to her task, keeping away from the tattoo. Like me, she was working us out as she went. I let her know exactly how I liked it. What felt most incredible. Which was pretty much everything.

In no time, my balls were tight and my hand was wedged in her hair, guiding her blow job. Trying to control myself. But it was no use. She turned me on too much to last.

"I'm going to come," I gritted out.

Breeze stayed exactly where she was, sucking harder.

My orgasm hit, then I came down her throat. She swallowed me then stopped when I gripped her hair tighter, the sensation too much.

Then I was floating on a cloud of bliss. I wrestled my jeans back in place then kissed her. Breeze let me, this time not avoiding the contact. I drove us home with a grin that wouldn't go, my worries pushed to the back of my mind.

We diverted to McInver's to pick up Thea's car. At the mansion, Breeze got into the little Kia, following me home.

On convoy, we neared the cabin, first passing the castle. A group stood outside—Gordain, there with two other men. I stopped and opened my window.

"Camden, I was just coming out to see ye. This is James and Sebastian, the people I was telling ye about." He gestured to the men, one his age, and one around thirty.

Shite. I'd figured that's who it might be, and I really wanted to talk to them. We needed allies, but I couldn't do it now. There was barely enough time to get back, get changed into a clean, long-sleeved shirt, then get back in the car and drive to Inverness.

I climbed out and shook their hands. "Grand to meet ye. I really want to talk to ye both, but there's somewhere I need to be this evening. I can't miss it."

Breeze pulled up in the car behind, her expression worried.

A sudden flash of concern hit me. I had to leave her alone. My family were all elsewhere, divided, and spread far and wide when I needed them close. Our focus had been split.

But there was no choice, I couldn't take her with me.

I shook off the feeling; this place was safer than anywhere I'd ever known.

"Will ye still be here tomorrow?" I asked the men.

"We will," the younger man said, Sebastian, I gathered. "I'm borrowing a heli for a flight. You can come with me. Bring your lass, too."

I thanked him and got on the road. At the cabin, I dressed in minutes then jogged back to Breeze, circling my arms around her as that same wild sense of concern grew. "Those restraints in your bag... I keep picturing tying ye up with them. Securing ye here."

I drove her backwards to the window seat. Beneath it ran a radiator, the metal pipework perfect for what I had in mind.

"You'd leave me here tied up?"

I growled, confused by my own instincts. "No. I want to but I wouldn't. That's the fucking worst part of my DNA talking."

Slowly, she inclined her head. "You need to channel McInver tonight. I get it."

She might understand, but I hated how badly the sense grew.

"Stay here, stay safe. I'll forward my family's phone numbers in case ye need them. I don't know when they'll be back. I don't know when I'll be back. Believe me." I pressed my forehead to hers. "I will do everything I can to find Summer."

She produced a sad smile. "And free Burn."

"That, too."

I kissed her, held back the ILY words that fought for release, and left.

28

Camden

The police station appeared ahead, a solid red-brick building that should've had me more on edge, ready, alert. But my thoughts had stayed with the fair-haired lass I'd left.

I parked in a visitor's spot and brought out my phone, dialling Struan.

"What's wrong?" he asked.

"I'm at the station but I'm worried about Breeze. She's at the cabin alone. When will ye be home?"

Struan said something in a mutter, presumably to Thea. "We'll drive back. It won't be quick. We're picking up food for Sin and Lottie then we're driving to deliver it to them. They're planning an all-night stakeout as there's no sign of Cassie yet, and none of the rest of us found a viable house. They don't need us to stay with them, though. We'll get home to your lass once that's done."

I watched the entranceway. Daniels, the chief of police, appeared, his fake smile installed when he spotted me.

"I need to go. About to head into the lion's den."

"Love ye, man. Come out fighting."

"The fuck did ye just say?"

Struan grumbled in annoyance. "Thea told me to say it. Some shite about men having to express their feelings. Say a word and I'll fucking brain ye."

Amusement broke into my wretched state. "Love ye, too, then, big brother."

He swore at me and hung up.

I gave myself a second more to wallow in my feelings. Worry for Breeze. Love for her that was taking me over. Devotion to my family. Fury over Burn being imprisoned behind the very walls ahead of me.

Then I got the fuck out of the car and put my game face on.

"Chief Daniels," I greeted the man.

He joined me, placing a hand on my shoulder. "Camden McInver. Your timing is perfect."

"I want to see the prisoner again."

"Voice down, please. Officially, he doesn't exist. If all goes well, I'll let you have at him again after the weekend. This time, do a better job. Cheeky little fuck hasn't been broken yet."

It hadn't been the plan to see Burn tonight, but getting in there again to hurt him enough for hospital treatment became a very real possibility. I couldn't imagine laying my fists into him. Still, I'd do anything to get him free.

Chief Daniels guided me to the Rolls-Royce. The lightness in his eyes blipped out, and seriousness came over him. "I understand your father permitted you to be raised away from him. I have some thoughts on why that might be, but that does leave us in a situation. As he is unable to guide you currently, as his closest friend, I will take on the mantle. Tonight will be…illuminating for you."

This man gave me the creeps. With his short beard, smattering of grey in his light-brown hair, and height a few inches beneath mine, there was nothing offensive to him. Until he spoke.

"I thought ye said this was a party," I said.

"It is. Toss your phone into the car."

My unease grew, but I did as the chief asked. Whatever he was about to show me, I needed to see.

Chief Daniels directed me to another vehicle. Then he drove me away to who the fuck knew where.

In the car, I sat tall, the sense of being out of control pounding my heart.

"Where are we going?" I asked finally.

The chief shot me a look. "Don't worry, your father would approve. From your habits, I'm certain you'll like what you find."

Wasn't that fucking ominous.

"My habits?"

"I know all about you, Camden Marshall."

My real name, not McInver's that I'd appropriated. My hackles rose.

"Born in Stirling, raised in poverty by a single mother with no help from your wealthy father. He left you there. Let the streets forge you. I like the sentiment. Wish I'd done it myself with my own boy, not let his useless mother influence him." The chief tapped the steering wheel with each point. "Injured by an assailant unknown, your own subsequent apprehension for knife crime."

Fuck. He'd done his homework on me then locked me inside his car. It was true that I'd been caught with a knife aged fourteen. No charges had been pressed, but it had been my go-to method for protecting myself in the shitty world I lived. I'd never hurt anyone, though.

"Guess that kind of background check is why ye made it to chief." I faked amusement.

He glanced over. "It would be wrong of me to take you into the fold without due diligence. Don't worry, though. If you're what I think you are, you'll fit in just fine."

Forty minutes on, we turned off a main road that pierced the dark Scottish countryside. Lit-up gateposts announced we were entering Kendrick Manor.

The name seemed familiar. I stared at the sign, then the memory clicked in my mind. Ick Manor. The envelope I'd taken from McInver's. Now I had the full name.

Ahead, through a row of trees, a vast stately home disturbed the landscape. Dark-grey stone and soaring towers.

My gut tightened, but I kept up my persona of McInver's son. "What is this place?"

"See? That you don't know my manor. So neglectful." The chief tutted.

His home, then. The chief of police had money as well as connections. My picture of him started shifting.

He stopped outside, and we climbed out. From the building, a man exited, my age or a little younger.

Chief Daniels presented me to him. "Camden McInver, brought into our midst at last. Can't you see his father's mark on him already? Camden, this is my son, Arran."

The son took me in, his expression inscrutable. His height matched mine, and muscular shoulders rounded out a designer shirt. His dark-blond hair had been cut into a neat style, but it was a rapid scowl, a flash of absolute disdain, that settled on me.

In a second, it had gone, and he produced a cool smile. "Great to meet you."

"What a moment," the chief continued. "It's such a shame that you and Arran didn't know each other growing up. I'm sure you would've been fast friends. You have much in common."

I nodded at the son. "Pleasure to meet ye, Arran."

The chief snorted. "Better manners than your father, which is a good start. Camden, I look forward to testing your mettle. Arran, take him inside and show him around. I have business to take care of so will find you later."

He strode away, leaving us alone.

I turned to the son. "What does testing my mettle mean?" Better to get this man on side by creating a personal connection.

Arran glowered at me, resentfulness returning.

"He told me to show you around, not chat," he complained.

He stomped away to the house, and I followed.

Inside, music came from behind closed doors to the right of the entrance. Like with McInver's place, opulence abounded. A broad staircase curved to a landing. Bright chandeliers lit the space with sparkling yellow light. No other people could be seen, or servants, though I bet they had them.

Arran turned to face me, his expression even more sour. "We already know about you. If you think that lawyer of yours is loyal, guess again. We know you're just like your dad, and that the first thing you did after becoming the heir was to spend his money on your shared hobby."

My unease tightened. I was stuck here, no phone, no transport, and with a hostile reception that could only get worse. And I knew exactly what that hobby looked like.

"I know what you are," Arran continued with his lip curled in disgust. "You're just another one of them. So go ahead, show him what he wants to see so he can get on with his plans. Excuse me if I don't join in."

"Don't assume ye know a fucking thing about me," I bit out, unable to stop myself.

"Yeah, right. Take it in, oh noble son of a decaying pervert."

Arran thrust open the double doors.

An unbelievable scene met my gaze.

In a formal receiving space, women draped over every surface. Naked, or nearly so, they chatted and laughed together, but the more I stared, the more I saw.

On a table in the centre of the room, under another sparkling chandelier, one woman lay on her back with another lass beside her feet. The second lass picked up her foot and kissed her ankle, her gaze locked on me and Arran. The one lying out arched her back, palming her tits like the single touch had her orgasmic.

Before I could glance away, the second woman bent between the first's legs and licked her pussy. Both moaned with fake pleasure.

I shuddered, repelled.

"Over here," a feminine voice called from the window.

A tall lass in a floaty see-through nightdress perched on the window seat. She picked up a hefty-looking dildo and slid it inside herself, no hesitation, her heel on the seat so nothing was hidden.

Another lass knelt beside her and enclosed her erect nipple in her mouth, taking over control of the dildo, fucking her with it slow but hard.

Beyond them, women groped each other; some danced in stilettos and nothing else.

It was an orgy, or the pretence of one. All the women were acting, waiting on us to join in.

None of them could pass for Summer, and I was certain I'd recognise her.

At my side, Arran heaved a sigh. "Don't just stand there. Get it over with."

I struggled to summon the words to tell him where to go. My mother had done this. She'd been part of sex parties at McInver's house. Whatever of him I'd inherited, it wasn't this.

I only wanted Breeze. No matter how she'd kickstarted my sexuality, with the sight of her spread out naked, this kind of shite was obscene. The realisation came in fast, staggering me.

I'd only wanted the woman, not the degradation.

I gave up a hard laugh. "So this has been laid on for my

benefit? Your da won't trust me until I've taken my pick?"

He glowered at me more, then turned back to the women, ignoring me.

As if activated by my rejection, the mood changed in the group. The sexy music changed to a slower, sleazier tune, the lights dimming around the edges of the space.

Where lasses had been standing together before, now, they moved it up a notch.

Two women held another by the arms and dragged her to the centre of the room. They lifted her onto the table, the other lasses clearing the space, then positioned her on her back with a blindfold hiding her eyes. She didn't fight them, her long brunette hair spilling off the table to brush the floor, but I guessed this was staged to test my kinks.

A woman with red hair in long curls strolled up in heels that defied physics. She came over and circled me, drawing a finger across my chest. She moved onto Arran, but he tutted and slapped away her hand.

She stalked back to the table, putting on a show.

Arran leaned into me, his voice low. "Not that one. My dad will kill you."

"She's his favourite?"

He laughed. "He calls them his wives for the night. Whichever whore he picks gets special privileges as the lady of Kendrick Manor. They fight over it."

This evening was getting more and more fucked up. Tonight's Lady Kendrick climbed onto the table and seized the much younger woman by the legs, opening her up. She held out a hand, and somebody placed a conical object into it.

"Bet she uses those butt plugs on my dad," Arran quipped. "Are you into guys? Dad doesn't order male whores in most of the time, not unless a guest specifies it. Let me know. He'd want me to arrange it."

"No, thanks. I'm good. Question, though. That lady title..."

"Dad's Lord Kendrick. Not widely known."

Fuck. I'd underestimated the police chief no end.

The wife drizzled lube from a bottle down onto the core of the woman beneath her. Like the other lasses, Lady Kendrick watched me and Arran, sweeping her red hair aside so we didn't miss a second of her show.

She ran the butt plug across the woman's clit then briefly inside her pussy, drawing it back out then down to her arse.

The younger woman gasped at the insertion, her hands and feet now held by others so she couldn't pull away.

Lady Kendrick put her hand out again, this time a long double-ended dildo given to her. At the same moment, someone forced a ball into the younger woman's mouth and clipped it into place with a harness around her head.

She whimpered.

I'd seen enough.

If the test was for me to pick someone to fuck in order to prove myself one of them, I'd fail. With all that was at stake, I couldn't do it. I couldn't betray Breeze, or the morality I'd built inside me as I'd grown up watching this kind of bullshit from the sidelines.

Heartsick, I turned to Arran, ready to make a play for this not being my thing. Act the imperious arsehole. Whatever I could do to get away.

Then movement at the back of the darkened room captured my attention.

Spread on a chaise longue, a blonde woman undulated under another, her tumble of hair long and luxurious. I squinted, horrible recognition forming.

Summer was here, and she was part of the show.

29

Breeze —*two hours before*

Alone, I sat in the middle of the bed, clutching a book. Last time I'd been here, I'd read part of this. *Wuthering Heights.*

I couldn't bring myself to open it now.

I didn't need the reminder of a dark and twisted relationship where the couple crashed into each other over and again but couldn't unite until they were both dead. What a crappy fate. What a terrible way to let yourself go on.

For my sake, Camden had gone tonight. The police chief had given him an in, but he didn't need to take it. He didn't need to go there with a second agenda that could lose him everything, that was all my doing because I wanted him to find my sister.

But my hope for Summer to still be alive after a month or more of nothing...I was a fool.

A cold tear slid down my cheek. I didn't cry easily, but this was worthy of despair. I'd sent Camden into danger. Given him the responsibility of returning to me and explaining all was lost.

I couldn't believe he'd find anything.

Instead, all I saw was him getting hurt. Losing his life as she'd lost hers.

Somehow, I'd fallen in love with him.

I pressed my balled-up fist to the centre of my chest, the ache unbearable. Camden was the best man I'd ever met. Selfless, kind, funny, and he gave himself entirely to others.

Instinctively, I'd known. I'd been careless with him, not just with risking pregnancy, but risking my heart, too. Except careless felt like carefree. Happy.

I didn't deserve him, and he didn't deserve me using him in the way I had.

In the car, he'd wanted to talk. I'd seduced him with the lessons I'd been given at my audition, and it had stopped him questioning me. What a thing to do just to avoid honesty.

My resolve formed, and I swiped at my damp face, sitting up taller. At least in one thing, I could be of use to him. The revelation I'd had regarding his scar.

The *moment choose, little whore* joined the dots in my mind.

Around the age of twelve or thirteen, I'd been a scared, knock-kneed, skinny girl, hiding in the bedroom I shared with my sister because Mum's boyfriend had friends around.

I'd never liked Jack, not from the minute we met, but I liked his friends even less. They came over to drink and take drugs in the flat, like they still did now, and would brag about their shitty activities, each trying to outdo the others.

Jack's brother was a wannabe gangster and had once brought a gun with him. I'd never seen a gun before, no one had one that I'd ever known, so I'd cracked the bedroom door to spy on the men.

Giving me complete access to hear their conversation.

They'd handed round the weapon, commenting on the weight and pretending to shoot each other. But one of the men sneered at it. He drank vodka neat from a bottle and weaved a story.

He'd told them that true masculine power came not in paltry things like guns, but in the way you struck fear into your victims, holding them in your grip before you did a thing.

He didn't have a knife, or knuckle-dusters, or any of the things the others had, but his words cut through me.

"You take their greatest fear and use it against them. Corner them when they're with the person they care about the most, then play on that love. Choose, I tell the little whores. Them or their kid. Whoever. Ninety-nine times out of a hundred, they give you what you want without a fight. All you use is words. Don't get your hands dirty unless they've really crossed you."

He'd gone on to illustrate his claim with a story of how he'd forced a woman to accept a beating, or watch him take it out on her elderly mother. His words were followed up with cruelty I'd been unable to comprehend.

He'd horrified me, but I'd assumed his were mainly sex crimes. It didn't occur to me that he would cut a child's face until Camden related that choose calling card.

It couldn't be a coincidence. Nor a copycat, as Camden's injury would already have been inflicted by that point. Plus Edinburgh wasn't far from Stirling.

But I couldn't tell Camden anything until I was completely sure.

If I was right, Jack still hung out with the guy. He'd been there when I'd visited the flat, looking for my mother—he'd said his favourite words to me then, inviting me to go inside or stop ringing the bell. But I didn't know his name.

I had to find out his identity.

Taking out my phone, I called Mum. I'd never had Jack's number, nor let him have mine.

"Breeze," my mother gasped as she answered. "Oh, Breeze. You won't believe it. Oh my God above. My baby girl."

I clutched the phone. "What's happened?"

My mother sniffed, her breathing shuddering. "It's the best news. The only thing I've wanted and been waiting for. My heart is so full. Jack, you tell her. I can't."

The phone rustled, then Jack came on the line. "Breeze, where are ye?"

"Not in Edinburgh. Why? What's happening with my mum?"

"We need ye back here, right now. Grab your bag, steal a car. Bring that boy of yours."

"Why? Will someone give me a straight answer?"

"Your sister's back."

My heart stopped. The world slowed. What had seemed impossible minutes ago was now a reality.

"Summer? There's no way," I started. Jack was a liar. He always had been. "Put my mother back on the line."

Mum sobbed. "It's true. Come home, come home. She

needs you. She—"

The call ended, but it was all the release I needed. I leapt up, grabbed my bag, and sprinted down the stairs, pausing only to jam my feet into my shoes and steal Thea's keys.

Summer was home, *alive,* but something was wrong.

I needed to get to her now.

30

Camden

Ignoring the live sex show, I stormed across the room to the couple writhing on the chaise longue.

"Get off her," I commanded the woman on top.

She smirked like she'd won the competition to capture my attention, and stood, in my way and with her naked body pressed to mine.

I was only interested in the lass under her.

Blonde hair, longer than Breeze's, but the same colour, the same weight to it. That was where the similarity ended.

A stranger stared back at me, no familiarity in her features.

Not Summer.

"She's wet and ready for you," the woman gripping me whispered. "She's brand-new, never had a man. Fill her up. Show her what she's missed out on."

The woman on the cushions spread her legs, sliding her fingers between them. "Please, I need you."

Fuck all of this. I shook off the cling-on, my hands out to ward them away.

"What's wrong with you?" Arran asked. "Why aren't you getting on with it?"

"Because this is bullshit."

His gaze suddenly held mine. Where before, he'd been dismissive, now, he was paying attention. "Yes. It is. But why the fuck would you think so?"

"Camden," a voice boomed across the room.

I swung around.

Chief Daniels entered, passing the women who posed for him, too.

I got it, they were being paid to do this. Didn't mean I had to like it.

He moved closer, sparing a second to ogle his pick for Lady Kendrick who was now double-ender deep in her partner.

Arran had been at my side the whole time I'd been in their sex den, but now he merged back to the shadowed wall, away from his dad.

"Which one?" the chief said, his words hard.

"What do ye mean?" I asked.

The blonde on her back stood, her hand up. "He picked me, sir."

The chief narrowed his eyes at the lass. He clapped once, and the other girls dutifully skittered from the room, barring the redhead and her partner who kept up their act with moans increasing in volume.

This was the weirdest shite I'd ever seen.

The house owner paced right up to me, trying and failing to intimidate me. "If you're intending to become one of us, I need that proof."

I shrugged. "Never claimed to be anything other than what I am."

The night was a fail. Summer wasn't here. The only part I could hope to salvage was staying in the police chief's good books so I'd get to see Burn.

The chief shook his head once. "Don't play dumb. Don't tell me you haven't discovered all your dad's dirty secrets. I know you stayed at the house. I know what he keeps there. So I'll ask again. Prove to me that you're your father's son and you'll continue in his footsteps. Uphold the business deal we made."

I had a horrible suspicion of where this was going. They'd made a deal. It had to be for women. Breeze's mother had been trafficked to the UK. Summer had turned vigilante to investigate it. What if there was a ring that funded trafficking, bringing in more girls to feed their habit?

That would take money and business to hide the activities behind. Police corruption to ensure they looked the other way.

I'd assumed it was just a group of dirty old men, but the facts started to look murkier.

He inched closer, his gaze fixed. Angry. "You bought the girl I wanted. I could forgive that of your father when he outbid me the first time. Did you know that was on purpose? Did you do the same? That little slut is exactly what I like. McInver knew that. Taunted me with it."

He meant Breeze. Adrenaline blitzed my veins, and my blood pumped faster, fury rising.

He gestured now to the woman who thought she'd won me. "Have this one. Have them all. Fuck, bruise, bury them all. I don't care. Give me back the one I want. I know she's still with you."

I opened my mouth to shout him down. To defend her.

From the open doors, another man hurried in, a servant at a guess. He stopped by the chief. "Forgive me, sir. I'm sorry to interrupt, but I just took the call you've been waiting for."

Chief Daniels glowered at the cowed, penguin-suited man then murmured a question in his ear. The servant whispered back, and the chief nodded, releasing him to hurry away. He turned to me, a new emotion present in his eyes.

"Your father is awake."

I stared at him, the room quiet, apart from the moaning Lady Kendrick who came in a loud, undulating cry.

"He woke from his coma an hour ago. Your lawyer is with him."

All of a sudden, I had nothing. I was here under false pretences, driving a car I had no right to, using a name that was of no use to me anymore. The second McInver called me out, I was in danger. I could only hope he hadn't spoken yet.

I needed to get out of here.

"Take me to him," I demanded.

Chief Daniels kept up his perusal, in no hurry to do anything. "All in due course. You were busy picking your lady and considering giving up mine." He snapped his gaze to the man behind me. "Arran."

His son stepped forwards, hiding worry behind deference. Or maybe fear. "Yes, Father?"

"Keep your new best friend occupied, will you? I'll return later tonight."

"Wait," I said. "Ye can't keep me from McInver. I need to see him."

But the chief only gave a thin smile. "You will. Trust me on that."

He walked away, closing the door behind him.

I was stuck. Caught here without any easy way of getting home. I could run and hitchhike, maybe, though no sane person would pick up a strange man in the dark Scottish countryside. Maybe I wouldn't even make it out of the house if there were guards or dogs present. I eyed the windows, muscles primed to make my escape.

But maybe there was another way.

I turned to Arran, drawing his attention onto me. "Honesty, now. What is this to ye?" I gestured to the room.

The three remaining working women huddled together, their show suspended, and the red-haired lass watching us like we were a threat to the others. Discarded dildos lay on tables, and the music had been switched off.

"All shades of fucked up," Arran breathed.

"It is, and I'm not one of them. I know you're not either, no matter what your da orders from ye. So listen up, I need to get out of here fast. Will ye help me?"

It was a risk. He feared the chief, that was for certain, but excuses could be made. His hatred had to equal mine.

Arran gifted me the first real smile. "Fuck, yeah, golden boy. Follow me."

He led me through a door at the back of the room and down a dark corridor that ran to the side of the house. Outside, I peered into the night.

Red taillights disappeared down the road to our right, the chief heading out, I guessed.

Either way, I needed to leave just as quickly.

"Here," Arran said, hushed, and gestured to a neat, dark-coloured sports car.

We climbed in, and he sped away from Kendrick Manor.

"I need a phone," I said.

"Here's mine." Arran handed his over. "I'm going to be fucking executed for this, but I don't care. I hate their shit with everything in me. My mother..." He trailed off.

The chief had mentioned something about Arran's mother, but I focused on remembering numbers, no time to ask his story now.

"Sorry about your ma. Don't go back," I muttered, stabbing at the buttons, praying I had Struan's number right.

"I don't have a choice," Arran muttered in reply.

The phone rang. The line was answered, but silence greeted me.

"It's me, on the chief's son's phone," I said.

"Fuck," Struan said, caution in his voice.

"Our father is awake," I said, sweating over how to handle this. I couldn't say too much, no matter how Arran seemed to be on my side. I needed my own phone and car back.

"Your lass has gone."

The bottom fell out of my world. I closed my eyes for a long moment, imagining the worst, slammed into by the loss.

"Any intel on where?" I managed.

"None. Get back here."

"I'll do my best."

I hung up then deleted the number from the call log. It didn't mean shite, but it was the best I could do.

"Take me back to the police station in Inverness so I can pick up my car," I requested.

The chief's son shot me a look, taking the phone I held out. "We're closer to the hospital. I'll play chauffeur so you can see McInver. Surely it'll be better if you visit him before my dad's been alone with him too long. You can trust me. I want to help."

That was debatable. I could only imagine what his father might do to find him if he realised he'd assisted me.

"I need my car," I said again. "And ye need to get back to the manor ahead of your da returning. Then claim I ran for it."

He worked his jaw.

In another life, I'd want to talk it out with him. Help the lad who was clearly stuck in a hell I'd only seen the very edge of. At a guess, he was exposed to as much shite as I had been growing up, but worse, as the chief ran the show. Had expectations of his son.

"Fine. But take my number in case you need it," Arran finally decided.

He rerouted our path to Inverness, giving me a pen to scrawl his phone number on a scrap of card. Down the street from the police station, I left him with thanks, jogging back to the Rolls-Royce and peeling away.

I didn't know why Breeze would leave me, or how I'd get her back, but beyond anything, she was my first thought and my last.

I knew without doubt that something was badly wrong.

At the cabin, I burst inside to find Struan and Thea not alone. Max, Struan's friend, was there, along with Sebastian, the Englishman I'd met outside the castle earlier with his father.

All four stared at me.

"What do we know?" I barked without hesitation.

"Only that she left before we got back, and she took Thea's car. Do ye not have a message from her?"

I shook my head. I'd checked my phone, called her with no answer, then threw myself in the driver's seat to get back here. On the way, I'd mentally calculated the time I'd left her and how far she could have driven. Why she might go.

Thea gestured to my phone. "Call her. It might be nothing."

"I tried her on the way here. What if someone took her? McInver's business partner wanted her." I pressed to dial her number, my heart thudding.

"What does it matter that your da woke from his coma?" Max asked Struan, presumably continuing the conversation I'd interrupted.

"Him versus us," Struan replied in the most accurate and basic fucking sum up of our lives.

The phone rang. I put it on loudspeaker.

"Hello," a voice answered.

It wasn't Breeze, but older and male.

"Who the fuck are ye?" I said.

"We've been introduced. I'm Jack, Breeze is my step-daughter."

I didn't like his tone. The steadiness and feeling of rehearsal in his words.

"You're nothing to her," I stated.

Jack tutted. "Actually, I'm everything to her right now. I own the little whore from her spoiled cunt to her pretty titties. If ye want her back, if ye want what's between her legs, you'll pay for it like any other punter."

I went deadly still, anger mixing with my pain.

"Don't talk about her like that." My words came out hard.

"I know ye fucked her already. Ye bought her from that same place that sold her ma time and again. Now tell me you're not a nice little rich boy who can afford to make a proper offer for outright ownership. I saw the car you're driving. You're good for it."

"I will end ye," I growled.

Struan leapt up and set his hands on my shoulders, forcing me to meet his gaze.

"Negotiate," he mouthed.

"You'll try, and she'll wind up facedown in the Water of Leith." Jack laughed back. "That's the fucking river, if ye miss my meaning. I'll drown the bitch like her ma should've done at birth."

"What do ye want?" I followed Struan's instruction, his

lead giving me a path through this.

"A million. For that, you'll get to own her forever. Do what ye like to her."

"Agree. Get a place to meet," Sebastian whispered from across the room.

Struan nodded agreement.

"Fine," I stated, hating myself and the words. "I'll pay. You'll bring her to me—"

"Get the cash by this time tomorrow, and I'll make the arrangements," Jack said.

The call disconnected.

I yelled in frustration, only just stopping myself from throwing my phone at the wall.

My brother raised his hands out to calm me. "They're in Edinburgh, right?"

My mind rushed with violent scenes. Jack hurting Breeze. Him luring her in. "That's where they live. We don't know if that's where she went."

He looked at the others.

"Max, tell him what ye just told us," Struan said.

The auburn-haired Highlander sat on the edge of his seat, muscles bunched as if ready for action. "That Kia she took has a tracker."

The Kia? I'd forgotten that car belonged to Max's family. Thea had borrowed it after hers died. "Seriously?"

"All our vehicles do. They're cheap but effective. We follow the principles of the mountain rescue service. Know where your resources are at all times. It's saved our arses any number of times."

He produced his phone and brought up an app, all of us crowding around as he selected the right tracker from a list.

A dot pulsed on a map, zooming out before homing in again. For a minute, it was blurry, not loading the location.

Then it resolved.

"Leith," I stated, soul sick. "You're right. For some reason, she went home."

"A reason engineered by her stepdad," Struan surmised. "What could possibly get her to go to him without waiting to say goodbye?"

There was only one thing I could imagine. One person she loved above anyone else. "Her sister," I guessed.

Max pressed something else on the screen. "The tracker stopped moving twenty minutes ago, so she only just arrived."

Which meant she was possibly still there. My mind whirred over what I could do. It was hours away. A minimum of two and a half, if the roads were quiet. I'd need to stop for fuel.

"They could move her anywhere." I jammed my fingers into my hair. "I can't get to her in time."

Max and Sebastian shared a look.

Sebastian, a stranger in almost all ways, stood. "I can fly us. I worked for Gordain for years. He'll lend me a helicopter."

In a series of stages that felt like I was in a dream, or nightmare, we got out to a hangar on a flat moor beyond the castle, loaded into a helicopter, and were airborne in no time.

"Hold tight," I told Breeze in my head, willing the miles away. "I love ye. I'll save ye. I'm coming for ye."

31

Breeze

Hot fury bubbled inside me. Beyond the locked door, Jack spoke to someone on his phone, his wheeze of delight making it through the wood.

I paced the narrow floorspace in my sister's bedsit, cursing myself for ever trusting the word of this man.

Summer hadn't come home. Jack had made it all up, and Mum had believed him, too. She was now doped up downstairs in her place, and I'd been half thrown through this door, the lock engaging when I finally worked out his ploy.

Jack thought I had a rich boyfriend who could set him up for life.

Jack was also as smart as a box of rocks.

I tapped my sister's spare key against my palm. Jack might have taken my phone and my bag, but he didn't know my sister had an extra key hidden, taped to the top of a drawer. If I wanted, I could march right up to the door, unlock it, pop my mother's boyfriend in the nose, and leave.

I'd probably even get away.

But there was a reason I was staying.

Up until now, no one would be missing me. Camden would be out for hours. I had time and access to the right person to find out the truth about the man I suspected of inflicting Camden's scar.

I'd resigned myself to expecting Camden to return to me with sadness because he hadn't found Summer. I'd come full circle from my enduring expectation of her being okay. Now it was my turn to bring something to the table. A small gift for the man who'd stolen my heart.

I thumped on the door. "Hey, Jack. Open up."

The muttering outside ended, then his voice returned louder. "Not until I've got my money."

I squared my shoulders, commencing my plan to provoke the asshole. "Whose idea was this anyway?"

"Mine. Now shut the fuck up."

"Liar. There's no way you could think of something like this on your own."

He smacked the door. "What do ye know, bitch?"

I held in a laugh. "I remember your training sessions, where your so-called friends came round to our place to talk up their big crimes. I know the only reason you did that was to get ideas, because you couldn't dream up anything on your own."

"Training? More like the other way around. I gave them the benefit of my experience."

I could almost imagine him preening in his fictitious role as a gangland boss.

"Your experience? What have you ever done beyond grabbing old ladies' handbags or nicking stuff from the corner shop? At least your friends are badass. Who was it who had a gun?"

"My brother, but he was only hiding it. Dumb bastard didn't know how to load it."

"And the one who used to make his victims choose who he beat up?"

I held my breath.

A longer pause came.

All I needed was a name. With that, I could ask around, use other sources of information.

"Sounds like the kid's got your number," a second voice came.

I froze.

Sickness soured my gut.

It was him. Even without seeing his face, the voice was unmistakable. The man who'd carved up Camden's skin really was in on it with Mum's boyfriend.

Jack grumbled something I couldn't hear.

I listened hard, trying to pick up their conversation.

"...dunno where he'll be coming in from," Jack was saying.

"Did you give him a deadline?" the second man queried. "Confirmed where to meet?"

"I'm not a fucking idiot. I know it takes time to get that amount of money together. I gave him until tomorrow."

"You were too greedy. A lesser amount would be easier. Now, you've given him time to mobilise around you."

"How? It's not like he's going to look for her here. No one would think I'd be that stupid."

Dismay gathered, crunching my stomach. Camden had already been told they had me. He would've left the party. He might even be driving down through Scotland now.

"The first place he'll come is here," the knifeman argued back.

"He won't, Gil. It's too obvious. That's the beauty of my thinking."

"You're wrong. We need to move her."

The voices drifted away, their argument continuing.

I stared into the darkness of Summer's bedsit, desperately trying to work out what to do. If Camden was on his way, how would he react to seeing Gil, as I now knew him to be named, or hearing his voice? It could throw him completely. Put him in danger.

If he brought his family with him, someone could get hurt.

I had to get out of here, fast.

Crossing the room, I readied the key and pressed my ear to the door. I listened hard.

Silence.

If they'd gone, this could be my only chance.

I'd run, then work out a way to contact Camden. Maybe call the owner of that big castle. Surely that would have a phone number listed somewhere.

I sucked in a breath, summoned my strength, and took the key to the lock.

The same second, the handle cranked down and the

door flew open, smacking into my head. The last thing I knew was Jack's beady eyes staring down at me as I went out cold.

32

Camden

The sprawling, bright city lights of Edinburgh passed by underneath us, the helicopter making no time of the trip down country. At the controls, Sebastian brought us into a swoop, homing in on our destination—a park in Leith.

Max's voice came over the headphones. "One minute until touchdown."

I simmered with rage, more than ready to go. "Once more with the plan. Sebastian will remain with the helicopter to avoid it getting picked over. Thea will stay with him. Struan, me, and Max are raiding that tower block. First stop, Breeze's mother's place. Next, her sister's room upstairs. If her ma can't tell us which number, we'll knock down every fucking door."

Everyone gave their okays.

Next to me in the spacious interior, Struan kissed Thea. I knew it hurt him to leave her behind with Sebastian at the helicopter, but it was safer for her not to go up against whatever criminal pack had been put together to hold Breeze.

"I'll talk to Sin and Lottie about going over to plan B," Thea said.

Shite. In all the worry and panic, the mess that already twisted our lives had taken a backseat. Yet McInver would be in the process of cutting me off. I'd lost the access Breeze needed and for me to reach Burn. We had no money to buy Cassie.

Which painted a future we'd been trying to avoid.

After this, after doing everything it took to retrieve our missing loved ones, Breeze included, we were on the run once again.

Fuck it. This was our life, and we'd make it work.

The ground neared, then Sebastian touched us down on an expanse of grass. I'd already examined my map and wasted no time in jumping out and taking off at a jog, my brother and Max at my side.

At the park fence, I leapt over then pelted down the street, passing small groups who'd gathered presumably at the sound of the helicopter.

We resembled a rescue party, or a raid.

Flat out, we took on Queen Charlotte Street without breaking a sweat, not slowing until we reached the tall, grey tower block where Breeze had shown me her world.

"This the place?" Struan asked, flying to a halt alongside me.

But my gaze was locked on the entrance.

Two men struggled under a flickering light, Breeze's abductor plus a stranger, carrying something wrapped in a floral quilt.

In a heartbeat, I was back on the cold grass of McInver's estate, watching with Sin as the guards carried this exact shape into the mansion. Back then, I'd said it looked like a body. But Breeze was small, and I hadn't been sure.

Now, I had absolutely no doubt.

With a guttural yell, I ran at them. The men backed up, but I was faster. I bowled into them, taking hold of the body. I didn't know if they'd hurt her. I didn't know anything except I needed to get her into my arms.

I grappled the quilt-covered body and pulled away. Max and Struan simultaneously took the men to the ground, landing hard with shouts of anger.

I fell to my knees, wrenching back the blanket.

Breeze's yellow curls appeared first, then her wide, panicked eyes. Silver tape hid her lips. She gave a muffled shriek, wrestled her arms free, which had more tape securing her wrists together, then flung them over my head to encircle my neck. I hugged her, pinning her to me for a moment where everything else fell away.

"Thought I'd lost ye," I breathed.

She made a sound of distress, and I stood, letting the blanket fall to carry her away from her kidnappers. A glance back showed me my brother and his friend had the men under control, pinning them down and growling threats to their ugly mugs.

With care, I slipped under Breeze's arms then peeled back the tape covering her mouth. "Are ye hurt?"

"I can't believe you came for me."

I kissed her, softly, but unable not to. "Always will. Tell me if they hurt ye."

"Only my pride. And maybe a small bump to the head.

But Camden, listen."

"Yes, Camden. Listen to your girlfriend," another voice came.

It rose like a spectre. The voice from my nightmares.

Still holding Breeze, I slowly turned.

Under Max's grip, the lean, older stranger with her ma's boyfriend leered at me.

Max shook him. "Shut your fucking mouth."

I held up a hand to pause my brother's friend. "No. Say something else."

"Know who I am, then?" the stranger drawled. "I remember ye. I remember your stupid bitch of a mother, too." He swung his head to address Jack. "This is your money maker? You're a joke. He's nothing. Just some little whore's kid from nowhere."

In the tower block's doorway, people gathered. Others peered from windows. A group rounded the corner of the road.

I was caught on dark memories. Reliving the horror I'd never forgotten.

But then Breeze palmed my cheek, covering the scar and bringing my attention back to her, where it should always be.

To linger here would be dangerous. We were the outsiders. Breeze's kidnappers could have friends coming. But I only saw her.

"He's Gil. A friend of Jack's. He's the one who hurt you. I guessed it after your story in the car, but I needed to be sure."

"Thank ye for working that out for me. Is that why ye came back?"

"No! I wouldn't leave you. They told me Summer returned. I believed them and couldn't do anything but drive here. I knew I had time before you finished so I could message later. I'm so sorry."

"Are ye sure you're okay?"

"Am I?" Her expression crumpled. "All I worried about was you. Jack is nothing. I could've taken him down myself, but his friend… It felt like a trap. I need you to understand something. He's nothing. A waste of space. The only power he held was in the fact a small boy and his terrified mum couldn't fight back."

I gave myself a second more to study the beautiful blue eyes of the woman I loved, then nodded, kissed her, and brought my gaze to Max.

"Switch."

The Highlander understood and dropped the man he was handling as I stepped away from Breeze.

"He had this." Max held up a knife.

Despite all the years that had passed, I recognised the handle of the knife that had cut me. I let him keep hold of it.

"Go to Breeze." I had to trust that he'd protect her in the short seconds I gave myself to finish what this man had started.

I took hold of Gil by his lapels. He grappled my wrist with both hands.

"Think you're in charge here, kid?" he snapped at me. "Guess again. Jack owns her ma. Don't think you're walking away without paying up."

With no pause, I dragged him to where Struan held Jack, pulled back my other fist, and punched the wannabe gangster stepdad right in his jaw. He fell, and my brother dropped him, snickering a laugh.

Struan stayed with me, having my back.

Then I addressed Gil, the man who'd tormented me for years. "I dreamt about killing ye one day. Ye threatened my mother and did fuck knows what else with her. Then, in the safety of our house, this happened by your hands." I drew a line along my scar, owning my identity. "Bet ye felt like a real villain. Roughing up women and children while playing the big man. You're weak. Nothing."

Gil stopped struggling. "Fucking little bastard. She begged. Offered her body. As if I'd take that over the money she owed. Dumb whore never stiffed me for my share of the cash again."

I grinned, knowing that it distorted my scar even more. I had my answer. He was her pimp and he'd cut me for money. What a sad, shitty life he led. "Bastard is right. The rest and everything I've become is nothing to do with ye. If I ever see ye again or hear of ye interfering with my family, including Breeze's ma, I will end your life. I'll take your own blade and slice right through your belly wall until ye have to hold your guts in as ye die in agony. Got it? Until then, rot in the hell you'll never be good enough to rise out of."

I reared back my fist once more, throwing all my power into breaking his face. Gil dropped to land in a heap across his partner in crime. Blood oozed from his nose, but he was out cold.

Breeze pushed under my arm, holding on to me like she never wanted to let go.

A bigger crowd had gathered, surrounding us. Breeze's mother weaved her way through. She stared with rounded, reddened eyes at the man on the floor. "Liar. Don't ever darken my door again." She spat on Jack's unconscious form.

Then she ran to her daughter and me, handing over Breeze's bag.

"What are you waiting for? Go!"

33

Breeze

We lifted from the grassy stretch of Leith Links in a helicopter, as if in a goddamned movie. We'd run, and I'd had no clue about destination, and I didn't care. Camden had found me. He'd managed it all with a combination of brute force and his brilliant brain.

Plus a little help from friends.

Thea had hugged me when we'd reached the aircraft. I hadn't had time for shock to set in. We were airborne and leaving Edinburgh in our wake.

Emotion crested in me, and I gave a splutter of a laugh, turning into Camden's hold. He hadn't taken his arm from around me since we'd strapped in.

"This is insane. I was on my own in that. I really believed Summer had returned. He had Mum fooled, too," I babbled. "But then you were there. Throwing down and owning it. That was hot as hell."

Camden kissed me, his attention fixed. His hand in my hair.

I couldn't get close enough. Pity we had an audience as I needed to climb on him.

"Got to love that adrenaline rush," the pilot said to Max who sat beside him. His voice was clear as day over the headphones, which meant mine had been to everyone else.

Max nodded. "High, horny, low."

Camden laughed and dragged his gaze off me to the man up front. "Horny what?"

"Adrenaline has that effect," Max replied. "Ye get euphoric, then horny as fuck, then don't be surprised to feel low tomorrow. I recommend hiding in bed for a couple of days. That'll take care of it all."

Camden held me closer, then he addressed his friend again. "Noted. Did ye keep hold of that knife?"

Max held out an object. Gil's knife in a leather case.

The mirth fled Camden's expression. He took it and turned it over, sliding it from the case halfway before changing his mind. "Can I open the window?"

We were above water now. The pilot gave him the okay, and Camden undid the latch. Then he jettisoned the blade to the sea below.

He took a long breath, shut the blustering air out, then addressed the cabin once more. "Can I talk to my lass in private for a second?"

Struan, Thea, and Max removed their headphones. The pilot flipped a switch on his controls, saying something which didn't come to our ears, which I guessed meant he'd isolated himself.

Camden brushed his thumb over my cheek. "I didn't find Summer. Not only that, McInver has woken up. I doubt

I'll get near his inner circle again."

Sadness gathered within me. "It's okay. After you left, I realised my hopes were unrealistic. She's been gone for so long. I have to accept I won't see her again."

"I'm so sorry."

"I am, too. There's something else I realised with that." Nerves jangled my senses, but I had to say this. "I've fallen in love with you."

My voice cracked, and Camden's shocked, happy expression nearly did me in. But I pushed on.

"I thought I was chasing down the only person I really cared about beyond my mother, but at the same time, there was you, giving me unconditional support. Being there for me when there was no reason for you to do so. You're the best person I've ever met. I know this is sudden, but I need you to know how I feel."

"It isn't sudden, or if it is, I'm way ahead of ye. I've loved ye for as long as I've known ye." His lips met mine for a long, drugging kiss that ended too soon.

I wilted into him. He held me close.

"You're mine," he continued. "But that brings with it trouble. I don't know how my life is going on from here. My family has tried to do things the good way, play it straight, build ourselves back up. It didn't work. There are too many people out there who want us to fail and are working against us. Which means from now on, we'll be in greater danger. We'll be pulling shite that will put us on the wrong side of the law, not least to free our brother. I think this is where we were always meant to be. Doing things our own way. The world is too corrupt for us not to. But you have—"

I pressed my fingers to his lips, silencing him. "Don't say I have a choice. Don't give me the option of walking away because I don't want it. Anything that comes our way, I can handle. My life has never been easy, but I've never really been happy either, not until you. I only want you, and the world can take us on together. Got it?"

That perfectly imperfect upside-down smile of his returned. "Good," he replied simply.

Struan gestured wildly from beside us. Everyone put on their headphones once more.

"Sin and Lottie have seen Cassie. She's there. It was the right place. But they failed in their attempt to rescue her."

I gasped while everyone chimed in with shouts on how to save the little girl.

In Camden's arms, I worried over his sister as I released the hope for mine. In one final surge of emotion, I took out my phone and logged in to our dating app. Added a second message to the one sent back when I thought I'd find her again, a final farewell forever.

Then I swiped away my tears, shut the phone down completely, and rejoined the conversation.

The helicopter powered on through the dark night, delivering us to a place where hard decisions would have to be made. We'd withstand it. We'd do whatever it took to reunite the last members of his family and make it on our own. Keep everyone safe from now on.

Together, we'd overcome every single scar.

Epilogue

Summer

Muffled voices wormed their way through the wall of my prison. Chained to the pipes of the boot room, and naked, I inched closer to the wall, listening to the servants chatter in the kitchen next door.

"...been in such a rage," a man said with a nervous laugh, dishes clattering in a sink. "He has since his friend was hospitalised."

There had been a party here this evening, though it had obviously finished early. In my room, I'd picked up the sounds of music and laughter.

"But you think that will change now the man's awake? I hope so. The chief's temper terrifies me," a woman replied.

"With any luck. He even smiled as he left earlier. I didn't think him capable."

They were talking about the chief of police. Their master. My captor. Terrifying didn't even start to describe him.

The woman replied something I couldn't hear, her voice obscured by their activities.

I strained to catch their words, needing any human contact after so long of being hidden away. Tied up and locked in. Ignored, even when I cried for help.

The man's voice came back a little louder, jokey, even, as if he'd suffered under his master's anger and the events of the evening were a relief. "That prisoner he's been ranting about will get it tonight."

"What prisoner?"

"Have you been living in a cave? The man he said burned down McInver's house. He's held the arsonist down at the station, breaking all kinds of rules to keep hold of him until he could take action."

"So? He owns the police. He can do what he likes."

"No kidding. He needed McInver to wake up. Something to do with a deal they made. Now the guy's conscious, the prisoner is dead meat."

I didn't know who these people were, the unconscious friend or the man in prison, though I felt bad for the latter. He and I shared a major fuck-up in common, both being in cages of our own making.

As it often did, my mind drifted off my desperate situation and to a happier place. The servant's words about an arsonist had me picturing the boy I'd long ago fallen in love with. The one who'd been obsessed with fire and told me of things he'd done to bad people involving his lighter and a wicked attitude.

Jamieson was my talisman in this dark place.

The flame that kept flickering inside me.

One of my biggest regrets, besides the obvious, was the fact we'd never met, and now, never would.

I adjusted my position, my handcuffs cutting into my wrists. The keys hung on a hook across the room, but they might as well have been miles away for all the good that did me. I didn't have the strength to break the pipes even if the door wasn't locked from the outside.

The man on the other side of the wall chattered on, "Tonight was always going to bring an end to it. Without McInver, he had the son. He was going to get him to make the decision."

"Camden McInver. Where the hell did that prodigal son come from?" the woman asked.

"No idea, but he doesn't need him now. McInver's back, the prisoner will be vanished, and life gets back to normal again."

"I hope so," was his response.

In the month of me being here, I had no clue of what 'life back to normal' looked like for the evil man who ruled this house. He bought and sold women. Hurt people.

It could only get worse from here. I knew, because he'd told me so.

The police chief had talked of breaking me. He seemed delighted by my fear and planning something evil.

I only had myself to blame.

I'd always been impulsive, but the action I'd taken had hidden dangers I'd never suspected. For that, my naïveté, everyone who loved me suffered. I could only imagine my sister, grief-stricken and endangering herself as I knew she would, because I'd do the same for her if she were missing.

Emotion rolled through me. I imagined her face. Her worry at me not coming home, and of hearing from our mother where I'd gone.

It was never meant to be like this.

By now, she probably assumed me dead.

Then again, from the servants' conversation, I was as good as that when the police chief returned. If his other distractions had been removed, he'd take the time to deal with me.

Just like his mystery prisoner, his arsonist, my sentence was coming to an end.

Footsteps sounded in the hall outside.

My breathing stuttered, and I swiped at my cheek with my bare shoulder, trying to hide the tracks of tears I didn't want him to see.

If it wasn't him, calling out was pointless. No one would help. He could do anything, and his staff would look the other way.

If it was him, my suffering was about to get a thousand times worse.

A key turned in the lock.

Terror gripped me.

The door swung open, and my vision flickered, my fear so extreme I was on the verge of passing out.

But a woman entered the room. Long, red curls and a baby-doll nightie did a poor job of concealing her otherwise nude skin. Glancing behind her, she closed the door.

Her gaze settled on me, her eyes rounding. "Tell me your name," she demanded.

I pressed my lips together, unwilling after everything I'd experienced.

The woman crouched beside me and brushed my blonde hair back from my face. "Please, tell me. I think I know but I have to be right."

Then she said something that burned away my hesitation.

"Your sister is hunting for you."

Shock jolted me. My words came out as the smallest whisper. "You know Breeze? Is she okay?"

Her shoulders sagged. "It is you. Holy fucking shitballs, sis. Yeah, she's great. Missing you, though."

I gawked at the stranger who somehow knew Breeze. "My name's Summer. You've heard of me. You know who I am."

"Got that right. I'm Divine." She eyed my constraints. The handcuffs holding my wrists to the wall. The silver tape around my ankles. "God. How long have you been a prisoner?"

"A while." My words came in a mumble. I shouldn't trust a stranger, even when she claimed to know my sister, but what else did I have? That she'd even entered the room was a miracle. "Why are you helping me?"

"Your sister was kind to me and stood up for me. I always pay my debts. If that's in freeing your ass, great."

An act of kindness sounded like Breeze. I swallowed back my hesitation. "Can you really get me out?"

She darted an anxious gaze over me, peeking at the door and taking a deep breath. "Maybe. I've been here a few times in the past, and tonight, he made me lady of the house. It means I stay here overnight so I can be ready for the chief whenever he wants me, amongst other...duties. It also means I have access to wander around."

My sob came out as a hiccup, emotion breaking free. "Help me, please."

"He'll kill me if he finds out I did this, but look at you. You're so young." Divine reached out to pick at the tape on my ankles. Quickly, she unwound it, not hesitating over ripping it from my skin.

I stood, unsteady like a fawn, and my handcuffs rattling on the pipe.

"Shh!" Divine hushed me, jabbing with her finger at the wall.

The servants had gone quiet, and panic rushed through me again. If they heard, they'd stop her from freeing me. None of them would dare risk angering the chief. I'd never get away.

"The key. Over there," I said with a head jerk to the hook by the door.

Divine darted for it, bringing it back to insert in the lock.

She fumbled it. It fell with a tinkle on the stone floor.

My panic spiked. I watched the door, certain someone would enter.

"Shit, sorry," Divine muttered. She tried again, this time rotating the key with a sweet click.

The handcuffs fell away. I gasped in relief and rubbed my wrists.

Neither of us stood still. Divine listened at the door then peered out, beckoning me to follow her. My heart sped. An old hunter's jacket hung next to where my key had been replaced, and I snatched it, shrugging it on my chilly body as I chased my rescuer down the hall, our bare feet padding on the tiles.

I didn't know how this was happening, but now wasn't the time for questions.

The hall joined a wider, bright corridor, a door to the outside just across the stretch.

"I have no idea how you'll get off the grounds, but that's the closest exit," Divine said, low.

Voices came from the right.

Divine walked straight out into the corridor and smiled at whoever was approaching, one hand hidden behind her back giving me the tiny signal to hide.

I darted through an open doorway into a darkened room and crouched behind a sofa. It looked to be a sitting room, but a not so formal one. Maybe for the servants.

The soft overtones of conversation met me, Divine causing a distraction, I hoped, the words inaudible over my breathing and the rushing of blood in my ears.

Slowly, my eyes adjusted to the gloom.

On a low table, dead ahead of me, someone's mobile phone sat. I gasped and grabbed it. It unlocked without a code, and I suppressed a squeal of delight at my second piece of luck.

Instantly, I went to dial the police.

Then I stopped, back spacing the 9-9-9.

There was no way the cops would come here and arrest their chief. Even if they believed me, he was the one with the power. I couldn't risk it. No, I needed to get away myself.

But I couldn't waste another second without letting my sister know I was alive.

I took the risk and dialled her number, my stomach somersaulting.

The call didn't connect.

I squinted at the screen. No service apart from the Wi-Fi.

I swore under my breath and deleted the number. Maybe this was a phone just used in the house and not on a network.

What could I do?

I couldn't call or text her, but I could send a message on another platform. Except Breeze didn't allow most notifications on her phone. The only one that she did was email.

Right.

That, I could do.

As quickly as my numb fingers would allow, I brought up a browser and logged in to my email.

Messages loaded. My gaze snagged on one containing my sister's name. It was from the dating app we used to amuse ourselves. Another appeared right behind it.

I opened the oldest, staring at the message she'd sent me weeks ago.

If you're out there, please let me know. I'm so worried. I'm staying with a guy called Camden, he's searching for his missing brother, Burn, or Jamieson, as they all have nicknames. I don't know why I'm telling you this because all I want is to find you. Please, Summer, talk to me.

My heart ached.

My blood chilled.

The servants mentioned the name Camden. He was the son of the unconscious man whose house had burned down. How common was that name? Surely it wasn't the same man she was staying with.

Then there was the other person. His brother, Jamieson.

Even in my frozen state, with my mind slow after so many weeks locked up, I couldn't deny something strange was going on.

I backed out of the email and loaded the second.

I know you were talking to a boy named Jamieson. He's in jail, being held illegally. We're praying he hasn't been killed. His brothers are trying to find ways to free him. I wish you were here. You were always so clever. I bet you would have come up with something brilliant. I love you and miss you so much. I always will. Goodbye, Summer.

Noise came at the door, and Divine entered, spotting me by the light of the phone.

"Hold fire here for a second," she whispered. "There's people in the hall. Give them a minute to clear, then go. I'll make a distraction."

I struggled with my thoughts. The impossible picture trying to form in my mind.

"Divine," I whispered to my saviour. "I overheard the servants talking about a man who's being held in jail. Some prisoner who'd committed arson. Do you know who that is?"

She gave a small nod, her gaze still on the hall. "The chief talks when he fucks. Not to me, but to himself, all this angry, crazy shit. He caught some man named Jamieson who he thinks is an arsonist. He's holding him in the station. Why?"

Because there was no possibility of this being wrong.

Because that was my Jamieson being held in a cell.

Because tonight would bring about an end to him like it should have me.

I took a fast breath, my dormant impulsiveness rushing back in the face of a threat against one of the people I held most dear.

"What police station?" I asked.

I was almost free, and walking straight back into danger was insanity. But for him, for Jamieson, I'd see the world burn.

The End.

Order the explosive finale to the series now in Burn (Dark Island Scots,#4).

https://www.amazon.com/dp/B0BM88FW7S

ACKNOWLEDGEMENTS

Dear reader,

Phew, three books in and the plot is so thick, it's a very tasty soup. Our tribe of found family is growing but still scattered, with the youngest siblings captured and in danger. So much is still up in the air, and I'm so grateful that you're enjoying the ride.

Camden had a journey to go on to realise his true strength. There was anger along the way, plus one or two tense acts and wild outbursts, but he's shaping up to be a mature and competent man. Nothing like his terrible father. Truth and good reasoning are his strengths, despite everything he went through that could've changed him for the worse. Likewise, Breeze needed to accept help and stop being an island, as well as not throwing herself in harm's way in her desperation to find her sister. She was right on the money about Summer's life being at risk, but no single person is ever going to bring down the conspiracy we're seeing the edges of.

Breeze and Scar complement each other.

They've also got one heck of a shock coming up.

I can't wait to dive into *Burn (Dark Island Scots, #4)*. The final episode of this rollercoaster of a story is going to be 100% wild.

Thanks go to Elle Thorpe and Zoe Ashwood, Sara Massery, Shellie M, and Liz Parker for being my core team. Hugs for you all. Cleo Moran makes amazing graphics, Natasha Snow provides sumptuous covers. Emmy Ellis edits each manuscript until it's shiny, and Lori Parks joins her to proofread to perfection. My ARC and Street Team are *chef's kisses* wonderful.

Thanks also to narrators Zara Hampton-Brown and Zachary Webber who are the voices of this series now and do an amazing job.

Join my Facebook reader group if you like to talk books (Jolie's Fall Hard Fans). Or add yourself to my newsletter to never miss a new release announcement.

My final words as always go to my husband and son. You are my whole world and a noisy pair of pests who took great delight in playing a raucous game behind me as I wrote these words.

Jolie <3

ALSO BY JOLIE VINES

Marry the Scot series

1) Storm the Castle

2) Love Most, Say Least

3) Hero

4) Picture This

5) Oh Baby

Wild Scots series

1) Hard Nox

2) Perfect Storm

3) Lion Heart

4) Fallen Snow

5) Stubborn Spark

Wild Mountain Scots series

1) Obsessed

2) Hunted

3) Stolen

4) Betrayed

5) Tormented

Dark Island Scots series

1) Ruin

2) Sin

3) Scar

4) Burn

Standalones

Cocky Kilt:

a Cocky Hero Club Novel

Race You:

An Office-Based Enemies-to-Lovers Romance

Fight For Us:

a Second-Chance Military Romantic Suspense

Visit and follow my Amazon page for all new releases
https://amazon.com/author/jolievines

Add yourself to my insider list to make sure you don't miss
my publishing news

https://www.jolievines.com/newsletter

ABOUT THE AUTHOR

JOLIE VINES is a romance author who lives in the UK with her husband and son.

Jolie loves her heroes to be one-woman guys.

Whether they are a brooding pilot (Gordain in Hero), a wrongfully imprisoned rich boy (Sebastian in Lion Heart), or a tormented twin (Max in Betrayed), they will adore their heroine until the end of time.

Her favourite pastime is wrecking emotions, then making up for it by giving her imaginary friends deep and meaningful happily ever afters.

Have you found all of Jolie's Scots?

Visit her page on Amazon and join her ever active Fall Hard Facebook group.

www.ingramcontent.com/pod-product-compliance
Lightning Source LLC
Chambersburg PA
CBHW051322190726
48290CB00001B/273